Would solving th
do anything at all

She had always been a big "fixer." The one people asked to organize dances, fund-raisers, the second-grade field trip. The one who gave her childhood friends advice on cheating boyfriends and broken hearts.

Ever since she'd learned the truth, she had felt disorganized and off center, angry and confused. But if she discovered her origins, she would finally understand the secret thoughts, like nightmares, that had haunted her for as long as she could remember.

She had been fearful and ashamed of those thoughts, because she had never known what they meant. But now she did. They weren't nightmares.

They were memories. Memories of real events, real people.

Memories she needed Tommy Lee McCall to help her chase down.

ABOUT THE AUTHOR

A One-Woman Man is author M.L. Gamble's seventh Intrigue novel. A huge fan of mystery, Ms. Gamble enjoys crafting interesting and memorable characters and a fast-paced plot. She currently resides in suburban Maryland with her husband and two children and works for a software company.

Books by M.L. Gamble

Don't miss any of our special offers. Write to us at the following address for information on our newest releases.

Harlequin Reader Service
U.S.: 3010 Walden Ave., P.O. Box 1325, Buffalo, NY 14269
Canadian: P.O. Box 609, Fort Erie, Ont. L2A 5X3

A One-Woman Man
M.L. Gamble

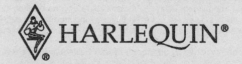

HARLEQUIN®

TORONTO • NEW YORK • LONDON
AMSTERDAM • PARIS • SYDNEY • HAMBURG
STOCKHOLM • ATHENS • TOKYO • MILAN • MADRID
PRAGUE • WARSAW • BUDAPEST • AUCKLAND

For Beth Harbison and Mary Ann Comparetto,
two women who could teach the world
about loving and supportive friends.

ISBN 0-373-22480-X

A ONE-WOMAN MAN

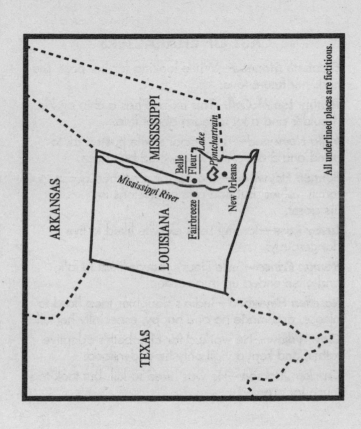

All underlined places are fictitious.

CAST OF CHARACTERS

Elizabeth Monette—While looking for her past, she finds her future love.

Tommy Lee McCall—This ex-cop has a chip on his shoulder and a lot to learn about fate.

India Heywood—This doctor's wife has an ax to grind and a daughter who would be queen.

Bennett Heywood—The doctor preached about family values, but had a few skeletons in his closet.

Luvey Rose—Tommy Lee's ex-wife liked to live dangerously.

Roman Prince—Belle Fleur's mayor liked to talk, and often ended up in a corner.

Rosellen Heywood—India's daughter tried hard to please, and made no one happy, especially herself.

Clay Willow—He worked for Elizabeth's adoptive father, and kept a vigil only he understood.

Cracker Jackson—He was hired to kill, but took too much for granted.

Prologue

December, twenty years ago...

The man in the white coat bent down and kissed his only child on the top of her head. "Be good for your mother in the morning, sweetheart. No crying about brushing your teeth."

"You going to be here when I wake up, Daddy?" the girl asked, her lips pursed expectantly.

"I'll try, baby, I'll try." His expression showed none of his turmoil as he hugged her close. He had promised himself he would always treat his only child as if theirs was a normal family. But he realized as she pulled out of his embrace that each day she got older and more aware, and that this charade could not last.

He had to do something. Something to end this limbo in which he and his daughter lived. And he had to do it soon.

Silently the man crossed the kitchen to the back door and let himself out. He ignored the child's mother who sat staring out the window at a stand of trees, outlined in silver blue, like a Christmas tree, by the moonlight. He could think of nothing to say to the woman that would not hurt her, or him. Not even "Good night."

Especially "Good night," as that well-worn phrase carried with it the full weight of his leaving them to reside in another woman's home.

"Daddy's going to try to be here in the morning," the girl announced when the sound of her father's footsteps had faded. She leaned her chubby arms against the dinette table as she peered into the empty wineglass clutched in her mother's pale hand. "I'm going to ask him to tell me the story about the girls in the beautiful dresses and the ball. That's my favorite."

Blue eyes met blue eyes.

The woman snapped awake from an open-eyed dream. She reached out to stroke her daughter's cheek. "Aren't you getting tired of poor old Cinderella? Midnight comes and all the fun is over."

"Not Cinderella, Mama. The new story about the Midnight Ball. Daddy told me it's real, not a fairy tale. One girl even gets to be the Queen of Midnight." The child's eyes shone as she put her hands around the goblet and licked the bitter-tasting edge. "Daddy said I might get to be the Queen when I'm a big girl. Did you get to go to the ball, Mama? Daddy said all the beautiful girls get to go to the Queen of Midnight Ball."

"No. No, I never went." A flush stained the woman's skin but she smiled and pulled the child to her. Her heart pounded with anger. The child's father should never have told her about the Queen of Midnight Ball, Belle Fleur, Louisiana's most revered social occasion. It was especially heartless to give her hope that she might someday be a part of it. Only girls with proper families and legitimately married parents were nominated as "electees" for Queen of Midnight.

She would give him a piece of her mind about this tomorrow and warn him never to mention it to their child again. She would not let hopeless dreams poison the child's spirit and set her up for such a big disappointment. "Come on, darling. It's time for bed. When Daddy comes back, we'll get him to tell you a lovely story. Just remember, though. He works long, long hours. So don't count too much on him being here first thing in the morning."

With a hug, the woman glanced back out at the magnolias. She had been thinking of the summer night when she had made love under those trees and become pregnant in the thick, sultry air of summer. A night six years ago last August.

If someone had asked her then, she would have agreed that her baby might well have a chance at being Queen of Midnight. But not now.

She kissed the spot on the soft blond hair where the man's lips had rested a moment before, wishing against reality that "happily ever after" existed in life like it did in fairy tales. "You need to get ready now, child. It's very late and we've got a big day tomorrow. We're going over to Fairbreeze."

"With Daddy?"

"No. No, just us girls."

"I want Daddy to come. We never go anyplace with him."

"Oh, but we'll have fun. I promise."

The child made a face. "Can we get lunch out? At that house with the strawberry ice cream?"

"It's not a house, it's called a restaurant. I don't know if they have strawberry ice cream so close to Christmas. But we'll get you something, okay? *If* you brush your teeth tonight for two whole minutes, then get right into bed and wait until I come up. Deal?''

''That's a deal, Mama.'' The girl shook her mother's outstretched hand excitedly, then scampered toward the doorway. Suddenly she stopped. ''You'll come up soon, won't you, Mama? I don't like it up-stairs at night when daddy's not here.''

''I'll be up in a bit to tuck you in, darling. You remember now, brush for two whole minutes. Watch the little blue fish clock on the wall till it moves two bubbles.''

The girl held up two plump fingers. ''This many bubbles?''

Her mother nodded and flashed two fingers back. ''That many. Very good. Now, hurry up. It's late.''

As her child disappeared up the back stairs, the woman stood and cleared the table, mulling over the next day's appointment. The woman shivered sud-denly. Deep in thought, she reached into the bottom drawer of the bureau that held her grandmother's china and fished out a small, velvet-covered box. She stroked the cover for a moment, then opened it. Inside, the diamond-studded pin sparkled and danced. Five small rubies glittered in the miniature crown. Tugging at the bottom of the box, she pulled up the lining to check that the child's birth certificate was still tucked inside. It was, the footprints on it impossibly small.

With tears in her eyes, she snapped the case shut and pushed it back into its hiding place. Was seeing an attorney the right thing to do, she wondered? Not for herself. Nothing she could think of seemed the right thing for herself. But for her daughter? Was it the best thing to hire a lawyer and force the girl's father to do what was only fair and right? To force him to do what he had once promised he would, without any urging or threats from her?

Her mood darkened as several possible results of her action—among them, his prominent family's retaliatory response—flashed through her thoughts. Belle Fleur was nothing if not small and devoted to gossip; the more shocking the rumor was, the quicker it was passed on.

She glanced upward toward her daughter's room. If their story came out, it might ruin the child's father. It would surely tar her own family name even blacker with the brush of scandal. As if that were possible.

Despite herself, she smiled grimly, then tossed the newspaper into the trash and shook her head. Those women she read so much about who talked up "power for females" might change some laws for women up north, but they couldn't change the way people in Belle Fleur judged other people, wouldn't change how those with money and a good name judged a woman with no living male kin or property who bore a child out of wedlock. No, there wasn't anything she could do to change that. There wasn't anything she could do to change anything in her life, it seemed.

Except try and make sure her daughter had more than she did. Who you were mattered the world in Belle Fleur. Who you *might* be would gain you nothing but whispers and finger-pointing. She knew firsthand how the ugliness of that treatment seeped into a person, ate away parts of your soul.

With a deep breath, the woman turned on the water and rinsed out the sink, mulling over her child's fascination with the story of the Queen of Midnight Ball. Was it just love of a good story, or did her daughter intuitively connect with the town's event of the season, at which several of her ancestors had danced and laughed and shone as members of the society "court"?

After all, the girl's grandmother had been a Queen of Midnight. The painting that hung in her lover's family's hallway sprang suddenly alive in the woman's mind. The smiling, lovely young face, the glittering ball gown, the crown of twinkling gems nestled in the blond hair so like her daughter's.

Tears of humiliation and frustration suddenly clouded the woman's vision. Angrily she pushed them away and filled her thoughts with simple tasks. She poured soap in the dishpan, ran the water till it steamed and plunged the few dishes off the counter into it with a splash. She furiously washed and rinsed and scrubbed, finally relaxing a bit as she held the crystal wineglass—a long-ago gift from her lover—up to the light to check for soap bubbles. As she did, a moving shadow from outside her window tossed a reflection against the curved, wet surface.

Someone was here, walking up the drive, she realized. It was too late for visitors. Besides, no one came to see them, except the child's father. Not ever.

She stood motionless as footsteps creaked the gray boards of the back porch. Why had he returned tonight, she wondered? She glanced at the table and searched it for keys, wallet, his hospital identification tag.

But the tabletop was bare. Nothing of his remained, which meant he had returned for...what? A word with her?

For an instant she wished—she hoped with a startling surge of emotion—that tonight might be like other, long-ago nights. As if his hand were on her face now, she remembered with a rush of sensation the warmth of his touch, the tenderness in his arms, the gentle way he had always kissed her, even in the heat of passion.

At the sounds of a brief knock and the back door opening, the woman dried one trembling hand against her skirt and turned, her mouth tense, lips parting to speak his name.

The first blast from the shotgun hit her in the chest. She cried out when hot lead from the second bit into her skin in a hundred stinging places, and she crumpled to the floor.

Beside her the goblet shattered, its pieces glimmering in the moonlight like a fairy-tale slipper in a little girl's dream.

Chapter One

December, twenty years later...

Elizabeth Monette pressed the pink linen napkin to her lips and whispered to the girl on her right. "I'm going to slip out in about five minutes, Aspen."

Aspen Carter's eyes narrowed as she worriedly scanned her friend's face. Elizabeth was, hands down, the most beautiful woman she knew, but today, despite the blue dress that brought out her lovely coloring and accentuated all the positives of her figure, Elizabeth looked like hell. She had circles under her eyes and none of the usual gaiety in her voice. "I'll cover for you. But why won't you tell me where you're going?"

Elizabeth shook her head, then with a forced smile murmured, "I can't right now. But don't worry. And don't tell Miss Lou about me leaving for an appointment. I don't want anything to ruin her day."

Both women's glances traveled to the tiny, elegantly dressed lady sitting ten feet away at the head banquet table. Luisa Monette—"Miss Lou" as she was fondly called by everyone who knew her for more than five minutes—was a past Queen of Midnight winner. As befitting this honor, today she sat at the head table when the Queen of Midnight Search Committee hosted their annual event honoring past queens.

This luncheon introduced the past "Royal Ladies of Belle Fleur, Louisiana," and formally invited them to place sealed envelopes containing the names of their nominees in the silver chest that sat prominently on the speaker's lectern.

It was a day of great happiness for Miss Lou, for her envelope held the name of her only child on the nominating ballot. Of the fifteen past Queens in the room, thirteen of their ballots held the names of blood kin to the Queens, so Miss Lou's choice would come as no surprise to the two hundred and fifty-odd guests gathered there.

What would come as a surprise, one of the guests sat thinking as she watched Elizabeth Monette chat with the mayor's niece, was that it was unlikely Elizabeth Monette would live to hear her name read at the Queen of Midnight Ball.

Across the room, Elizabeth shivered from a sudden chill and glanced around to determine if she was being stared at. With a nearsighted squint, she saw no one. As she gave Aspen's hand a quick squeeze, she cast a last glance at Miss Lou. "I'll see you later."

"Your hands are like ice, Elizabeth," Aspen replied. "Are you sure you're not ill?"

Elizabeth smiled at the girl who had attended nursery school with her. Though they had been separated when Elizabeth moved to Maryland, they had kept up a correspondence. Aspen was really the only friend she had in the town where she was born. She looked at Aspen with affection and winked. "I'm fine. It's all the excitement."

Aspen made a face. "Right. You're excited about

being in the running for queen. Miss 'I'm Not Interested,' who said no to Miss Lou six—count them—six times in the past. Tell me another lie, and I'll not believe that, either.''

Elizabeth gave a self-deprecating shake of her head and discreetly fished around under her seat for her purse. Locating it, she eased it onto her lap and again scanned the room. She couldn't shake the feeling that someone was staring at her, but without her glasses she wouldn't have been able to see Kevin Costner blowing kisses from the next table. As far as she could tell, everyone's attention appeared to be concentrated on the speaker, Dr. Bennett Heywood, chairman of the Midnight Ball Committee.

The tall, bald president and chief of surgery of the town's hospital was halfway through his speech, regaling the gathering with stories of past Queen of Midnight Pageants and the honors they had bestowed on the women who had led them. For the most part, Elizabeth felt it was a lot of foolery to treat what was basically a small Louisiana town's society party of the year as if it meant anything significant, but she mentally gave herself a shake.

In this crazy old scary world, there was a lot to be said for tradition, and besides, it meant a lot to her mom and dad that she'd agreed to move home for a while and take part in something that had been a high point in Miss Lou's life.

Besides, Elizabeth reminded herself, since she didn't have a snowball's chance in hell of winning, she didn't have to worry about upholding the Belle Fleur civic agenda for the next year. All she had to give up was a couple of weeks of nights spent at parties and glad-handing the folks of Belle Fleur and Fairbreeze, the two tiny cities in Farquier County that made the Queen of Midnight Ball the event of the year. Even she could do that for her folks, her brain lectured. She might as well just relax and enjoy it. Let her mom and dad wish upon a star. Then get on with life.

As Dr. Heywood finished his remarks with a joke, the room broke into laughter, led by the loud, squeaky voice of Belle Fleur's mayor for the past six years, Paris Prince. Elizabeth saw her chance and grabbed it. Rising gracefully, she slipped out of her seat and mouthed the words, "I'll see you tonight at the party," to Aspen. Without attracting too much attention, she crossed the room and had exited before her mother noticed. Elizabeth hurried through the lobby, past one of the young women she recognized from the banquet. The so-called Queen "electee" was deep in conversation with an older, foreign-looking man standing near a darkened phone booth.

Elizabeth looked away before she had to make any kind of an explanation to one of the girls on the court. As she hurried past, she experienced another odd intuition that the furtive-looking pair did not wish to be spoken to any more than she did. *I'm being a bit paranoid,* Elizabeth chided herself, realizing her overly active imagination was probably due to the appointment she was secretly rushing to keep.

Reminded of that errand, she clenched her teeth and continued through the revolving doors, emerging nervous, once again, into the chilly winter air. If she thought about it too much, she'd probably postpone this meeting until after all the Queen of Midnight nonsense, and then maybe forever.

Could she live the rest of her life not knowing? *No,*

her mind replied. *No, you couldn't.* With that conclusion, Elizabeth retrieved her gym bag from the bellman and stood patiently while he beckoned the cabbie waiting beside the curb. In a moment she was off on a trip that might change her life forever.

With a smile she leaned into the leather seat, not once noticing the rusty pickup parked across the street, or the thin, gray-haired man sitting inside who had waited for three hours just to catch a glimpse of her.

TEN MINUTES LATER, Elizabeth's cab pulled into another hotel parking lot in an older, less charming section of Belle Fleur and deposited her at the door. Elizabeth stared at the office building across the street for a moment, tucked her purse under her arm, settled her gym bag over her shoulder and set off.

She had never met a private detective before, never even considered meeting one before last week. To tell the truth, if anyone she knew had said they were going to hire one, she would have smiled politely and wondered what on earth a nice, well-bred person like her friend was doing going to a private detective.

Ordinary people didn't need private detectives, she would have thought. "What a difference a few weeks makes," Elizabeth whispered to herself as she stepped out of the creaking elevator on the second floor of the Montrose Building. She walked slowly toward the door on which were hand painted the words D. Betts, Investigations and rapped sharply.

There was no answer.

With a thud, the elevator doors across the small hallway shut and the slow, whining sound of the car's cables filled Elizabeth's ears. She began to feel a sense of panic, almost of foreboding. From the edge of her consciousness a piece of a memory surfaced, like a ripple on dark water. The echo of her knocking, of knuckles against wood, were followed in her mind by the sound of...of what?

Of a horrendous popping sound. Of glass breaking and a woman screaming. Of a little girl sobbing, and calling out for her mother.

It wasn't the first time she'd had this memory, but as they had a hundred times in the past, sadness and fear overwhelmed her. Blinking back the static terror that accompanied these haunting thoughts, Elizabeth took a breath and forced her concentration back to the present. Though her palms were damp and her heart was racing, she silently thought of the words the psychologist had told her when she'd first been treated for panic attacks years before.

"It's only imagination. It's only imagination. You're safe. You're safe. Don't push to remember what it means, Elizabeth. When your mind is ready—if it ever is ready—the memory will return."

She knocked again, this time more firmly.

No answer.

Elizabeth looked behind her at the elevator doors, reassuring herself she was alone, though suddenly not reassured by that thought. Where was Dorothy Betts, the investigator she had talked to yesterday evening? Why wasn't she in her office? The woman had told her to stop in today. "I'm always there at two. Typing up notes, or on the phone. Don't bother to call ahead, just come on by no later than two or you'll have to wait a couple of weeks to see me, " the woman had told Elizabeth.

Elizabeth leaned closer to the door and listened again. Had she heard something inside? The muffled sounds of talking? Was Dottie Betts on the phone? If she was, perhaps she hadn't heard her knock. With that thought, Elizabeth turned the doorknob and opened the door.

And came face-to-face with a man who looked every bit as surprised to see her as she was to see him.

"Oh, I'm sorry," Elizabeth said in a rush, her voice too loud to her own ears. "I didn't mean to intrude...."

"No problem," the man replied, taking a step back toward the desk he had been leaning against when she'd entered into the room. "Can I help you find someone?"

"I'm looking for Ms. Betts." Elizabeth smiled. She had been expecting to find the friendly-voiced woman whose gentle manner had reached out to her through the phone lines. She had been expecting to find the ex-legal-secretary-turned-private-detective, whose specialty was tracing the birth parents of adopted people through public records.

But instead of the kind Ms. Betts, Elizabeth was confronted with a tall, big-boned, firm-jawed man whose black hair needed combing, mustache needed smoothing and blue jeans needed mending.

It was a wholly disconcerting turn of events, and Elizabeth felt her face flush from the man's open scrutiny of her. She didn't feel threatened, for his appearance wasn't unsavory or ill-groomed, except for the holey blue jeans. If anything, he looked scrubbed, a tiny nick on his chin evidence of the very recent pass of a razor. But though he looked civil enough, the man had an almost-animal-like air of watchfulness about him. Like a pet dog an owner tells you to go ahead and pat, but when you reach a hand toward the animal, it responds with a growl, or a bark, or worse.

Elizabeth stood her ground and met the man's brown eyes with her own steady gaze. "Do you know where Ms. Betts is?"

"Yes, I do. Why don't you have a seat?"

The man motioned to a straight-backed chair and surprised Elizabeth by walking behind the desk and settling into what was presumably Dorothy Betts's chair.

"Excuse me, but where is Ms. Betts?"

"In the hospital."

Elizabeth gasped. "Oh, my. Is she all right?" Several lurid scenes from television detective dramas flashed into her mind.

The dark-haired man smiled and put his feet up on the desk. "Yes. Or at least she will be in a bit. As soon as those two rascals she's fixing to give birth to are ready to make an appearance, I'm sure she'll be her old hell-raising self."

"Oh, then she wasn't hurt on the job." Elizabeth sat down and sighed. "I'm glad to hear that."

The man shot her a look, then smiled. "No. No crazy ex-husband or maniac creditor took a gun after her, if that's what you mean. Though if one did, I'm here to tell you they'd be the ones ending up in the hospital." He grinned again, more kindly than watchful this time, then abruptly stood and extended his hand across the desk. "I'm Tommy Lee McCall, Dottie's brother."

Elizabeth accepted Tommy Lee's firm, warm handshake. "Elizabeth Monette. Nice to meet you, Mr. McCall."

"And you, Miss Monette." He sat back down, his

eyes seeming to measure her in every way imaginable. "Now, what can I help you with?"

"You?" she said quickly.

"Yes, me. You see, last night when Dottie found out her doctor was sending her to the hospital in New Orleans, I agreed to help out here until she can come back. So unless you can wait for help for three or four months, I'm it."

Elizabeth now took a closer look at Tommy Lee. The first thing she decided was that he was impatient. Several things about his quick movements and penetrating gaze told her he was a man who made instant judgments, who never walked if he could run. He probably never chatted or shot the breeze with his neighbors, and when he wanted to ask a woman out, he spent little time working up to the question.

This last thought surprised her, and quite suddenly Elizabeth couldn't imagine discussing with Tommy Lee McCall anything as intimate, or as painful, as what she had come to confide to Dottie Betts.

"Well, Miss Monette, whenever you're ready," Tommy Lee said.

"I'm sorry, Mr. McCall. It's just that I was expecting to meet with your sister. We've talked several times on the phone. I've just two weeks ago moved back to Belle Fleur from Baltimore, and before I arrived I contacted her to look into a, uh, situation with my family, and I guess maybe I'd better wait—"

"Suit yourself," Tommy Lee answered abruptly. He leaned back in the chair, which creaked with his weight, then shifted one boot-clad foot onto the desk and looked up at the painted ceiling, as if mentally counting to ten. "But as I told you, Dottie's not going to be back in business for four or five months, if you ask me. So if what you need help on can wait until spring, that's fine. I'll tell her you stopped in.''

Elizabeth cleared her throat. "Did your sister mention my name at all to you when she passed her duties over?''

"Not that I recall. But then she didn't exactly have time to give me much detail on anything. Her husband was hovering, as was her little girl. Also, her bigshot doctor was pacing up and down, looking like Dracula's kin ready to suck some more blood out of her arm.'' He smiled. "Your name didn't come up, but I'm ready to listen as soon as you're ready to talk.''

"Yes. Well, it's not that simple.''

"It's not?''

"No.'' Their eyes locked for a moment, then she turned away. Elizabeth debated with herself as she stared out the second-story window at a massive magnolia tree, its branches black against the gray December sky. The city Christmas ornaments seemed cheerless, devoid of color, and hung limp from the overhead wires. "You should put a note on the front door, warning people that your sister is out for a while.''

"Good idea,'' he replied easily. "'Beware of Tommy Lee, All Ye Who Enter Here.'''

Tommy Lee chuckled, but was irked a bit by this woman's attitude. He had seen people beat around the bush to avoid talking about painful issues hundreds of times in his thirteen years as a cop, but this woman was a champ at avoidance. Tommy Lee glanced over her head at the clock. It was time to move her out of here, then call up Dottie and let her know his spur-of-the-moment agreement to baby-sit her private-investigation business was a bad idea.

He wasn't cut out for patiently waiting for someone

to spill their guts. He had realized this all morning while fielding calls and meeting with Dottie's other visitor, a sixty-year-old woman who wanted him to investigate her seventy-year-old neighbor, Miss Leticia Prince, who happened to be the mayor's aunt, for flirting with the postman and "delaying the official business of the federal government for several minutes every day."

He was a cop, ready to investigate, act and react. Actually an ex-cop now, as all those damned disability folks had insisted on calling him on their computerized forms. But he still felt and thought like a cop. And he realized as he stared at the gorgeous-but-closemouthed Miss Elizabeth Monette that he would muck up this private-investigator thing in short order if she and the other woman were typical of the clients his sister dealt with.

That decided, Tommy Lee moved swiftly. He stood and motioned toward the door. "May I walk you to your car?"

Elizabeth snapped out of her mulling and stared at him. "Excuse me?"

"Your car. If it's parked downstairs, I'd be glad to walk you to it."

"But our meeting..."

"I thought that was over, Miss Monette."

Flushing, Elizabeth stood and dropped her purse. She bent to get it, annoyed that Tommy Lee McCall watched, or rather stared, at her when she bent down. She retrieved her purse and stuck it into the gym bag. Standing quickly, she stiffened her back and glared at him, while she couldn't help noting that the man was well over six feet tall and not at her eye level, like most men. The blood ran warmer in her cheeks. He was incredibly attractive, and openly appraising her. She thought suddenly of what kissing a man with a mustache would be like, how the silky hair would feel on her lips, on her tongue.

Elizabeth experienced a moment of mental dizziness and blinked to regain her composure. She was not used to having this type of elevated physical reaction to a man, but as she met his glance straight on, she realized she had never really met anyone quite like Tommy Lee.

"Well, no. Our meeting's not over. I mean, well, I have some business and…" Her voice drifted off. She looked out at the dismal winter grayness. She didn't want to leave, but she was suddenly afraid he might just laugh at her if she began confiding her worries to him.

But the letter she carried in her purse was no laughing matter—not after what had happened in Baltimore. Twenty sleepless nights of worry overruled her generally cautious nature, and Elizabeth decided to take the plunge. She snapped open her purse and removed a folded white paper. Handing it to Tommy Lee, she said, "I received this three weeks ago."

He took it from her, unfolded it, frowning as he read. Before he could say anything, she handed him a second, smaller sheet, inside a pale yellow envelope. "This came yesterday. It was stuck under the front door of my parents' home, not sent through the post office like the other."

Still silent, Tommy Lee took the second note and scanned it, his face expressionless, but the playful light in his brown eyes disappeared. "What else?"

Elizabeth realized she'd been right about Tommy Lee's inability to make small talk. "Three weeks ago, before I moved here from Baltimore, someone may have tampered with my car. My brakes failed. According to the mechanic I took it to, it looked as if someone may have cut the brake line and the fluid drained out.''

"Were you hurt?" Tommy Lee asked dispassionately, though his eyes were gentle as he again inventoried her from head to toe.

Elizabeth touched her forehead, smoothing her heavy bangs. "A little bump. I always wear my seat belt. The telephone pole I hit took the worst of it."

"What did the police say?"

"Nothing. I—"

"What do you mean, 'nothing'?" he interrupted. "They didn't investigate? They have tests they can do easily to tell if the line was deliberately cut."

Elizabeth put her purse on the desk and sat down, turning her face away. She was suddenly more than tired; she was frightened. "I didn't call the police."

"Why the hell not?"

"Because I couldn't believe it was done deliberately," Elizabeth replied, her voice rising. "I don't have any enemies. It just didn't make sense. I mean, I assumed it was a prank, or some kids who went further than they meant to..." Her voice trailed off and she turned her eyes back to Tommy Lee. "But then I got those letters and I thought maybe it wasn't an accident."

Tommy Lee handed her back the letters. "Call the police. Now." He jerked his head toward the phone on the edge of the desk. "Use that one. Ask for Chief Foley. He'll probably come out himself, considering that second letter."

Elizabeth stared at the note Tommy Lee passed back

to her. The words were scrawled in feverish black felt-tip slashes and cut-up pieces of printed ads. "The Queen of Midnight means death for you. Leave town now," it read. The first letter's contents were identical, though the ink was blue. They were as insane looking and meanspirited a thing as she could imagine.

"I don't think I want the police involved," she said softly.

"Are you running for Queen of Midnight?" Tommy Lee replied, trying not to allow his personal opinion of the overhyped New Year's Eve event to seep out.

"Yes, well, I am 'running,' I guess you call it. I haven't lived in Belle Fleur for ages, but my parents moved back two years ago and got all involved in the committee again. It means a lot to them," she added. "You know what the Pageant is?"

"I know," he said in a controlled voice. Tommy Lee sat down behind the desk and picked up the phone. "Look, let's get the police down here and go forward from there." He began to dial but stopped when Elizabeth clicked the disconnect button.

"No."

Tommy Lee hung up the handset and crossed his arms over his broad chest. He stared angrily into Elizabeth Monette's vivid blue eyes. "This is serious, Miss Monette. If I were you, I'd be worried about my safety and that of my parents, and do what is right by them. This person came to your house, or sent someone. Either way, they know where you live. Who are your parents, by the way?"

She lifted her chin defensively. "Baylor and Luisa Monette. Of Fairbreeze."

Tommy Lee snorted and shook his head. "Judge

Baylor Monette, retired federal circuit-court judge? I'll bet he doesn't know anything about this little mess.''

"No. He doesn't. He's not been well lately, Mr. McCall, which is why I was hoping that your sister could quietly look into this and—'' She stopped abruptly and leaned forward to look him directly in the eye. "Listen, I'm not going to be elected Queen— some girl who has lived here her whole life and is planning on staying forever will be. That's certainly not me. So I think in another month, when the Pageant is over, this nonsense will stop. This is probably just some prank. But I don't want my parents to have to deal with a scandal, and bad publicity, which in a town like Belle Fleur will last for years. And I especially do not want my father worried silly over this.''

"So what exactly do you want?''

"I want to find out who is sending these notes and stop them from sending any more to my parents' house. Reason with them. Discuss it. Or at least let them know I know who they are. Surely that alone will stop it.''

Tommy Lee couldn't help himself from frowning over this woman's naiveté, but he kept silent. It wasn't his place to lecture Elizabeth Monette, socialite and babe in the woods, about the psychosis of anger and jealousy that usually prompted people to send hate mail and sabotage cars. "And if it doesn't stop when we find this person and confront them?''

"Well, we'll go to the police then. But I need to try this my way first.''

"And what's your way, exactly?''

"Discreetly ask around, I guess. Find out if anyone else who has been nominated has received letters like this. After all, I was thinking, I might not be the only one.'' It sounded lame to her and under the ex-cop's scrutiny, Elizabeth's felt her face begin to grow hot. ''I don't really know. I just want you to stop this hate mail.''

''Well, what do you suggest? Should I get a list of Queen of Midnight electees and ask around to see who is green-eyed jealous and crazy enough to try and kill her competition? Then I can sit them down and say 'No, no,' and put an end to this?'' Tommy Lee leaned back in the chair, his eyes full of challenge.

Elizabeth frowned and stood up. ''I'm not an investigator, Mr. McCall. If I was, I wouldn't be here talking to you. Of course I don't want you to go directly to the other women's houses. How discreet would that be?''

He pulled at the corner of his mustache and scowled. ''So you suggest what? I go talk to the maids who work at these young ladies' houses, spread the word around the street that someone snuck up to your door with a poison-pen letter? Do you honestly think in a small town like Belle Fleur that this kind of stuff is going to stay a secret?''

Elizabeth paled, thinking of the other matter she had wanted Dottie Betts to look into for her—one even more prone to be gossiped about if it became known. She pursed her lips together and grasped the strap of her gym bag. ''You're right. Maybe we should just forget this whole thing, Mr. McCall, if you can't handle this without creating a scandal. I'm sorry I bothered you.''

Tommy Lee leaned forward. ''What if another attempt is made to hurt you? One that's more serious. Or more successful?''

Elizabeth swallowed, stood and stared into his face. ''I'll deal with that when and if it happens. But I don't think it's going to, Mr. McCall.'' She held out her hand. "It was nice to meet you. Please try to figure out some way to discreetly look into this matter. If you can, please call me at my parents' tonight. We're in the book. I'll be home by six. If you can't come up with a way to do this, then please mention this matter to no one.''

"And if I say no, will you go to the police?'' he snapped back. Tommy Lee watched as she seemed to consider her words carefully.

"No. No, I won't.'' She walked toward the door and opened it, then flashed him the first real smile he'd seen on her face.

It electrified him. And unsettled him. Because he would bet a girl with a smile like that was born to be Queen of Midnight, despite her view on her chances. He scrambled to his feet and grabbed the door, then followed her outside to the elevator. Suddenly unable to concentrate, he felt mentally clumsy and physically on alert, as if something was ready to ambush him. He stabbed at a round red button on the wall, and for a few awkward seconds they stood and waited.

"When are they sealing the tally this year?'' he finally managed to ask.

Elizabeth raised her eyebrows at his depth of knowledge of the Queen of Midnight routine, but didn't ask how he knew so much. She would assume, if he was a native Belle Fleur resident, that he'd been raised on the lore of the ball and would be familiar with the procedure whereby the votes of the nine committee members were officially counted by the Caretaker, who was the only one who knew the identity of the Queen of Midnight until New Year's.

"Tonight, actually. There's a party for the debs at

the mayor's and the committee is meeting at the chairman's home for dinner. Then a round of dances, teas and parties for the next couple of weeks. Then the ball on New Year's Eve. But something tells me you know all that.''

The elevator pinged and the doors whooshed open. Tommy Lee nodded his head. He knew firsthand, but tried not to remember when he'd been personally involved in that phony ballyhoo. ''I'll be in touch tonight, Miss Monette. But don't count on my help. I'm not sure I'm going to continue to handle Dottie's business.''

''I'm sure you'll do what's right—for yourself, if not for your sister. I'll look forward to hearing from you.'' She nodded, the doors slid closed, and she was gone.

Tommy Lee's mouth dropped at her measured sarcasm. He stood there for a moment, then turned and let out a whistle. Elizabeth Monette might look like Alice in Wonderland, but she had a mouth like a high-school principal. He grinned, though he had to admit her implication that he was being selfish with his sister was correct. His cop instincts kicked his brain into a fast-moving scenario of what he would do if this were a police case he was investigating. Judge Monette was a high-profile, ex-federal official who probably had made a lot of enemies through the years. Had one of them set their sights on his daughter to even up an old score?

If they had, the Queen thing could be a smoke screen. And the culprit would have to be considered a much more serious threat than pretty little Miss Elizabeth seemed to be willing to consider.

Aggravated by the unfamiliar experience of having

no "official" capacity to act on his instincts, Tommy Lee slammed Dottie's door and hurried to the window to get a last look at Elizabeth. She was heading away from the office toward the crosswalk across from the Bonaparte Hotel parking lot where he figured she was going to catch a taxi.

Keeping her in his sight, Tommy Lee picked up the phone and dialed the hospital. Elizabeth Monette was a fine-looking woman. Dark blue eyes full of life. A perfect complexion. Streaky blond hair thick and shiny and swishy like silk against her shoulders. She was as tall as most men and straight-backed, with curvy legs and wide hips. Not one bit fat, but shapely. Carried her weight proudly, not worried about it. He liked that in a woman.

Tommy Lee chuckled. Too bad she was spooky as a horse with barn smoke up its nose. "Room 213," he said into the phone, then leaned back against the windowsill to watch. Elizabeth waited by the curb and dug into her purse for a tissue. *The two-minute-long traffic signal will tick her off,* he thought. He decided her profile was as nice as her rear view. She definitely would fill out a bathing suit to good advantage.

Or that empty space in your arms, a voice in his head added.

His annoyance at the thought was pushed aside by the "Hello?" from a female voice speaking into the receiver against his ear.

"Hey, baby, how are you?" Tommy Lee responded.

"I feel like day-old bread, kid," Dottie Betts replied. "Rich and Olivia are going to bring me some supper, then they're driving home for a few days. I don't want Olivia missing much school. I don't know what we're going to do for the holidays.''

His sister's voice sounded unusually vulnerable, almost as if she might cry—something he hadn't heard her do in more years than he could remember. Suddenly Tommy Lee knew Elizabeth's remark was on target. He was going to have to go through with his spur-of-the-moment agreement to help his sister out, at least until Dottie was emotionally stronger. ''Hey, just rest up. You know when those twin boys are born in a few weeks you won't be getting back-to-back hours of sleep for a long time. It's going to be fine, darling. You just rest.''

''I will, Tommy Lee. Are you in my office? Did you check my messages? Oh, and I think a woman named Elizabeth Monette might be dropping by any time.''

Tommy Lee glanced back out the window. ''She just left, as a matter of fact. Wants me to look into that hate mail she received.''

''Hate mail? Did she call the police or the feds? Sending crap like that through the mail is a federal offense, you know.''

''Yes, darling, I know,'' Tommy Lee said. ''I'm the cop, remember? But to answer your question, she did not call anyone but me. Wants me to discreetly check around. Thinks it might have something to do with the Queen of Midnight Pageant, for which she is an electee.''

Dottie started to laugh. ''Hmm. You think maybe your ex-wife and her little sister have gotten a little more determined to bring the crown into their family?''

Tommy Lee winced at the mention of his ex-wife

as he stared out the window at Elizabeth. She was tapping her foot impatiently, but had so far honored the red light's directive to stay put. Which showed good sense, since Government Boulevard was the widest, and usually the busiest, street in downtown Belle Fleur.

"I doubt Luvey Rose would stoop to murder so little Tammy would be Queen. She'd be too jealous. If she didn't risk the electric chair for herself a few years back, I can't see her doing it for Tammy."

"You never know about a woman's secret ambition, Tommy Lee." Dottie chuckled. "I think I told you that the night you married her."

Tommy Lee scowled. "I didn't call to rehash my pitiful one-year so-called marriage, Dottie. Now, what can you tell me about Miss Monette? She said she spoke to you a couple of times."

"She told me quite a bit concerning another issue she wanted me to look into for her. She didn't mention anything else to you?"

"No. So why don't you?"

Dottie hesitated for a moment. "Well, I guess I'm not breaking any confidences since you're working with me now. She asked about how hard it was to trace the birth parents of someone who had been legally adopted. She never said anything about hate mail, though."

"Adopted? Elizabeth Monette wanted to hire you because she was adopted?" Tommy Lee asked, completely baffled. Downstairs he saw the light on the opposite corner turn yellow and Elizabeth stepped from the curb. A man on the street across from her, wearing an army-fatigue jacket and a Walkman radio, appeared to be watching her as closely as he was.

Tommy Lee tuned Dottie out and rubbed the back
of his neck. Something about the guy was familiar,
and whatever it was struck a bad chord in his memory.

Dottie's voice distracted him again. "Yes, she knew
I had luck tracing adoptees. Hers is a pretty interesting
story. She said something tragic had happened to her
as a child, that she had blacked out the entire first few
years of her life because she'd witnessed something
horrid, but that 'repressed memories,' I think she
called them, kept reminding her of a woman she
thought might be her mother. She wanted me to find
out about her father because she was sure her mother
was dead."

"Pretty damn dramatic," he replied. "Do you think
she was telling you the truth about any of it?"

"She seemed on the level, but I haven't had much
success in checking out her story. She hadn't yet gone
to her parents about looking into the past, though she
said something about knowing the name of the lawyer
who handled things. Peach, I think his name was. I
tried him once, and talked to Dr. Heywood's daughter
in the hospital birth-records office. There's a file with
Miss Monette's name on it in my office, though...."

Dottie's voice filled Tommy Lee's head. But before
he could ask anything more, his eye caught the movement of a black sedan two blocks farther up Government. Though approaching the red light that had just
blinked on at the intersection, it appeared to be picking
up speed instead of slowing down.

Elizabeth was headed for the middle of the four
lanes of traffic. On the opposite side, the man with the
headphones suddenly turned away and hurried up the
street. The sedan was now in the farthest oncoming

lane, heading right for the place the blonde would be walking into a few moments from now.

Tommy Lee dropped the phone receiver, which crashed against the side of the desk, pushed open the groaning window and drew his lungs full of air. In a piece of a second he realized that if Elizabeth heard her name, she would stop and turn around.

And his voice would be the last thing she ever heard.

He threw his leg over the windowsill and glanced at the ground below. He hoped it wasn't more than the nine or ten feet it looked, hoped the thick bank of brown and woody azaleas were more comfortable than they looked, and with an eye on Elizabeth Monette, he started a quick prayer that his rebuilt left knee would hold him.

Then he jumped.

Chapter Two

Henry "Cracker" Jackson, ex-Belle Fleur cop, knelt on the oil-free garage floor and carefully replaced the stolen New York State license plates with the rightful Louisiana set. He stood, favoring his left hip, and tossed the white plates to his partner, Petey Connor. Petey sat on a folding chair watching and drinking directly from a bottle of tequila.

"Put these away, Petey. Hide them good. I think someone may have gotten the number, and we don't want them turning up in your possession."

Petey nodded and stared at the tinted windows of the Lincoln. "Think the dude got a good enough look to ID the driver?"

"What dude?"

"That cop, McCall. The one you said pulled the bitch out of the way."

"I don't know. McCall was a hotshot cop, but he ain't no Superman with X-ray vision or anything." Cracker walked around and stared at the driver's side of the car. "I think she's safe. She was wearing her 'disguise,' don't forget. Ray told me he saw the whole thing—said he didn't hear McCall give the pig on the scene any description at all, except of the car."

The two men shared a sarcastic chuckle over the silly hat and huge sunglasses their employer had donned before driving away in the car that nearly ran down Elizabeth Monette.

Petey got to his feet. "She's got company coming soon. Wants us gone. You ready?"

"We're not invited to her tea party, huh?"

Petey grinned, his gold-capped front tooth gleaming, and patted the pockets of the army-fatigue jacket for the keys to his van. "No way. We're gum on her shoes, partner. She don't even like that we're on her property at all, you ask me."

"Tough," Cracker replied, pushing a wad of gum into his mouth. He looked across the wide, neat lawn at the rear of the elegant white Colonial home. A purple silk banner, black fringed and sporting the silver mask logo of the Midnight Ball Society slouched against a flagpole in the weak December breeze.

Through French doors, adorned inside and out with red velvet bows, Cracker looked into the dining room where hundreds of tiny white lights twinkled on an enormous evergreen. Next to the tree, a black woman, in formal uniform and white apron, was setting a table.

"You get the money?" Petey asked, screwing on the lid of the bottle and tucking it into his coat.

Cracker tapped a thick, callused finger on the pocket of his jacket. "Five thousand dollars cash. But I'm still thinking maybe Ray should go over to the hospital tonight and visit." Cracker pulled his leather gloves on and motioned for Petey to follow him. "Come on. And don't forget those damn plates."

Petey nodded, a small shudder shaking through him at Cracker's second mention of Ray Robinson, the third man in on their three-man job. Petey didn't like

Ray. Didn't trust him. "I don't know about old Ray, Cracker. I watched him take a big notch out of that girl's brake line in Baltimore a couple of weeks ago. Big enough cut to have really hurt her, not just scared her like you told him."

"Didn't kill Miss Monette, though, did it?"

"Good thing. I'm not doing no time for a killing, Cracker. You never said nothing about a killing when you explained this deal to me." Petey rubbed his jaw, where a jagged scar marked the entry of his cellmate's blade during a prison fight three years before. The feel of the smooth scar tissue increased Petey's anxiety. "I can't do no more time. I can't."

Cracker stared at him hard. He hadn't said anything about a killing because that hadn't been the plan. The original plan, that is. As he stared at his partner, Cracker considered telling Petey their employer had told him that plan might have to change, but decided against it. Petey had been drinking a lot lately. He might shoot off his mouth at the wrong time. Better to wait a bit.

"Nobody's going to get killed and nobody's going to do no time, as long as they listen to what I say. Stop yapping. We got to go."

The two men shut the garage door and hurried around the back of the building to an alley where Petey had left his van. Lost in their separate thoughts, they drove slowly down the back street of Belle Fleur's most exclusive neighborhood.

FROM BEHIND THE UPSTAIRS curtains, the woman who had hired Cracker watched the two men drive off in the faded blue van.

As soon as they were out of sight, she sighed and

moved away from the window. Silently she wrapped her arms around her body, suddenly chilled. It was foolish of her to have agreed to drive the car today. She wouldn't make that mistake again. After all, she was paying Cracker Jackson more than enough money to do things without making herself vulnerable to exposure, like today.

Pushing Cracker and his cohort from her mind, she hurried out of her bathroom thinking of the only thing that mattered—the Queen of Midnight coronation, and the much-delayed glory of her family.

ELIZABETH'S BRUSH WITH death came so quickly and was so unanticipated, that it was only after she landed, hands and knees akimbo and forehead lightly scraping the concrete foundation of the streetlight at the corner of Government and Magnolia, that she experienced fear.

Which, when it came, flooded her body with hot shock as it filled her mind with cold, cramping terror. Before her brain could state a full sentence of disbelief, she heard the thud of another body and an accompanying groan from Tommy Lee McCall as he crashed into the curb beside her. The car that had thrown him there like so much roadkill sped off. She smelled the rubber of the auto tires and saw blood, and after those two sensations registered she cried out and crawled to Tommy Lee on her bruised and cut knees without feeling the pain.

"My God, are you okay?"

He lifted his bleeding chin up off the asphalt and tried to look behind him in the direction of the car that had sent them flying.

"The number! Can you make it out?"

Elizabeth turned her head but saw only the street and cars and people—people running and holding their hands over their mouths and pointing at her and at Tommy Lee. The shock on their faces scared her even more, as did the amount of blood she realized was on her blouse, dripping from the painful area over her left brow. Tommy Lee was white-faced except where his jaw was beginning to swell and bruise. He held his shoulder at an odd angle and continued to stare down the street, as if he could will the car that had nearly killed them both back onto the scene.

"I can't see anything," she said.

He looked at her, then gingerly reached into his jeans pocket and withdrew a clean handkerchief, neatly laundered. With a gentle move, he reached toward her and dabbed at the wound on her forehead.

Elizabeth blinked when he pressed the soft white cloth to her skin, then murmured, "Thank you, Mr. McCall. Thank you for pushing me out of the way." Elizabeth shut her eyes against the wave of pain that overcame her, while the surreal memory of the minute before replayed itself at fast-forward speed in her head. One moment she had been in the crosswalk of a busy boulevard, planning a workout at the gym followed by a long soak in a hot bath, the next moment she had heard the rush of an approaching car. She'd turned to see the steel grill of what seemed a monster-size sedan less than five yards away. Before she could scream, a hard-muscled arm had grabbed her around the waist and literally tossed her through the air to safety.

Her eyes flew open and she met Tommy Lee's anxious stare. "But where did you come from? Did you follow me downstairs?"

"I'm Superman. I flew." Tommy Lee grinned, then grimaced as his swollen cheek complained about his choice of facial expression.

Elizabeth's gaze darted across the street and she stared at the open second-floor window. "You jumped out the window. You jumped out the window?" she repeated.

"Don't go making a big deal out of that, Miss Monette. It ain't that high a window."

Before Elizabeth could express any more disbelief, or gratitude, which frankly made him uncomfortable as hell, Tommy Lee struggled to stand. He started ordering the bystanders around, directing them to get to a phone, call for an ambulance, and to, "Please stand back and give the lady some air." His gruffness belied his concern and helped him fight off dizziness. He stretched out his hand to help Elizabeth Monette to her feet.

Her pale skin was dry and taut as an eggshell, and it looked to him like her pupils were different sizes, which could mean a concussion or worse. An elderly gentleman was removing his topcoat and offering it to Elizabeth, who was turning him down, but Tommy Lee took the coat and draped it around her shoulders.

She slumped against him and he held her, feeling surprised at the jolt of pleasure he got from her soft body molding up against his aching ribs.

"I called the police, sir. They're on their way," a young woman told him, clutching a portable phone.

"Thank you, miss," he replied, heartened by the approaching wail of sirens. "Did you happen to see the car that nearly killed us?"

"Sorry, no," the young woman said. She handed

Tommy Lee Elizabeth's gym bag, which had an ugly oil stain down the side.

The crowd had grown to about twenty now, and they all began talking at once. It didn't sound like anyone had seen anything much that would help, Tommy Lee realized.

"I think the plates were out of state," Elizabeth said in a small voice. "Maybe New York."

Tommy Lee squeezed her gently. "Good job. How you doing?"

"Okay. A little shaky, but okay."

She showed no sign of moving away from him, which filled Tommy Lee with more pleasure than he'd felt for a long while. As the crowd murmured and the first emergency vehicle pulled up to the scene, Tommy Lee realized he was going to remember this day for the rest of his life.

But he couldn't say if that was because of playing superhero or because of meeting up with Miss Elizabeth Monette. With a snort of surprise at that thought, Tommy Lee turned his attention to the pair of paramedics now shouting orders at him, and grudgingly released Elizabeth to their care.

"How's BELLE FLEUR treating you, Miss Monette? I hear you've only been here a couple of weeks."

Elizabeth smiled grimly at the white-coated woman walking into her hospital room. "Great. I have sore knees, three stitches in my elbow and a goose egg the size of a moon pie on my forehead." It was an accurate summation of her rotten afternoon, though it left out her nitwit performance with Tommy Lee McCall.

That would have taken more time, and explaining, than Elizabeth had any intention of dealing with. A person had only so much stamina. And today had been almost as horrible as the day a few weeks ago when her parents had told her she had been adopted at the age of five.

As the memory of that scene flew into her mind, Elizabeth lowered her eyes, the fear and hurt of that day still fresh enough to bring tears. She kept her gaze averted, unwilling to share this pain with a stranger.

Elizabeth had never been any good at lying, and the last thing she wanted to do was explain to this efficient-looking doctor why she was about to cry. She touched the lump on her head, which pulsed under her fingers, hoping that injury would be a logical excuse. "All in all, I guess I'm lucky I wasn't hurt worse. No broken bones, I hope?"

The woman, who introduced herself as Dr. Katherine Smiths, clicked on the light behind the viewing screen and stared at the greenish X ray. "No, ma'am, not a single one." The tawny-skinned woman snapped off the light and turned to stare at Elizabeth.
"You look like someone I know. You got kin in Belle Fleur?"

Elizabeth flushed. Her first instinct was to ask, "Who do I look like?" but the reality of where that question might lead could not be answered without more preparation. "My family's over in Fairbreeze. There's no one here in Belle Fleur. Not that I know of."

"Humph. You put me in mind of someone, I just can't say who." Dr. Smiths shook her head and reached down to take Elizabeth's pulse. "I'm going to keep you overnight. Just to be sure you have no concussion. Wouldn't want you passing out at the Midnight Ball in a couple of weeks, would I?"

Surprised that even someone as sensible looking as Dr. Smiths was consumed with thinking about the ball, Elizabeth kept her voice neutral. "I'll stay tonight if you think it's necessary, but I'd really rather go home."

"You stay put." Dr. Smiths glanced around the empty room, then locked her dark eyes on Elizabeth's face. "Did you get a chance yet to call your family and let them know what happened?"

"No, not yet. I don't want them to worry."

The doctor's mouth tightened. Her deep voice, clipped and accent free a moment before, took on the drawl of those born and raised on the sultry Gulf Coast. "If you were my child, I'd want to hear two hours ago—not later—all about how you came to be nearly run down by a car and then tackled by a six-foot-tall brute smack into a Belle Fleur light pole. Worry or not, I'd call them."

"Thank you for your concern, Dr. Smiths. But my mother is out for the evening and my father has been ill, and he's the type who'll be bellowing to the police and ordering the FBI in here before he sees I'm okay. I'll be fine. They'll do better to hear this from me later tonight when I can assure them it's all over with."

Dr. Smiths crossed her arms over her chest and frowned.

Elizabeth quickly added, "I promise I'll call. They'll be home late tonight. I'll call them then."

The doctor stared for a moment longer but finally smiled. "Well, then, let me get another look at you."

While the woman's gentle hands completed their examination of her, Elizabeth marveled at the effectiveness of hospital grapevines in Belle Fleur, if Dr. Smith's knowledge of the day's events was common.

"Okay, now let me see those knees," Dr. Smiths said, pulling the sheet back. "Bend them for me, please."

Elizabeth winced as the adhesive bandages stretched unwillingly over her skin, but she obediently bent both knees. Dr. Smiths's requests had a way of sounding like orders. Even Tommy Lee McCall had seemed meek when the woman was sticking an IV needle into his hand in the emergency room. The looks and banter she'd observed Tommy Lee and the doctor exchange indicated they had a relationship that predated today's accident, but what that relationship was, Elizabeth couldn't guess.

She peered closely at the doctor, remembering when one of the emergency-room staff had announced, "Tommy Lee McCall really is something," to Dr. Smiths.

The doctor had ignored the nurse and turned to Tommy Lee. In a voice loud enough to be heard behind all the partitions, she'd said, "I see you're still living by the slash-and-burn version of police behavior. Leave your body to science when you die, Mr. McCall. I'm sure some eager little researcher can do her entire thesis on how your skull is harder than any other known human specimen."

This comment confirmed Elizabeth's conclusion that Tommy Lee McCall was considered by most who knew him as somewhat of a "character." Though in her book, the man who jumped out a window to save her would also always be considered a hero with a capital *H*.

"Can I get you anything from the gift shop before they close? You need a magazine or newspaper?" Dr. Smiths asked in a kind voice.

"No, thank you."

"What about a bottle of Coca-Cola?"

Elizabeth smiled, loving the familiar way the people she grew up around pronounced the soft drink with three syllables as "cok-cola." "No. No, thank you. I ate a big breakfast this morning and had lunch right before the accident. But thanks."

"All right, why don't you get some rest. I'll check on you later this evening." She smiled and turned to go.

Mustering her nerve, Elizabeth ventured, "Excuse me, Doctor, but before you leave, can you tell me how Mr. McCall is?"

Dr. Smiths slowly turned. "He'll live. This time. But don't you go spending any of your time worrying about him. This town is full of folks, especially female folks, who've worried about him for years, but he keeps on putting himself in death's sights. I don't think he'll be happy till he nails Satan or the devil nails his sorry behind. So you rest, and don't spend one single second worrying about Mr. Tommy Lee McCall!"

With that amazing advice, Dr. Smiths stomped out.

Elizabeth shut her eyes and tried not to think how bad her head and shoulder and elbow and knees hurt, while the surreal memory of the afternoon happenings replayed themselves at fast-forward speed in her head.

Elizabeth turned off the thoughts and reminded herself she had been delivered to safety. She touched the bruise on her head. Well, not exactly to safety, considering she had fallen onto the curb with both knees and almost crashed headfirst into the base of a concrete light pole. But Tommy Lee had saved her from certainly more serious injuries from the car.

"Thank you," she had managed to tell him, but she wasn't sure now if he had heard her. He'd been too busy directing people to see if they could catch a glimpse of the car license. When he had finally looked at her he'd grinned and said, "You okay?" then had reached out and gently wiped some grit off her cheek.

For some reason, she felt she would never forget this day as long as she lived. Though she realized she couldn't say if that was because of nearly being killed, or meeting Mr. Tommy Lee McCall.

With a snort of surprise at that thought, Elizabeth smiled, goofy from the pain medication she had swallowed earlier. "What a crazy man," she murmured, leaning back into her pillows.

"I bet I know who you're talking about."

Elizabeth's eyelids darted open and she turned toward the female voice floating through the warm hospital air. Standing in the doorway was a red-haired nurse, with green eyes and a drop-dead figure. She was beautiful and looked very familiar, though Elizabeth didn't think they'd ever met.

Elizabeth quickly turned to get out of bed, only to be stunned motionless by twin rushes of pain from the wounds on her legs. "Hello," she managed to say as she eased back down onto the pillow. "I'm sorry, what did you say?"

"I said if you're calling someone crazy, it's ten-to-one odds that it's Tommy Lee McCall." The redhead smiled wider and walked over to Elizabeth's bed. "Sorry to bust in on you hon. I'm Luvey Rose. Tammy's sister. When I heard one of the Queen of Midnight electees had nearly been run down, I decided to come up and see if there's anything I could do."

Tammy Rose. The pretty, petite, auburn-haired ballet dancer who was one of those most favored by the gossips to win this year's title. Except for their coloring, and the fact that this woman was about six inches taller than Tammy, they could be twins.

"That's very nice of you, Luvey. Thank you."

"It's a hell of a welcome back to Belle Fleur, Elizabeth Monette."

"That's true, but thankfully I'm okay." Elizabeth pulled the covers straight and patted the bed. "Please sit."

Luvey glanced at her watch. "I think I will take a load off. I've been on since six this morning. I'm in charge of public relations for the hospital. Give tours to the kids, fill them in on the story of how Dr. Bennett Heywood started this hospital with his little bother Tyler and built it into the best on the Gulf Coast." She smiled and leaned closer. "Of course, I don't tell them about how the two boys had a terrible falling-out some years back and the baby brother disappeared. Can't muddy up the public image, you know."

The woman's eyes, though tired, twinkled with interest. "Now that I've told you all that, why don't we order us some good old hospital food and you can tell me all about what the hell prompted my husband to jump out a window for you?"

"Your husband?" Elizabeth gasped and felt her skin glow warm.

"Well, ex-husband is probably more the truth, but I'm not one to give up claim to a man just because of a little old piece of paper. Though I did take my name back. Luvey McCall sounded like a cowgirl, where Luvey Rose is a little more dear, don't you think?"

Before Elizabeth could answer, Luvey launched into a series of stories starring the very same man Elizabeth had been ready to dream about. She found them all very interesting, which was how, she realized, she also found the man.

INDIA HEYWOOD HURRIED from her bedroom, her mind filled with all the work left to do downstairs. She had to check that there was enough mushroom quiche cut into bites for the appetizer trays she was to serve to her Midnight Ball Committee members. She had to remind Justine to brush egg whites on the rolls and make sure Noonie had put the tiny, crown-shaped pats of butter out on the buffet to soften.

Things had to be perfect for the committee. To-night's meeting was the night the secret ballot would be taken to elect the Queen of Midnight. India inhaled deeply to keep her excitement from overwhelming her and walked down the hallway.

Rapping sharply against the freshly painted door of the room next to her bedroom, she called out, "About ready, baby? Let me see how you look."

"Come on in, Mama."

She walked in and caught her breath. Her daughter, Rosellen, stood preening in front of the mirror. The white satin off-the-shoulder gown glowed against her pale olive skin. The young woman's green eyes spar-kled and her black hair bounced as she twirled in front of her mother's approving gaze.

"What do you think, Mama? Didn't Miss Hattie do a fabulous job altering this dress?"

India clasped her left hand against her constricting throat. She felt she might collapse, that she would have to at least cry. Not with pleasure over the sight of her only child's beauty, which she did not notice, but at the memories welling up inside her. She, India Sewell

Heywood, had worn that very dress twenty-four years ago to the day. Her mother had purchased it for her in London, from Norman Hartnell, the designer who had created Queen Elizabeth II's wedding dress.

It had been almost at this very minute, on that day, that her daddy had given her Grandmother Sewell's necklace—the very one grandmother had worn when she was Queen of Midnight in 1937—to wear with the dress. India moved her hand from her throat to her collarbone. She caressed the warm, familiar roundness of the pearls she was never without.

"You look a vision, darling," she told her daughter. Now, put your shoes on and come on downstairs and check the table with me."

Rosellen grabbed her mother's arm and pulled her over in front of the mirror. She laid her head on India's shoulder and smiled. "You *should* have been Queen of Midnight, Mother. You're still the most beautiful woman in town, just as Daddy says."

India's stomach tightened and a vein at her temple seemed to throb with her heartbeat. Her eyes misted over with the pain she still felt from the terrible injustice all those years ago, the disappointment that stung as if it had just happened. India reached over and patted Rosellen's hair. "You'll be Queen for both of us, darling. That's all that matters now."

"I don't think my winning is such a sure thing, if you want to know the truth." The girl's words tumbled out in a nervous rush. "Daisy's mama told us that Judge Monette's daughter had so many admirers, and now that Miss Lou, who was a Queen, has convinced her to let them put Elizabeth's name into nomination—"

"Stop it!" India's eyes blazed and she glared at her

daughter. "Don't listen to that foolish Daisy Gambeaux or anyone else. *You* will be Queen of Midnight this year. No one is going to rob me again. No one, no matter how sweet their mama."

Her mother's snarling comment froze Rosellen into silence. The young woman took a step away. "All I meant was that I don't want you to get upset. It doesn't really matter so very much to me, for myself, I mean—"

"It matters the world to me, as I've told you a hundred times!" India shouted, grabbing Rosellen's elbow. The woman's fingers bruised her daughter and left a damp crease on the filmy silk. "It's a birthright in our family. There have been three Queens in my family, and two in your daddy's! Who else do you know in this town with that kind of pedigree? Not Luisa Monette, or poor, pitiful Elizabeth. Not anyone else."

"I know, Mama. But it's not such a big deal like when you were young—"

"Shut up, Rosellen. Don't you see that if a girl's been Queen, she has that honor to recommend her for the rest of her life. She's set. She was *Queen. Queen!* Queen of two cities, Queen of the whole county. Can't you understand the significance of that yet?"

Rosellen looked down at the soft mauve carpeting. "Yes, Mama, I do. I just won't be able to bear it if you're disappointed. I couldn't live with that."

"Well, that's one thing you won't have to live with. Believe me, I'm doing everything I can to make sure that won't happen. Now, that's enough of this talk." India took a deep breath and reached up to correct an errant hair on Rosellen's head. "Hurry and get ready."

Rosellen smiled, but without any conviction. The

child was upset, India could see that. And if she could see it, then the others could, too. Which just wouldn't do. India felt in the pocket of her silk skirt and pulled out an unmarked prescription bottle and popped off the lid. She poured two tiny white pills into her palm and handed them to her daughter. "First, take these. They'll calm you down. We've got to make sure everything's perfect tonight, especially you."

Unenthusiastically, Rosellen took the pills from her mother. "Whatever you say, Mama."

"And wear those diamond ear studs instead of these silly little pearls you've got on now. You've got to sparkle, child. Mama can do only so much." With that comment, India hurried downstairs, leaving her daughter staring into space.

Once out of her presence, India no longer thought of Rosellen. Her mind was fully absorbed with her guests, all leading members of Farquier County society. She wondered how many of them had daughters who didn't seem to have a clue just how important, and necessary, it was to be named Queen of Midnight when it was your rightful God-given turn to reign. One more thing wasted on the young.

She shook her head. Her mother had made certain she understood the importance of it. They'd dieted for a whole year when it was India's year to be nominated. Both had lost enough weight to be size fives with nineteen-inch waistlines.

But India had lost, and her mother had never forgiven her for not being Queen.

Her face flushed with the shame of it. She knew people still whispered that her mama had died years before her time because of the scandal between India's daddy and that Elaine Gibbs woman. The killing of

Gibbs's husband, even though her father had proved self-defense, had robbed India of her crown. Her mother had threatened to kill the girl named Queen instead of her daughter. That caused another little brouhaha that was blown totally out of proportion. Her mother wouldn't have hurt a fly, everybody knew that. It was spite that got her sent away to the hospital.

Spite and Malice.

Well, those two handmaids of the Devil weren't going to rob Rosellen, India swore as she blinked away tears and hurried into her kitchen.

Some day Rosellen would understand. When she had a daughter of her own. Then she would see that sometimes a mother had to be willing to do things—whatever it took—to see that justice was meted out.

Even murder? a voice taunted inside India's head.

"Whatever," India whispered, having proved already that she was a much stronger woman than her own mama had ever been.

DOWNSTAIRS IN THE emergency room of Belle Fleur General, the afternoon traffic was thinning out. Only one patient remained in one of the curtained cubicles lining the examination room.

That one patient had a visitor who also wanted the complete details on what had happened out on Government Boulevard a few hours before.

"Not so fast, Tommy Lee. Hold on a minute." Frank Foley, the skinny chief of the Belle Fleur Police Department, licked the point of his eraserless pencil. "You say the car was a black four-door sedan with New York plates and tinted windows. Did you get any of the numbers?"

"No." Tommy Lee moved his lower jaw and tried

to sit up, then glared at the IV stuck in his left hand. "I didn't catch any numbers but there was some kind of parking decal on the left rear fender. Silver circle, with a seal of some kind."

"I understand you told Patrolman Duval in the ambulance that it looked like the car made a deliberate attempt to hit the girl. Is that true?"

"Yes."

Foley made an impatient noise. "Tommy Lee, I'm surprised you'd say something like that to Duval. You know his sister Binnie works for the *Press Register*. This damn story, starring a young lady I hear is in the running to be Queen of Midnight, is going to be splashed all over the front page tomorrow. You trying to give Belle Fleur as much bad publicity as you can?"

"Maybe the story will knock the debutantes back into the nineteenth century where they belong."

Chief Foley grinned. "All right, now. You know as well as I do that the Midnight Ball and New Year's Festival are the biggest moneymakers Farquier County has. Ain't nothing wrong with those gals and their mamas making a big fuss about it. It helps everyone, even you."

"Right. My ex-wife gets to buy a dress that I pay for with my disability cheque. That's a huge benefit to me. That and the strings of plastic beads I find in the bushes of my sister's house that the festival float-people throw with their drunken aim."

"Don't be disrespectful about the floats now, Tommy Lee. Remember, I ride on one." The chief glanced around him. "As do most of the doctors in this place. You'd better be quiet or they'll remove something from you by accident."

Tommy Lee grinned. "Don't all you boys have to keep it a secret that you're members of any of those float "societies"? I always thought the real reason for that was that you were a little nervous admitting how much you all enjoyed wearing glitter and masks and makeup."

"Just stop your teasing, Tommy Lee. I'm here to talk to you about this hit-and-run case, not encourage your twisted sentiments about the Queen of Midnight Ball or any of the festivities."

"Whatever you say, Chief."

"Right," he replied in a sarcastic tone. "Now, you told Duval you thought the car sped up. You're sure the driver wasn't maybe having brake trouble? Maybe he didn't see the light go red?"

"Yeah. What about the guy I saw watching Elizabeth from across the street? I'm telling you, it wasn't any damn accident."

"So you say."

"So I say. I know. *I* was there." Plus, Elizabeth Monette had told him about her other "accidents." His heart pounded in his ears as he pictured the lovely young woman lying bloodied on the street. He clenched his jaw and reminded himself there was no way he could bring up any of what he knew about Elizabeth Monette's other close calls without opening the "confidentiality" can of worms Dottie had warned him of.

"Okay. So give me a description of the guy you saw standing on the street." Foley made a scoffing sound but resumed writing.

"Five-foot-eight or -nine, skinny, maybe one hundred twenty-five pounds. Black hair, dark skin. Maybe a scar on his chin. Wearing a pea-green fatigue jacket with a red patch on the pocket, blue jeans and scuffed running shoes. Italian or Mexican, I'd guess. Had on headphones to a cassette player, or something.''

"Something?" The chief stopped scribbling. Tommy Lee winced. He knew the chief thought highly of Tommy Lee's great natural instincts for knowing something was getting ready to happen before it came down. Some of the men on the force said that it was because Tommy Lee had a bit of Cajun blood and could smell trouble like it was swamp gas. Foley thought it was something different called "talent." Many a time, he'd said Tommy Lee McCall was the most skilled cop he'd ever worked with.

"Something like what?" the chief asked.

"I don't know for sure, but it could have been a walkie-talkie, or a phone, even. My take now is that I think he was talking to the car. Directing it. Telling them where Elizabeth was.''

Foley swore softly. "Sounds pretty sophisticated for little old Belle Fleur, unless this gal is a Mafia princess or the President's daughter, or something. As far as you know, is Miss Monette any of those things?''

"She's in the running for Queen of Midnight. That's real important, according to you.''

"This is serious, Tommy Lee. Maybe the girl's involved with drugs.''

"She looks more like Alice in Wonderland than a drug courier.''

Foley ignored the statement. "You heard that Cracker Jackson's been spotted back in town?''

"He's out of jail already?''

"Yep. Bad cops do the minimum time required, just like all the other slimeballs we send away. I'm wondering if we should look him up. Ex-cops are the first place citizens go to hire a hit on someone.''

"You think Miss Monette's a hired hit?"

"Don't you?"

Tommy Lee avoided the chief's eyes. The first thing he was going to do when he got out of this bed was ask Elizabeth what story her parents had given her about her birth relatives. Maybe a clue there could explain this whole mess. "Might be worth someone's time to have a talk to old Cracker Jack, but I never saw him anywhere around today."

"You said the guy with the headphones was familiar, though. Any name coming to mind?"

"No. Maybe. Roy. Ray, maybe. I'm not thinking real clear." Tommy Lee put Elizabeth Monette out of his thoughts for the moment and flexed his left hand into a fist with a grimace. "Chief, can you call Katie Smiths back here and tell her to get this damn thing out of my hand. I swear, I told them there was no reason for this in the first place."

"Hang on, son. You've been in here enough times to know it's standard procedure for them to do a drip on a possible internal-injury case. Dr. Smiths will be here when she's good and ready. Told me she had to check Miss Monette first. Which is what I should do as soon as we're through. Now, what about the driver of the car?"

Tommy Lee closed his eyes and pictured the car. The windows were tinted, but when he'd swerved his body away from the racing hulk of metal, he had the impression of a hat and sunglasses. "Might have been a woman driving. Can't be sure. Couldn't pick the sucker out in a lineup of one, though."

"Too bad." Foley snapped his notebook shut. "I guess they'll keep Miss Monette overnight."

"Good. I shoved her pretty good. She's probably calling her lawyer right now."

"Look out, son."

Tommy Lee chuckled. "Wouldn't be the first woman to drag my sorry hide before a judge."

"Or the last." Foley laughed and shook his head. "I don't know about your way with the ladies, son. Miss Monette was shook up good when they brought her in, but she did ask about you. I'd be real surprised if she didn't realize by now you saved her life."

"All in a day's work."

"Right. All the ex-cops I know jump out of second-story windows to save strange women from hit-and-run hit men." The veteran cop folded his arms across his narrow chest. "What's the story with this little gal, anyway? She told Duval her family moved back over to Fairbreeze after living in Maryland for several years. Also told him she was on Government Boulevard because she'd had an appointment with your sister."

Tommy Lee managed a shrug despite the pinch in his arm. He knew his body was overreacting to being in the hospital, but there was nothing he could do to stop the little flames of panic from flaring up inside his gut. He wiped a bead of sweat from his forehead and beat down the memories of when he'd nearly died in the same emergency room.

He forced himself to meet Foley's sharp gaze. "She's looking for some information about her relatives."

"Information she needs to get from a private detective?"

"I guess so."

Foley stared harder. "I know we Southerners have a reputation for eccentric families, but that sounds pretty odd, you ask me."

"You'll have to ask her if you want anything more," Tommy Lee retorted.

"Why's that? Is the rumor I hear you're taking on Dottie's practice true? You claiming client-detective privilege on me, son?"

Tommy Lee scowled. "No. If I can't work as a legitimate cop, I'll stick with my oyster business. So if you want any more of Miss Monette's story, you'd better go ask her, or her daddy."

"Who's her daddy?"

Tommy Lee had a bad moment wondering if he had revealed something privileged, but decided the matter of Elizabeth Monette's parents wasn't going to be kept quiet long. He also realized Foley wasn't going to like his answer one bit. "Baylor Monette of Fairbreeze."

"Judge Monette?" Foley bellowed. "I thought his only child lived in the East."

"She did. Until a couple of weeks ago. Poor choice of relocation, it looks like."

"Hellfire, Tommy Lee. Why didn't you tell me this before? I'm going to have all kinds of people on my ass, once Judge Monette gets wind of this. You never were any good at handling the public-relations side of being a cop, you know that?"

"I know."

"Does Duval know who her daddy is?"

"I don't think so."

"Well, that's one small favor." He took a step to leave, then turned. "I'll give you a lift, soon as Doc Smiths says you can go. Your leg's not busted, is it?"

Tommy Lee stared down at his jeans, which had been slit from hem to mid-thigh on his left leg, and rapped his knuckles against the exposed knee. "Nope. Cut up like hell from those azaleas under Dottie's window, but I didn't break anything."

"Ribs?"

He felt the adhesive on his right chest. "Naw. Just pulled a couple of muscles."

"What about the bullet?"

The chief's question was spoken quietly, but the words seemed to roar in Tommy Lee's ears. The bullet Foley asked about was a piece of a .38 slug embedded in the bone behind Tommy Lee's right shoulder blade, three quarters of an inch from his spine. It had been fired a few months ago from a gun held by one Petey Conner, a local piece of work Tommy Lee had come upon in the parking garage of the Bonaparte Hotel. Petey hadn't taken to being surprised in the middle of holding up a couple from Indiana.

Petey had gotten away in the tourists' 1992 Cadillac.

Tommy Lee had gotten away with his life.

But he'd lost his career because of a disinclination on the part of the police department's medical review staff to allow him to continue on active duty. The bullet could move—and paralyze or even kill him—at an "inconvenient time," they'd argued.

"Regulations," the mayor had said in a phone call to Tommy Lee, breaking the news.

"Lawsuits," Chief Foley had offered, by way of consolation.

"Crap," had been Tommy Lee's response on both occasions.

But he knew there was nothing he could do about

any of it, then or now. Tommy Lee cut his eyes away from Foley. "Nothing on the X ray shows it has moved. Hooray. Hooray. I think Smiths was disappointed. She keeps telling me she's already bought a dress for my funeral."

"That was a damn fool thing to do today, man."

Tired and hurting, Tommy Lee felt his temper flare at his old friend. "I don't need you to tell me how to live my life, Frank. No one's paying you to do that anymore. I'm retired, remember?"

"It seems I remember that better than you do," Foley replied. "I'll get one of the patrolmen to bring your truck over from Dottie's parking lot and leave it out here for you. You stay put, though, until I get back. I just might drive you home myself." The chief stalked off like a hunting dog who had lost his duck in the smoke.

"Don't bother. I'll walk home," Tommy Lee called after him, but his voice sounded more tired than angry. He loved the wiry old cop like a father. He knew it had pained Foley when the forced-retirement ruling had come down—almost as much as it pained him to have lost his job as a cop.

Trouble was, even though he wasn't employed as a cop, he still felt and thought and instinctively acted like one. With a sigh, he stared at the clock on the wall opposite his bed. It read 4:47 p.m. He wondered if Elizabeth Monette had gotten herself something to eat. One of the three things she'd said to him from the time he had knocked her down to the time she had been wheeled away into the cubicle next to him was, "I'm really hungry."

The second had been, "Your boot is in the street."

The last was, "Thank you. I really owe you."

That remark, accompanied by her gentle fingers pressing a kiss onto his bruised face, was particularly nice. Tommy Lee grinned and felt his equilibrium restore itself a bit as the anxiety over the bullet finally took a step or two back into his unconscious.

Nothing like having a pretty woman thank a man. Especially that woman. She was special, with a one-of-a kind type of sweetness.

It never hurt to have a woman like Elizabeth Monette owe a favor. He could think of a few ways he'd like to collect it, once the blond beauty was back on her feet.

With a grin, Tommy Lee glanced back at the clock and wondered where that pain-in-the-butt Katie Smiths was. He was hungry now, too. He wanted out of this place. He pulled on the IV tube. The yank was repaid with a pain like an eel bite that didn't budge the needle at all. He decided to lie back and wait.

To his surprise, it felt good. Tommy Lee closed his eyes to shut out the pain and the past, but not before remembering how soft Elizabeth Monette's hair had felt when it had brushed against his face.

Chapter Three

"What are *you* doing here?" Tommy Lee asked, holding the door of Elizabeth's hospital room open with a bandaged hand. His torn jeans flapped around his banged-up left leg like a banner and his cowboy boots clicked against the tile floor. He walked toward Elizabeth's bedside without waiting for an answer from her or his ex-wife, whose glee at finding herself smack in the middle of his private life was obvious.

Luvey was sitting cross-legged on one bed, and Elizabeth was lying on her side on the second bed, facing the red-haired nurse. The two women had been giggling over empty dinner dishes as if they were a couple of sorority sisters at a slumber party.

"Tommy Lee!" Luvey exclaimed in a seductive voice. "I love your pants. Is that the new peekaboo style?"

Tommy Lee shot a chagrined look at Elizabeth, then pointed his finger at Luvey. "I don't know what you've been telling Miss Monette, but she is supposed to be resting."

Luvey stretched her long legs out in front of her and reclined. "How attentive of you to point that out.

But don't worry yourself too much about what we girls have been chatting over. I've been very discreet.''

"That would be a first," he retorted.

"How are you feeling, Mr. McCall?" Elizabeth interjected.

Tommy Lee turned toward Elizabeth. His pique changed to concern. The blonde had a lump the size of a crab cake on her forehead and the beginnings of a shiner the color of a Louisiana catfish under her eye. Her lip was cut, her arm had a swollen, wiggly black clump of stitches and her knees were wrapped in gauze that showed drying blood beneath.

"I'm fine, Miss Monette, but you look like you've been in a train wreck." He walked a step closer, feeling a tug of conscience at noticing she didn't have much on under the flimsy, blue-flowered hospital gown, mostly because he was enjoying the sight. "I'm really sorry about today, I didn't see any other way to get you out from—"

"No, no, please don't say you're sorry!" Elizabeth interrupted, pulling the sheet over her legs. "You saved my life! I was just telling Luvey all about it. If you hadn't—"

"Don't start gushing, Miss Monette. I didn't do anything any other person wouldn't have done."

"That's right, Elizabeth," Luvey chimed in. "Belle Fleur men are famous for throwing themselves out of windows and in front of cars. I've been telling Mayor Prince we should put out a special brochure advertising the fact."

"Luvey—" Tommy Lee pointed his finger again "—don't you think you should be getting back to work?"

"Work's over, darling. I'm on my way to a party."

She stood and stretched languidly. "But I know when I'm not welcome." She smiled at Elizabeth, openly appraising the young woman's charms. "You take care, now. Are you sure I can't fetch Miss Lou over here for you?"

"No, no, really. I'll wait and call my parents later. Thank you so much for coming to see me. It really is wonderful to meet you."

"The treat was mine. Anytime a member of the Queen of Midnight court is in trouble, all her sisters need to rally round." Luvey walked past Tommy Lee, but stopped and turned, a smile on her lipsticked mouth. "Have you taken over for Dottie, like I've heard, honey? I thought you always said you'd never be a private hire."

"Things change, Luvey. But the fact of the matter is…"

Tommy Lee pulled at his mustache. He felt uncomfortable about doing this in front of Elizabeth, but he realized he'd better speak now, so that both women would go to bed expecting nothing much from him tomorrow. "I'm not going to be handling Miss Monette's case, or anyone else's."

"But why?" Elizabeth blurted out, her blue eyes wide.

"I decided I don't have the time. I'm going to be tied up with the oyster business, and I can't see running into town every few minutes to check on things, or people. Besides, I don't have the temperament—"

"For god's sake, Tommy Lee. It's December. You can't oyster full-time in the winter! How are you going to earn enough money?"

"Shows what you know, Luvey. You harvest oysters in any month with an *R* in it. It's the shrimpers that work in the summer. So don't go worrying about my business. I'll be sure you get your check every month.''

The harsh-edged exchange drained Elizabeth of any energy she had remaining. She closed her eyes, wishing they would both leave.

"I'll be going, darling," Luvey called out. "You take care, now."

Elizabeth smiled weakly as Luvey sauntered out. She noted that Tommy Lee looked as miserable as she felt, which cheered her a little.

"I'm really sorry about this, Elizabeth," he began.

"It's okay. I wouldn't want you to rearrange your life on my account. I was trying to tell you I—"

"Will you quit yakking and hush up!" Tommy Lee yelled while holding both his arms in the air. "Please!" he said, turning toward her. "Let me assure you I'm not quitting Dottie's business because of our meeting earlier. But while I'm thinking of it, the reason I walked in here tonight was to tell you I've filled in Belle Fleur's police chief, Frank Foley, about the accident today. But I didn't tell him about Baltimore. I think you should, right away so he can advise the police in Maryland. I also think you should not try to go poking around in Belle Fleur till he gets a chance to look into things. You need to get over to your folks' in Fairbreeze and stay put for a while."

The room became very still.

"I'm not going to the police in Baltimore," Elizabeth announced, feeling let down that the reason Tommy Lee McCall had come into her room wasn't to see how she was doing. This small hurt gave a huffy edge to her voice. "I'm sure what happened in Baltimore has no connection to today. It was just a crazy coincidence. Besides, my reason for moving back to Louisiana was to find some things out about my family, and I don't think you have any right to suggest I leave. I intend to leave when I—''

"You obviously haven't thought real hard about what happened today. If you had, I think you'd see it's clear you should go home,'' he argued. "Especially since it's clear to anyone with a brain that what happened today wasn't any coincidence or an accident!''

Tommy Lee saw the shock and fear register. He was aggravated and light-headed, pain and hunger undercutting his concentration. He threw a look of regret at the empty plates and pushed on. "Look, Chief Foley will explain all this to you.'' He felt a wrench in his gut, but he wasn't sure if it was because of being hungry or because Elizabeth Monette, that strong young lady, was looking like she might cry.

He sat on the edge of the bed. "Don't worry about anything more happening, Elizabeth. Has Chief Foley been in at all yet?''

Elizabeth's color heightened. "No, he hasn't. I thought the other policeman, Patrolman Duval, took my report in the ambulance.''

Tommy Lee locked his eyes with Elizabeth's. "That was just a preliminary. Now, if you want my feelings on this, I think someone followed you, possibly all the way from Baltimore, to Dottie's office, watched for you to come out, then somehow signaled the car.''

"But, but why?'' Elizabeth gasped. "Why would anyone want to—''

"That's what I was just going to ask you,'' he replied grimly. "Why don't you tell me who you know that would like to see you dead?''

"Dead?" Elizabeth repeated, her voice nearly a shriek.

He stared at her. Her lips were stretched taut and her face was scrunched up as if she were trying to hold back tears. He gentled his voice, knowing his words would surely bruise, but his exasperation was getting the best of him. "Dead. They weren't playing touch football out there today. So I need you to do what I'm telling you. This isn't a matter you can brush off or ignore at this point. Dottie told me that you came here to find information about your birth parents. Could that have anything to do with what happened to you today?"

"But how could it? I...I don't even know who they are. They don't know I'm looking for them—I mean him, my father. My mother is deceased, so I'm told." Elizabeth stopped and twisted her sheet in her hand. "I haven't talked to anyone. My folks knew in September I was coming here to be in the Queen of Midnight Pageant and to decide about going for my master's degree, but they haven't said much to anyone except maybe to the..." Elizabeth's voice trailed off. Her mother and father had nominated her for Queen of Midnight, announcing, no doubt, that she was coming home in November in time for the luncheons and dinners and dances held in conjunction with that affair.

The warning letters in her purse suddenly seemed even more ominous.

"Except maybe to the what?" Tommy Lee pressed.

"Just the executive committee."

"Who are they this year?"

She sighed in irritation. "Nine members serve on it, all pillars of the community. The president of the bank, the mayor, the owner of this hospital, Dr. Bennett

Heywood, the publisher of the *Press Register,* lawyers. Surely you don't think one of them could...?''

Tommy Lee stared back. He had that feeling he knew too well. The buzzing, itchy sensation up the back of his neck that told him to be on guard. He felt behind him for the gun he'd stuck in his waistband under his jacket. Illegal as hell, now that he was retired, but the hard shape against his fingers made him relax a bit.

"Anyone is capable of anything, from what I've seen in life. It just takes the right circumstances, the once-in-a-lifetime situation, for some things to go wrong."

"Or right," Elizabeth blurted out. Tommy Lee was smiling at her.

"Or right. Like today. It was right for me to meet you, and everything else that happened was worth it." He pulled on the sides of his jacket to smooth it, embarrassed that he'd said too much.

"Thank you. I'm glad I met you today. Superman to the rescue."

"I'm just an ex-cop, Elizabeth. Now look, you try and get some rest. I'm going to go find out where the hell Chief Foley is. Soon as he gets his report done, you and I can decide how best to get you over to Fairbreeze, maybe even back to Maryland for a while."

"I'm not leaving Louisiana now. Too much has happened."

He liked what she might be implying, on a personal level, but he felt his temper heating up that she was taking such a blasé view of the danger. "You're damn right too much has happened, so—"

She held up a scratched hand to silence him.

"While you are talking to the chief, make sure he understands that I'm not going to let this scare me off. In case you hadn't noticed, Mr. McCall, I'm well past legal age. If I choose to stay in Belle Fleur, there's nothing you can do about it."

"I noticed, Miss Monette. But eighteen is the legal age in Louisiana, and I've got blue jeans older than that. It doesn't mean they're smart."

"Excuse me. I'm twenty-five, a college graduate, a teacher, and I resent..." Elizabeth allowed her voice to trail off as she realized he was baiting her. His brown eyes were gleaming and a grin was lurking under the mustache.

She sat up straighter in bed and gave him the look she reserved for really naughty eight-year-old boys. "Thank you for your concern. And for what you did today. But I'm staying put. I'll talk to Chief Foley and file whatever reports are necessary. If you aren't doing Dottie's detective work for her, that's fine, I can do what needs to be done myself. When I left the office today, I'd already decided that."

Elizabeth crossed her arms and stuck out her chin. "But in my opinion, nothing happened today that should change my mind."

Tommy Lee rested his weight on his hands at the edge of the bed. He moved so close to her that his dark hair brushed the skin on Elizabeth's naked arm, and she shivered.

"Nothing except your butt nearly got flattened like an empty soda can on Government Boulevard by some nutcase who's still out there." He threw a glance at the night sky darkening her window. "And he knows you, probably even knows you're in here getting patched up, but we don't have a clue about him. How safe does that make you feel?''

Elizabeth felt the heat from his skin and from his breath, saw the muscles tighten in his neck and felt her face warm even more from his nearness. She had an urge to kiss him to make him shut up.

But instead she pulled her arms tighter around her chest and told herself not to let the fear pumping along with the blood through her veins show in her voice. ''Don't try to scare me, Tommy Lee.''

For three seconds, which felt a hundred times longer, Tommy Lee stared at her. Suddenly he stood, touched his bandaged hand gingerly to his right rib-cage, and sighed. ''This conversation isn't over.'' He turned and limped out, his shredded pant waving against his bare leg.

Elizabeth watched him. When the door closed she shuddered. She felt exhilarated, determined, and exhausted. She closed her eyes, stopped fighting the medication she had taken an hour ago, and fell immediately asleep.

WITH A JOLT, ELIZABETH woke. Her room was dark and the dinner dishes had been cleared off the table at her bedside. Her heart was racing and a pulse was pounding in her ears as she turned to look at the clock mounted on the wall opposite the foot of the bed. It read 8:25 p.m.

She had slept nearly two hours! Elizabeth took a shaky breath and felt her forehead. The knot seemed to be smaller. Her stiff body relaxed a bit as she woke up completely. She looked toward the open door. The low sounds of people talking, a metal tray scraping against a cart and the hum of television noise drifted in. Elizabeth wondered if Chief Foley had come to see her yet.

Slowly she got out of bed and went into the bathroom. Her face was puffy and unbelievably bruised, so she closed her eyes against the reflection and washed. She brushed her teeth and gave herself a cautious rubdown with washcloth and soap, too weary to even think of standing in the shower. Digging through her gym bag, she pulled out clean panties and a pair of sweat shorts, a T-shirt and socks.

She stared down at her knees and shook her head, aware of a fleeting memory of a blond woman hugging her and saying she was going to be all right. Throughout her life Elizabeth had experienced memories of a blond woman helping her, and had not had an explanation for who the woman was.

For some reason, she'd never asked her parents about it.

Now, in her heart, Elizabeth thought it must be her mother.

The possibility made her smile, though just as quickly the smile faded because there was no way she'd ever know for sure. Wearily she clicked off the light in the bathroom and crawled back into bed.

Hunger clawed at her stomach. Deciding she did have enough energy to eat something, Elizabeth reached for the pad beside her to signal a nurse, but before she could press it, she heard someone walk into the room.

A tall, olive-skinned doctor walked toward her. He was smiling. She noted he had a terrible scar, and found herself wondering why he hadn't had surgery to hide it.

The doctor was carrying a stainless-steel tray with

a napkin draped over it, and she thought that he looked more like a waiter than a physician. The dim light glinted off his wire-framed glasses.

"Miss Monette?" he said in a voice that carried a strong accent that marked him as a native of the Southwest or Mexico. "Good, you're awake. I'm Dr. Swan. How are you feeling?"

"Better. Thank you." Elizabeth was unsettled by the doctor's presence. Something about him reminded her of someone else, someone she did not like, though at that moment couldn't attach a name to him. She looked beyond the white-coated man toward the door, noting he had closed it behind him.

"Where is Dr. Smiths? I thought she was coming by to see me tonight."

"She'll be by later, I expect, during the ten-o'clock rounds," Dr. Swan replied. He walked purposefully around the bed and set the tray on the swing-top table beside her. Dr. Swan stared at Elizabeth for a moment, then removed a small penlight from his pocket, hit it against the palm of his hand twice, then flipped it on. "Let's get a look at those eyes."

Elizabeth sat back and stared dutifully into the light that Dr. Swan shone into her left eye, then her right.

The doctor stood away from her and said, "Uh-huh," slipped the penlight into his coat pocket and removed a thermometer. "Open up, now. Don't bite down with your teeth. This will just take a couple of minutes."

Elizabeth felt the cool stick of glass slide under her tongue. It surprised her Dr. Swan was taking her temperature the "old-fashioned" way. He hadn't shaken the thermometer down, or wiped it off with anything.

Earlier, the nurses had used the Digitemp machine on the wall, which gave instant readouts.

Uneasy, Elizabeth watched as the man looked around the room, glanced at his wristwatch, then at the door. He rocked back and forth on his heels, as if he were in a hurry. She thought it odd he didn't look at the chart at the end of her bed, but then scolded herself for being jittery.

Elizabeth's gaze fell to his hands. They were small and bony. He wore a ring with a black stone and a heavy gold band. His fingernails were dirty!

She gasped and nearly choked on the thermometer before she managed to pull it from her mouth. A doctor with dirty hands? Panic bubbled in her brain as she tried to think clearly what to do.

"I don't think that's done yet, kiddo," Dr. Swan said, his eyes sharp behind his glasses. He reached for the thermometer but Elizabeth tossed it onto the tray. She slid from the bed onto the floor, putting the hospital bed between them.

"Who are you?" she demanded, wishing she could reach the signal pad, fighting an inclination to scream.

"Why, I'm Dr. Swan. What's the matter, kid? You feeling a little nervous after your close call?" He leaned toward her and patted the bed, darting a glance behind Elizabeth at the closed door. "Just jump back up under these covers, and I'll give you your shot and you can go to sleep. You'll forget all about this in the morning."

For a moment Elizabeth felt doubtful. Then foolish. Of course, Dr. Swan was a real doctor. Who else would he be? She was being silly. "I'm sorry. I guess I'm—"

A loud knocking on the door to her room cut off her words.

"Elizabeth? Elizabeth, open the door!"

She turned and stared in the direction of Tommy Lee McCall's voice. The door must be locked. At the same instant that Elizabeth realized Dr. Swan was the only one who could have locked it, and that there was no good reason for him to have done such a thing, the man leaped across the bed and grabbed her by the hair.

Elizabeth screamed with pain as she and the man fell to the floor. She kicked and clawed at him, while the pounding on the door got louder.

He struck her in the face and she cried out. Desperate to make him let go, she bit the back of his hand. The man howled and pulled her hair again, then forced them both down flat on the floor. With one hand, he held both of her hands against the cold linoleum. She wiggled and yelled, then saw the syringe.

With his free hand he was pressing his thumb against the end, readying it.

Good Lord, she thought. This man was here to kill her!

"No!" Elizabeth screamed, kicking into his arm with both her bandaged knees. The force of her movement sent the syringe flying through the air and crashing into the wall where it splintered with a tinkling, brittle sound.

"You bitch!" the man hissed, then raised his fist to hit her but she yanked her hands free and rolled away just as the door was kicked open and a wild-eyed Tommy Lee McCall rushed into the room.

"Tommy Lee!" she screamed in terror.

His handsome face was contorted with anger. He held a drawn pistol in his hand and his voice was deadly. "Don't even think of moving, you sorry son of—"

"My God!" Dr. Katherine Smiths screamed out behind him, obliterating his last words. "What on earth—?"

Dr. Smiths's arrival was all the distraction the man in the doctor's jacket needed. He grabbed Elizabeth again and pulled her in front of him like a shield, the broken stem of the thermometer pointed at her throat. "Your bullets are going to have to go through this little honey first. Back off, tough guy!"

Tommy Lee stayed where he was inside the doorway, and heard Katie Smiths run down the hallway for help. He knew the man in front of him. Ray Robinson, local small-time felon, had evidently been hired for some big-time mischief. The guy was scared. And Tommy Lee knew from experience that scared punks acted without thinking. Slowly he lowered the gun. "I won't shoot. But I'm not letting you take her out of here."

"Not my plan, man. I wasn't paid to tumble on a kidnapping beef." Robinson pulled Elizabeth, who was glaring fearfully at him, to her feet and dragged her with him as he walked backward in the direction of the bathroom. Before Tommy Lee could react, the man shoved Elizabeth to the floor and ducked into the lavatory, slamming and locking the door behind him.

Tommy Lee rushed to Elizabeth, his arms gently lifting her in a hug against his body. He kept his gun trained on the bathroom door as he moved them both back in the direction of the hallway. "Watch the glass on the floor, now. When I get you to the hallway, run like hell to the nurses' station and make sure Katie called the police."

Elizabeth shook her head and tried to catch her breath, then realized she was crying and shaking and bleeding all over Tommy Lee's jacket. When they got to the doorway she took off, but didn't have to go far. Two hospital security guards and a uniformed Belle Fleur cop were running down the hallway toward her room, trailing two men in green scrubs along with a winded Dr. Smiths.

Katie Smiths embraced her and sat her down in a chair, then started shouting orders to two nurses who stood hugging each other in front of the reception desk. A few seconds later the cop and the two guards ran past her in the opposite direction toward the elevators, followed by one of the interns and Tommy Lee McCall.

"Is he still inside?" Elizabeth asked in a shaking voice as Tommy Lee came to a halt beside her chair.

"Nope. Slimeball took a ride down the laundry chute in your bathroom to the basement. Probably headed back to the rock he crawled out from under by now." Tommy Lee looked Elizabeth up and down, then wiped a tiny glass chip from her cheek. "You doing okay? He didn't hurt you before I got there, did he?"

"No, no. I'm fine," she replied, unable to control her shivers.

"Leave her alone, Tommy Lee," Dr. Smiths said. "I'm going to put her in another room and examine her. Come on, Miss—"

"Let her go, Katie," he interrupted. He put his arm around Elizabeth and darted a glance in both directions of the hallway. Her arm was bleeding where her stitches had been pulled, and she had a scrape on the side of the face, but all in all she seemed no more badly damaged than earlier. "Anything feel broken?"

"I don't think so," she said. One of the gauze bandages had been pulled off her knee and she tried to tape it back on. "I may never wear shorts in public again, but I'm sure these will heal."

He let go of her and jammed his pistol into the front of his jeans, and then took off his jacket and draped it around her shoulders. He told the intern standing beside him to run and get Elizabeth's things out of her room, then checked out her feet. She was only wearing a pair of pink bobby socks, but he wasn't waiting around to find shoes.

Without another word he slipped one arm around her back and a second under her legs and picked Elizabeth up in his arms. She was tall but light enough for him to hold her without breathing hard. "Let's give those knees a rest. We're going out the back way. My truck's parked there. Dr. Smiths, tell Chief Foley I'll call him when I get Miss Monette tucked away somewhere safe."

"Put her down this instant, Tommy Lee McCall!" the doctor yelled back, her hand slapping against his elbow. "Are you crazy? You can't take her out of the hospital. She needs medical care!" He appeared not to hear her, and slammed the door behind him.

Chapter Four

Elizabeth pulled the blanket Tommy Lee had produced from the back of the pickup closer around her shoulders and tried to keep her shivering to herself, but Tommy Lee must have heard her teeth rattle. He looked at her closely in the darkened space and turned on the truck's heater.

Every inch of her ached, but she felt the exhilaration of someone who had gotten away with something unlikely. She was supposed to be at a dinner party with a lot of people she hardly knew and a couple she didn't like, but instead, here she was, in a pickup truck with a handsome stranger, on a dark road heading who knew where, and it seemed almost like fun.

You're losing it, Elizabeth, she said to herself.

"I bet you wonder where the devil I'm taking you," Tommy Lee said suddenly, flashing her a sideways look. "Don't worry," he continued, dead serious. "No one will find you where we're headed."

"That's exactly what I am worried about," she said, a nervous laugh erupting from her throat. "After what's happened today, I think I need to ask you to tell me."

"My place."

Oh, good, she thought, not feeling safe at all, but liking it. They were on the causeway, crossing the dark, foamy water of the Mississippi River. The truck's heater crackled and the tires rumbled, gently vibrating under the old pickup's frame. Tommy Lee pointed to the lights on her right. The Fairbreeze Marina and Yacht Club hosted an annual Christmas parade on the river, and the boats were all decked out with sparkling gold-and-white lights, or the traditional multicolored bulbs. The reflected liquid rainbow against the glassy blackness of the water was as mysterious and thrilling as the northern lights.

"My house is about six miles that way, beyond the boats. My housekeeper, Mrs. Lane, will get you something to eat and you can call your folks. You should probably stay here instead of going home."

"Why?"

Tommy Lee seemed to try not to frown, but she could see he felt her question was pretty dumb. "Why?" he echoed. "Because someone has tried twice to kill you today, in my ex professional opinion. If the third time's the charm, wouldn't it be smart to not be where they'd expect you to be tonight?"

"I don't appreciate your sarcasm, Mr. McCall."

"And I don't appreciate your holding out on me, Elizabeth," he retorted. "Why didn't you tell me you were looking for your birth parents earlier today? Why keep the main reason for coming to Dottie a secret from me?"

Elizabeth opened her mouth to tell him it was none of his business, but closed it and snuggled closer to the passenger door. "I'm sorry. I got cold feet. You see, this whole thing about being adopted is new to me. I guess I'm not being very mature."

He was quiet for a few seconds. "I think it's pretty mature to do what you're trying to do. Not very smart, maybe, but clearheaded, at least."

She grinned, a little annoyed with herself for feeling so pleased that he approved. "I take it you talked to your sister. How is she?"

"She's great. Just great. Don't change the subject," he added.

She didn't blame him for being irritated; she was irritated herself by her own behavior and lack of coherent explanation when they had first met this afternoon. She was also more than a bit baffled by how quickly her rather boring but well-ordered life had been turned on its ear almost the instant she had been told the news she was adopted.

For a moment Elizabeth had felt a rush of anger at Miss Lou and the judge. They shouldn't have waited all these years to tell her. They shouldn't have hidden the truth. It had made it much more shocking and thrown her into turmoil to discover the facts at twenty-five, facts she should have known at age ten and maybe should have guessed at even earlier.

She shook her head in wonder at the events of the past few weeks. She had left a secure job, in a city she felt much more at home in than Fairbreeze, primarily to track down a mystery she had little hope of solving.

And for what reason? she asked herself silently. What would solving the mystery of her birth fix? Was her urge to know so great that it was worth placing herself in danger, digging around in issues that were best left buried? Elizabeth had always been a big "fixer." She was the one people asked to organize dances, fund-raisers, the second-grade field trip.

She was the one who had been together enough—on the outside, at least—at age ten, to give her girlfriends advice on cheating boyfriends and broken hearts. She had lately even begun to take care of things for her parents, hiring movers for Miss Lou when they migrated back to Fairbreeze, seeing to it that her father's medical records were sent to Tulane's best heart doctors in New Orleans before they left Baltimore.

But ever since she'd learned about her adoption, she had felt disorganized, off-balance, off-center, as well as angry and confused. Mostly confused. Confused about what she really wanted to find out. Did it matter who her birth parents—her biological mother and father—were? No, not in any way that would affect her identity to herself, or her self-confidence about her place in the world.

But it did matter, and suddenly, sitting in Tommy Lee McCall's drafty, rattling heap, Elizabeth felt her heart present the answer to her own question. If she found out the facts about her own origins, she would understand once and for all the memories, half-formed and nightmarish, that had intruded into her life for as long as she could remember.

Since she'd heard Miss Lou and the judge say the words that she was adopted, she had known that the secret thoughts she had been fearful and ashamed of did define her in a way that was unhealthy—because she had never known what they meant. But now she did. She now knew for a fact that they weren't nightmares.

They were memories.

Memories of real events, real people.

Memories of her life. Memories she had hired

Tommy Lee McCall to help her chase down, without telling him what he should be looking for.

"I'm sorry for all this," she again said to Tommy Lee softly. "I thought about telling you the whole truth today, but the hate mail and the accident with my car seemed more pressing, and less personal. I didn't mean to mislead you as to why I had originally called Dottie. But it is really hard to discuss."

"You've got nothing to be ashamed of," he told her, accurately reading her emotions. "You were just a kid, with no choice in the matter of what happened in your life. It's natural to want to know who your kin are."

"Even if they've proved they don't give a damn about you?"

He made a sound in his throat, nonjudgmental and serious. "It's hard to read intentions when all you're looking at is the outcome of something. I wouldn't jump to any conclusions that your family didn't give a damn, just because you were adopted."

Her skin grew clammy. Suddenly she didn't feel ready at all to take on the past. "Look, I can't see having you go looking into that issue right now, what with what happened today. So why don't we just drop it."

"Why?" Tommy Lee's voice had gentled.

Elizabeth, however, was unable to calm herself. "Well, because it's obvious that what's really going on here is that someone's trying to scare off a Queen of Midnight contestant, for some sick or jealous reason. But a reason that has nothing to do with who my parents were."

"I agree it's fairly illogical to think it's all connected, but we've got to consider it, Elizabeth. It's a mighty weird coincidence.''

She lost her train of thought again and let herself smile over the fact that Tommy Lee had said "we." Then she forced herself to concentrate on the issue at hand. "I don't think so. It's just coincidence. One has nothing to do with the other. Probably."

"Hey, I'm trying to figure out how to do what you asked me to do today. That's all. If you don't like my suggestions, you're the boss. Fire me. But if you can see the sense in what I'm saying, then think it over. Real carefully. Start with telling me if the guy tonight was familiar in any way."

Elizabeth felt the tension go out of her arms. She nodded. "Okay. I'll consider it." Turning her thoughts back to the events of the day, panic again began to build as she remembered the dark car bearing down on her, and the fake doctor's grimy hands on her throat. "The man posing as a doctor might have been at the accident today. He seemed familiar."

"What about the car? Ever notice one like it parked near your place in Baltimore, or out by your daddy's place in Fairbreeze?"

"No, but I thought they were New York plates."

"Yeah. Do you know anyone in New York?"

"No."

"Did your parents mention that anyone in New York was connected to your adoption?"

"No."

"Do you think you could testify that the guy in your room tonight was the same man standing across the street today right before the accident?"

A hazy picture of someone wearing earphones flitted through her brain, but no discernible memory of a face came into focus. "Sorry, Tommy Lee. I don't usually stare at strange men."

"Right. Not good manners for you debutante electees," he teased.

"I told you, I'm not a debutante. I'm only going along with this Queen thing because of my folks." Elizabeth crossed her arms over her breasts. "And by the way, I don't think you have any room to tease me about the Queen of Midnight Pageant. Your ex-wife told me you are no stranger to the electee scene in Belle Fleur. I think she mentioned you two met at a ball one New Year's Eve."

Even in the truck's darkened cab she could see his tan cheeks glow. Since having met the gorgeous Luvey, Elizabeth hadn't been able to stop wondering if he was still carrying a torch for her.

Not that it mattered, she told herself, but held her breath in order to hear every intonation in his voice when he replied.

Tommy Lee disappointed her by making no comment on his ex-wife's tales. "When did your folks tell you about the adoption?"

"Early September. They came to do some bank business and we went out to dinner. They both seemed so nervous about something, I took them to my apartment for dessert and coffee. They told me while I was cutting a pie." She swallowed hard, remembering her inability to eat a bite after the news and the odd, floating, disengaged way she felt.

"Did they say why they told you, after all those years?"

"My dad said since he was sick, he was worried he wasn't going to get a chance to explain things to me. Mama said they had always intended to tell me when

I was a teenager, but it had never seemed the right time.''

Tommy Lee braked for a cat that raced across the road. ''When did you call Dottie? Do you remember the date?''

''Yes. I decided before the middle of September not to return to my teaching job. I thought I'd better come to Belle Fleur and see what I could find out. I called Dottie on October 31. I remember the kids trick-or-treating when we were talking. Why?''

''And when did the car trouble happen, exactly?''

She blinked hard, trying to remember. ''November 8th. The movers came to drop off boxes.''

''And the first letter arrived when?''

''I don't know. Maybe that day, or the next. What are you getting at with this time line?'' Elizabeth demanded, sitting upright against the cold vinyl seat.

''You've only known about the adoption for a few weeks, Elizabeth. It just looks to me like as soon as you contacted Dottie, things started to happen. I'm not sure your looking for your parents isn't connected to these mishaps.''

''What are you saying? Someone is trying to kill me because I talked to your sister a couple of times about looking into the whereabouts of my parents? Why would they mention the Queen of Midnight Ball in the letters, then?''

Tommy Lee chewed that over, then spoke simply. ''Maybe they thought it would be easier to warn you off that way.''

''Warn me off? Who would care about me looking for my parents?''

He glanced at her. ''Maybe they don't want to be found.''

Elizabeth's skin grew hot and her stomach churned. She didn't know why, but his cruel hypothesis was too much to think about. "That's absurd. There's no reason to think anyone but you knows I spoke to your sister about all this."

"Maybe," he repeated.

"Besides, what kind of people would try to kill their own flesh and blood just because they came looking for information?"

He let out a breath. "I've been a cop for thirteen years, Elizabeth. I've come across plenty of families who have done as bad, or worse. You know what they say—crimes of the heart are the cruelest, and the most common."

"I can't believe this. I just can't believe this."

"Well, maybe I'm wrong. Why don't you tell me what you know about your biological parents? Dottie says you told her you thought your mama was dead."

A dull roaring had begun in Elizabeth's ears. She felt the familiar panic and loss of equilibrium. Inside her skull she heard a woman screaming, far-off and lonely. Elizabeth blinked quickly and tried to push away the thoughts she had been haunted by forever.

"All I know is that Miss Lou and the judge were approached by a business associate, an attorney named Emmett Peach. Mr. Peach told them he knew of a child he said had been orphaned in a violent incident in Alabama who needed a good home. He knew they were interested in adoption, and they took me. According to them, Peach said he wasn't at liberty to discuss anything further with them about my background, as the courts had sealed my birth certificate."

"How old were you?"

"Five."

"Do you know if this Peach guy is still around?"

"No." She took a deep breath. "Actually, that's where I was hoping Dottie would start to look for me. I gave her his name. We'll have to check if she tried to contact him. Maybe if he is retired or something, he won't be so closemouthed about telling us more details about the adoption. Especially when we explain about what's been happening."

"Don't count on it," Tommy Lee replied. "Most lawyers I know fit the joke about the skunks."

"What joke?"

"What's the difference between a dead skunk in the road and a dead lawyer in the road?"

"Tell me, if you must." Elizabeth smiled, despite their bleak discussion.

"There're skid marks in front of the skunk."

She laughed, amused as much by his grin as the slanderous joke. So Tommy Lee McCall, for all his tough-guy image, enjoyed a little corn. She liked that about him.

Another mile of causeway asphalt rolled beneath them before Tommy Lee spoke again. "Dottie also mentioned you have some specific memories. Can you tell me about them, or anything else you do know about your folks?"

Elizabeth sighed. The night, which only moments ago had seemed so full of adventure and promise, now seemed oppressively chill and bleak, as if the stars in the December sky had receded farther away from Earth, leaving it a dimmer, colder place. The roller-coaster effect made her suddenly realize she was exhausted. "I have a couple of pictures in my head— probably repressed memories, according to a psychiatrist—that are pretty horrible. They almost make me feel like I'm going to black out, they're so vivid, but unreal, somehow, like I'm watching them from up high, or far away. They're of a woman screaming. But I don't remember anything else. Except a tall man, wearing white. Who read to me. And maybe…''

Her whispered words hung between them in the car. Tommy Lee pulled off the interstate and headed down a gravel road. The sound of his turn signal clicking and the old tires slipping against the crushed stone echoed inside the truck.

''Maybe what?'' he finally prodded as a small, white wood-frame house came into view.

''I think the woman screaming was blond, like me. And I think she was my mother.'' Elizabeth added, then surprised them both by bursting into tears.

TWO OF THE FOUR IMPOSING residences on Kings Landing Road, sporting regal purple-and-black Midnight Ball Committee banners and Christmas wreaths with opulent red velvet bows, were lit up and full of partygoers.

The executive committee—all nine voting delegates—and their wives were in India and Bennett Heywood's home at Number Nine, Kings Landing. The house looked stunning, the food was delicious, the drinks generous and topped off when each committee member took so much as a sniff from his champagne glass. *Which is how things should be,* India thought to herself as she shooed Rosellen out the door to the party at the house next to theirs.

She watched as her daughter slowly walked away like a beautiful ghost, her white satin shoes glimmering against the flagstone like Cinderella's.

India smiled. Her dream was within her grasp. All

the events of the day had not gone completely as planned, she acknowledged, but nothing had gone so wrong as to threaten the dream. She went back into the living room, where the clock on the mantel read 10:50.

In an hour and ten minutes she would close the members into her husband's den for the tally. In an hour and twenty minutes, she was sure Rosellen Heywood would be named Queen on the small, gold-inked card that the Caretaker of the Tally would lock into a box and read aloud at midnight on New Year's Eve.

No other decision was imaginable.

AT THE PARTY at Number Eleven Kings Landing Road, Paris Prince and his sister, Madrid "Mattie" Carter, along with Mattie's daughter, twenty-two-year-old Aspen, were greeting the electees and their dates.

Tammy Rose, accompanied by her date, arrived at the door just as Rosellen Heywood scurried up the steps. Without a wrap, the dark-haired girl was clutching her arms to keep warm.

"Hey, Tammy," Rosellen greeted, buzzing the doorbell.

"Hi, Rosellen," replied Tammy, staring at Rosellen's huge diamond earrings but not commenting on them. She pulled on her boyfriend's arm. "Come on, honey. I'm dying to get inside and have some punch."

"Good to see you," the young man said, nodding to Rosellen. "You look cold. But very, very pretty."

"Thank you," Rosellen replied. She glanced down at her slim, diamond-encrusted wristwatch. "Only another hour to go before the Caretaker knows the tally."

Tammy rolled her eyes. "Like we don't all know you're going to win, Rosellen."

Paris Prince himself threw open the front door. He was wearing a white tux, which made his red hair look positively carrot-colored.

"Well, it's two of my last missing rosebuds," Paris purred as he admitted the girls. "And two of the prettiest. Rosellen, you are an absolute picture in that dress. I'm dying, isn't that your mama's very same coronation dress?"

Rosellen grinned and pushed her bangs off her forehead nervously. "You know Mama. It wouldn't do to not wear the sacred family heirloom."

"Mattie, look at this," he called over his tuxedoed shoulder to his sister.

Aspen smiled stiffly and Tammy looked bored while Mattie and Paris clucked over Rosellen. "Darling Rosellen, you look every bit as yummy as your mama and grandma!"

"Thank you, Mayor Prince. But why are you here? I thought you'd be with the committee at my house."

"Oh, I just ran over for a second to see all you darling girls. Don't worry, I'll slip back before your mama knows I'm being rude."

While her uncle prattled on, Aspen took Tammy and her young man by the hands and turned her back on her mother and uncle, leaving them to fuss over Rosellen, whose eyes were blank and glassy as usual.

"Looks like little Miss Medicine Lady has popped herself up for her big night," Tammy whispered. The three shared a smirk at Rosellen's well-known "problem" and hurried off to join the other young people.

After a few more overly generous compliments from Mattie and Paris, Rosellen and the pair went along into the living room, where thirty glittering, chattering people were lounging and partying. The tension as twelve of the thirteen electees stood pretending not to watch one another for signs of nerves was so high, Rosellen swore she heard a humming sound in her ears, like electric lines singing on a summer night. She let herself think for a moment how it would feel if she won, a leaping feeling of joy that was quickly extinguished by the fear of what would happen if she did not.

Her boyfriend, Paul deAngelis, was sitting in front of the fire, his face rosy with warmth and booze, alongside Aspen.

"Miss Rosellen," Paris directed, patting Rosellen's arm, "you had better get your pretty self over there and remind that boy of his obligations."

He took a quick look at the mantel clock. "It's five after eleven. All you beauties are here except for Elizabeth Monette." Turning from Rosellen, he called out, "Does anyone know where our lovely Miss Monette has gotten herself tonight?"

The door chimes sounded and Paris, grabbing Aspen by the arm to help him greet his late arrival, hurried from the room. Rosellen crossed to the sofa, a bit unsteady on the four-inch heels India had demanded she wear, and was pulled down onto Paul's lap. He planted a kiss on her neck.

The smell of rum was heavy on his breath. "Hey, gorgeous. How's the dragon lady doing next door? Has she had to kill any of the committee members yet?"

Rosellen made a face at him. "Very funny. Mama is doing great. I just hope she doesn't fall apart the next couple of weeks."

"Fall apart? Your mama? A bomb could go off in that woman's powder box and she'd stay calm."

His speech was slurred, but Rosellen liked it when Paul was drunk. He was much nicer than when sober. "Mama will be fine." She let her gaze wander over to the doorway where Aspen had returned, hoping to gain her attention, but Rosellen found Elizabeth Monette's best friend staring at her with a wary look on her face.

"Hey, Aspen. Where's Elizabeth? She's not going to stand us all up, is she?"

"I'm sure she'll be here."

"Hope so," Rosellen drawled. "You know Elizabeth's a favorite to win this whole shooting match. She needs to show up at these parties, or people are going to think she's overconfident."

"I'm sure she'll be here," Aspen repeated. "Once Elizabeth decides to do something, she does it."

"Well, that's a good quality to have. Let's hope she is as good as her word, because Paris prides himself on having all the electees here so he can compare them to one another. Though, once he sees for himself how much better looking Elizabeth is than some of us, he's liable to have a sick headache and retire for the night."

Several guests laughed at this not-so-subtle dig at Aspen and their host. It was well-known that Paris Prince had always hoped Madrid's daughter would follow in her footsteps and be elected Queen of Midnight. But the small matter a few months ago—of rumors that he was about to be indicted for a nasty little real-estate scheme—had tainted Aspen's chances.

It was unfair, everyone agreed, to hold the girl responsible for her uncle's poor business judgment and even poorer moral fiber, but the Queen of Midnight *was* Farquier County, Louisiana, as Dr. Heywood was fond of saying. And it wouldn't do at all to have people remembering the mayor's unpleasantness when the newspaper printed its Queen's biography on the front page the first day of the New Year. If one had to have a scandal in one's family, it had better be at least ten years ago—long enough to be well-known but certainly not news.

"Forty-five minutes," Tammy Rose suddenly announced, and the crystal mantel clock chimed the quarter hour. An excited buzz filled the room.

"You ready to be Queen the rest of your life, sweet cheeks?" Paul whispered into Rosellen's ear.

"We'll have to wait a couple of weeks to see who's Queen, Paul, so don't go counting your chickens," she replied with a smile. For a moment an almost-overwhelming sorrow welled up inside her chest, as if she had just been told she had lost the Pageant and could see the look on India's face. Rosellen blinked and reached for Paul's glass and gulped down the rest of the amber liquid.

It wasn't wise to mix her medicine with liquor, but tonight had to be some kind of medical necessity.

"Don't kid yourself. Don't you think your mama will know who has won as soon as those votes are counted?"

"No, I don't. Only one person knows, remember? And as far as I've ever heard, the secret's never ever been revealed by the Caretaker. One year they had to have another vote because the Caretaker died and no one could read what he'd written on the card."

"If anyone can break that little tradition, she will," Paul said with a smirk.

"Hush. I don't want to talk about Mama." She

turned and kissed him, willing to do anything to not think about what her mama would do to claim a victory in this year's Queen of Midnight Pageant.

"Attention. Attention, everyone! I have news!" Their host stood in his most dramatic pose, one arm around a late arrival, Tammy's sister, Luvey.

Luvey wore a black dress with a V neck cut dangerously low. Her red hair was swept up off her face to show off her lovely neck and well-endowed chest. She looked, thought Rosellen, like the cat who had swallowed the canary. It was known she was seeing Paul's father, Philip deAngelis, on the sly, and Rosellen could see her boyfriend's attention shift to the woman.

"What's the news?" Tammy begged.

Paris tittered and turned to the roomful of guests hanging on his next words. "Elizabeth Monette was nearly murdered this afternoon, and now she's been kidnapped from the hospital!"

"By my ex-husband, Tommy Lee McCall, no less," Luvey chimed in. "Poor man, once he lost me he had to kidnap a girl!"

A two-second beat of stunned silence greeted this news, then everyone began to talk at once.

All but Rosellen, the only electee in the room dreading a recitation of the scandalous details, and praying they didn't involve anyone too close to her.

Chapter Five

"I thought you might want to call your folks now," Tommy Lee said matter-of-factly, handing Elizabeth a portable phone.

She was sitting on the edge of a soft, bouncy bed with noisy springs in Tommy Lee's guest room. Wrapped in his heavy red-plaid woolen robe, she held a cup of Sissy Lane's steaming hot chocolate.

"Thank you," she replied and set the phone on the bed beside her. It immediately fell onto the floor with a bang, and she and Tommy Lee nearly bumped heads reaching for it.

"Sorry," Elizabeth offered, letting him retrieve it. She noticed he was moving pretty stiffly and remembered, with a small shock, that it had just been a matter of hours since he'd been thrown like a bundle of newsprint onto the pavement of Government Boulevard.

No wonder he was moving slowly, she thought. She was feeling like she had been hit by a linebacker herself. She stared at the big man in the room with her, admiring his tall, well-shaped body. It was hard, disciplined, and no-nonsense, but sensuous enough to indulge a woman's every fantasy. He looked at her quickly, as if something of her thoughts showed on her face.

She turned away, aware of his eyes. Unconsciously Elizabeth rotated both shoulders, managing to slosh chocolate onto her hands and his robe. She looked out of the corner of her eye at her host as she blotted up the mess with the supply of napkins Tommy Lee's efficient housekeeper had left on the tray.

He was grinning at her clumsiness, which made her heart race with something she couldn't name. She wondered if he'd trust her to rub his back. She wondered if she could trust herself. "Sorry," she repeated. "I'll rinse this out. How are you feeling? Pretty sore?"

"Naw. I'm fine," he said. He sat gingerly on the chair next to the bed and studied Elizabeth's face in the rosy light. "You look none the worse for wear, considering. How're the knees?"

She flashed open the robe and they both stared at her scabbed legs.

"It's a good thing most of the events over the next couple of weeks are formal. I can't see these things looking too great in short dresses." Elizabeth smiled and was taken aback by the intense look in Tommy Lee's eyes.

"I wouldn't worry about that," he said, his deep voice quiet and serious. "Now, why don't you call your folks. I want you to tell them you're okay before they hear tell some gossip and worry themselves sick."

"Thank you," Elizabeth replied. But she was not looking forward to the call at all. She dialed the number and listened for her mother's voice, noting that the clock beside the bed read twelve-twenty.

"You missed your party," Tommy Lee said suddenly.

"Yes. The ballots have been tallied, people are a little drunk, everyone's excited."

"I thought you never were involved in those parties before," Tommy Lee said.

"Oh, I went to one or two over the years. I enjoyed them. As a spectator they are great fun, but the actual Queen and her family go nuts with running around. To say nothing of going broke with all the entertaining."

"Yeah. Well, for what it's worth, I can't imagine a more beautiful Queen." His eyes traveled the length of her. "Skinned knees and all."

Her skin flushed down her neck. "I don't have a chance in hell, but thanks. I'm hoping my friend Aspen wins."

Her parents' phone rang a fifth and sixth time in her ear, and she focused on leaving a message. Since her father was a voting member of the committee, they probably weren't even home yet, she realized. Her parents' answering machine picked up and she felt a childish sense of relief that she could break her news to them electronically, without having to answer their questions just yet. So much for Tommy Lee thinking she was mature.

"This is Elizabeth. I'm not going to be home tonight. Please don't worry about me. I was involved in a little traffic accident today. But I'm fine. I'll call first thing tomorrow and explain where I am and why—it's kind of complicated. Just don't let the judge get upset. The number where I'm staying is—"

"Elizabeth? Are you okay?"

The male voice breaking in on her phone call was

softly Southern and very concerned. Those words from an unidentified stranger inside her parents' home shocked her and she gasped. It wasn't the judge's booming tone, and for a moment Elizabeth couldn't imagine who could be answering their phone. "Mr. Willow?"

"Yes, hello, Elizabeth," he stammered. "I was staying up at the main house till your folks got in tonight. Picked up when I heard your voice. I'm sorry to intrude on your private call, but I just had to be sure you were safe, that you were okay."

Clay Willow was the handyman who had shown up and offered his services to the Monettes within a few weeks of their return to Fairbreeze. Her father had hired him to help him as a caretaker, and over time, the judge had grown to depend on him more and more for errands, drives into Belle Fleur and, Elizabeth thought, companionship. Her mother and father had a very loving, but very traditional relationship, with somewhat separate private lives.

"Who is it? Is everything okay with your parents?" Tommy Lee interrupted, moving close enough to her that Elizabeth felt his warm breath on her cheek.

His question, and the notched-up energy in his voice, reminded Elizabeth of his earlier warning that her parents might be in danger. She nodded and put her hand over the receiver. "It's fine. It's my father's caretaker. I'm going to tell him a bit about what happened and have him make sure the gates and house are locked."

Tommy Lee nodded. His agreement had the peculiar effect of making her feel more in control than she had for several days. She liked his approval and felt, oddly, as if they were a team. "Uh, Mr. Willow. Thank you for picking up the call. Are my folks still over in Belle Fleur at the party?"

"Yes, Elizabeth. They're being dropped off by one of the other couples who were going to the party. A friend of Miss Lou's who lives over in Bayou Pines."

"Good. I'm glad the judge isn't driving so late at night. Anyway, like I was saying in my message, I was involved in a near hit-and-run accident today—"

"Then you're not at the mayor's party? Are you okay?"

He certainly paid attention to what was going on in her family, Elizabeth thought. "Yes. Really, I am fine. Please don't go into all this with my parents, Mr. Willow. I'll give them the whole story tomorrow when I see them. But the police think someone may have done this because of my involvement with the Queen of Midnight Pageant—"

"You mean like a stalker or something?"

"I...I don't really know yet, Mr. Willow. But to be on the safe side, would you please see to it that the front gate is closed up tonight, and that the house is locked after my folks get in?"

"Of course. I've been sleeping in the room downstairs by the kitchen, on and off this winter. I'll bunk down there for a couple of days. Miss Lou worries I'm not warm enough out back in the cottage, anyway, so I won't be upsetting her by doing that."

"Great. That's really great, Mr. Willow. Thank you. Now if you could write down the number of where I am, in case of an emergency. Tell my parents to please not bother to call, though. Everyone here is pretty tired." Her eyes met Tommy Lee's and she again took a measure of the fatigue and pain lines in his face. But another emotion showed clearly, one that made her catch her breath. Need. His dark eyes burned with it and she felt her body respond.

"What's the name of the family you're staying with, Elizabeth? Are you in Belle Fleur?"

Willow's questions pulled her thoughts away from Tommy Lee. "McCall. I'm not in Belle Fleur, but a few miles past the marina."

"Okay," Clay replied. "You get some rest, Elizabeth. I'll see you tomorrow. Don't worry at all about the judge and Miss Lou. You lock your door and get some sleep, okay?"

Elizabeth smiled, touched by the man's concern. "I will. Thank you." She clicked the button on the phone and passed it to Tommy Lee, who was still standing inches from her.

"What's the caretaker's name? Willow?"

"Clay Willow," she supplied, crossing her arms over her chest. Her skin felt moist and feverish, and she wondered if it was from her injuries, or from her close proximity to Tommy Lee McCall.

"Why did you tell him where you were staying?"

She sat up straighter, a little annoyed. "Because he asked, Tommy Lee. Let's not be too paranoid, here."

"You know that guy pretty well, then? I mean, you're sure he's okay?"

"Okay? Mr. Willow? Well, no, I don't know him all that well personally. But my folks have taken to him in a big way, and they're pretty choosy about people. He's worked for them the last two years and become more like a member of the family than hired help. I trust him to do what I asked."

"Does he have kin in Belle Fleur? I don't know anyone with that name."

"I think he's originally from Mobile, or Birmingham. Stop thinking like a cop. He's not a suspect, Tommy Lee.''

For a moment he stared at her hard, then gently reached out and squeezed her shoulder. ''I can't stop thinking like a cop.''

The regret in his voice made her wince. Elizabeth covered his hand with her own, ''I'm sorry, I didn't mean to bring up anything so personal. I know you're upset about—''

''About what? Losing my job? Look, I don't know what Luvey shot her mouth off about, but it's none of your concern. I don't need anyone's pity, Elizabeth,'' he snapped.

''I'm not pitying you,'' she retorted. ''Look, you're tired. I'm tired. Let me say thanks again. I'll be out of your hair first thing tomorrow.'' She sat down on the bed and eased herself back against the fluffy pillows, hoping he would just leave. But he didn't. He was staring at her. Meeting his gaze, Elizabeth was suddenly aware of her bare legs and scanty attire. She closed the robe and tried to cross her legs, but the movement made her knees smart.

Tommy Lee stepped next to the bed, touching her right calf tenderly. ''You need anything for the pain? You're not moving too easy there.''

''What have you got for pain?'' she asked with a small smile.

Before she could blink, his mouth was on hers. The kiss was brief and hard, and by the time she reached up to hold him to her, he had pulled away.

His dark eyes rested on her banged-up knees, then traveled up her body like a searchlight. ''I'd rather you stayed here at the house for a while in the morning. I want to talk to Frank Foley, maybe get him out here.

And you and I need to have a talk about where, and if, we're going on with this.''

"With what?" she asked, holding her breath, praying he'd kiss her again, wondering if he would if she asked him to.

"Your investigation. I'd say that attorney, Peach, is the best place to start. I'll call Dottie and see what she found out, then we'll talk to your daddy and see if he knows anything more.''

Elizabeth blinked as if she had been slapped, and blushed slowly from her hairline, down her face and neck to her breasts. She felt light-headed and stupid and incredibly naive. What in the hell did she think he meant by that little kiss, she scolded herself. He was just being friendly, and she was just being dumb.

She jerked her borrowed robe snugly around herself and ducked her head down, hoping he wouldn't notice her blush. "Fine. That sounds fine. Although I'd rather talk to the judge by myself. He doesn't know about the stupid letters and such and I want to be sure he doesn't get too upset.''

"Upset? You were nearly struck by a car and drugged by a man impersonating a doctor today. He needs to be upset. This is serious, in case you hadn't noticed.''

"Don't lecture me," she sputtered. Elizabeth squared her shoulders and met his eyes, no longer feeling much like a team member but more like a schoolgirl being bossed by her teacher. "I'm okay. Those were bizarre things, but as far as we know, someone is just trying to scare me, not kill me. The judge has a heart condition. I'm not going to let anyone throw him into a panic. So since you're working for me, I call the shots, okay?''

"You that good at controlling other people?" he challenged, the color back in his face.

Elizabeth noticed, not for the first time, how he clenched and unclenched his jaw when he stared at a person, and how big and strong-looking his hands were. "I don't make it a habit to control, or bully people, Mr. McCall. How about you?"

Tommy Lee wanted to yell at her, but he didn't. He didn't have the energy. Tommy Lee sighed and pulled on the left side of his mustache, as if that would help him keep his temper.

Outside, the foghorn blew eight miles away on the sandbars at Green Point. It was nearly one o'clock and he felt a hundred years old. He shouldn't have kissed this woman, his mind chided. She was the kind you kissed once and got hooked, like a fish on the line.

And the very last thing Miss Elizabeth Monette needed right now was a love affair with a guy who didn't know for sure where his life was going to be six months from now. "You'd better get some rest. Can I get you anything more before I hit the sack? Something to eat? Or some more cocoa."

"No, thanks. I'm fine."

He looked her up and down and nodded. She was miffed at him. Good. It would cut down on the possibility she'd ask him for another kiss. 'Cause if she asked, he wasn't going to refuse. "Good night, then. I'll see you at breakfast."

"Thank you again, Tommy Lee. I mean that."

He flashed a smile.

Smug old thing, Elizabeth said to herself once he'd left. But she wondered what he would have done if she had patted the bed beside her and asked the ex-cop to stay awhile. Though they hardly knew each other, and both of them were physical wrecks, there had been something real in that kiss. Something not just fooling-around about it, Elizabeth decided. Something she wanted to find out about.

If he hadn't made her feel confused and flustered and angry and happy all at once, she could have handled this little scene better. Barely suppressing the urge to blow a kiss to the empty doorway, Elizabeth instead flipped off the light. For a moment her body would not relax, and her senses replayed the feeling of Tommy Lee's mustache brushing her mouth. It had felt soft and sexy, scratchy but nice.

Finally, she closed her eyes and let relief and fatigue wash over her body like a warm bath. Her last coherent thought was of Tommy Lee jumping out his window to save her.

"My hero," she whispered with a grin. Elizabeth fell sound asleep, for the first time in weeks not afraid of dreams or memories or of what the morning might bring.

TEN MILES AWAY, in Belle Fleur, Paris Prince's guests mingled with the Queen of Midnight Committee members filing out of Bennett and India Heywood's mansion.

Aspen made a beeline for the judge and Miss Lou, determined to be the one to tell them about Elizabeth and reassure the older couple that their only daughter was in no danger.

"But I don't understand," Miss Lou replied after listening to Aspen's story. "Why didn't someone from the hospital call us?"

"Bennett!" Judge Monette barked toward the door, where Rosellen Heywood stood in animated conversation with her parents. "Bennett, can I have a moment, please?"

Aspen cleared her throat. "Judge, I'm sure everything is fine. Luvey said Elizabeth was staying with a policeman," she added, hoping that would make the judge feel better. "I'm sure he's very respectable, sir."

"I don't understand any of this," Miss Lou repeated, as Bennett Heywood walked up to the small crowd, his wife, India, in tow.

"Judge, you and Miss Lou please come back inside with us."

"Hang on a minute, Bennett," the judge challenged. "Do you know what the hell happened to my daughter at your hospital?"

"No sir, I don't. Let's go in and I'll call and find out what in the blue blazes is going on." With a huff, he took the judge's arm and headed back toward the front door.

"Come along, Lou," the judge yelled over his shoulder.

Miss Lou looked toward the house, then back at the group of young people. "You go ahead, Baylor. I'll help India get these folks on their way. Please see if you can find out where Elizabeth is so we can go get her."

The judge nodded, then continued on with Bennett. Dora and Harold Eckles, the Monettes' friends who were going to drive them home, trailed after the two men.

Miss Lou and India moved farther down the walkway.

"Can I do anything?" Aspen asked, squeezing Miss

Lou's hand. "Do you want me to take you folks home?"

"No, darling, you go get some sleep. We'll have Elizabeth call you tomorrow," Miss Lou replied, kissing her daughter's friend. "Come on, now, don't be so glum. You know as well as I do that Elizabeth can take care of herself. Now, you go on home, and give your mama my love."

"You sure you don't want me to come back after I get everyone to go home?"

Miss Lou noticed Luvey and Tammy, who lived on the other side of Paris Prince, at Number Five, Kings Landing, and she wondered why they were still outside. India Heywood was right; Luvey Rose had a terrible reputation for causing trouble.

"No, that won't be necessary, Aspen. India will take care of us."

"I certainly will," the evening's hostess muttered as she stood glaring at Luvey, who had turned away from her chattering group of fans and was looking over at them. "If you want to help things, Aspen, you get that bigmouthed sister of Tammy Rose to stop stoking the gossip fires. We don't need this kind of nonsense on a night when a new Queen's been chosen."

Aspen grimaced and hurried off. A second later, Luvey and Tammy Rose joined India and Miss Lou.

"Miss Lou!" Luvey exclaimed. "Don't you worry a thing about Elizabeth. I'm sure she's safe with Tommy Lee. He's basically a goodhearted type."

"He jumped out the window to save her life," Tammy gushed, her cornflower-blue eyes wide with adoration. "Can you believe it!"

"Is this some kind of joke?" India demanded, shaking her finger at the thirty-year-old Luvey as if she were five. "What kind of nonsense are you talking about—someone jumping out a window?"

Luvey gave India a barely civil look and then launched into an abbreviated version of the story. "So then, according to Katie Smiths, Tommy Lee just carried Elizabeth out of there. Chief Foley's boys are still looking for the black car that nearly killed them earlier today, to say nothing of the lunatic who was playing doctor. Hope they catch him, too, in case he's planning to go after one of the other electees."

"That's enough, Luvey!" India shouted, an edge of hysteria in her voice. "I won't have you suggesting that what happened to Elizabeth has anything to do with Queen of Midnight Pageant. And I wouldn't go repeating it, if I were you. You'll be hurting everyone here, including Tammy. You don't want her expelled from the Pageant because of your talk, do you?"

"I hardly think that could happen, India," Luvey retorted, her green eyes flashing. "Besides, since the tally's already been taken, Tammy might just be Queen. I've never heard the Midnight Ball Committee expel a Queen before she's been crowned. Although maybe you have, since you've been around for a lot more scandals than I have."

"If that's some kind of veiled remark—"

"Ladies, ladies," Miss Lou interrupted, placing an arm around India while shooting Luvey a look of warning. "Thank you for the details, Luvey. Now, why don't you and your sister go home and get out of this cold."

Luvey and India exchanged a last, hostile look. The young woman then kissed Miss Lou on the cheek and hustled Tammy off. Luvey knew better than to challenge India on her home ground. India Heywood's temper was as legendary as her supper parties.

"That redhead's a monster," India hissed, allowing Miss Lou to turn her around and head toward her own front door.

"Now, don't be so hard on Luvey, India," Miss Lou said softly, as she and India walked up the front steps and through the doors of the hundred-year-old Colonial. "I'm sure she was just excited."

"That girl's always had a big mouth," India replied. "Her mother, Tela Goughis, was the same way. Tela just couldn't wait to spread all kinds of gossip about me the year I was supposed to be Queen. When she died, I didn't even send flowers. Just a card."

Miss Lou was concerned about India. She could see the woman was upset, and knew how much pressure she'd been under to make the night a triumph. Miss Lou, despite her distaste for gossip, had heard from several sources that India's tirades and obsession with the Queen of Midnight election had grown more pronounced during the years she and the judge had lived in Baltimore.

If the exchange she had just heard between Luvey and India was the norm, she would have to admit the gossip was true. It was time to change the subject, Miss Lou decided. Get the woman refocused. "Thank you so much for letting us come back in, India. Do you have any idea where Bennett and the judge have gone off to?"

"I'm sure they're in Bennett's study. Come."

Miss Lou followed India down the center hallway. As they approached the study door, the sound of Dr. Bennett Heywood yelling clearly filled the room.

"And when I tell you to call me if something sensitive happens, I mean *call me*. Not my service, not my maid! Is that clear?''

Miss Lou and the judge, who was sitting on the leather sofa by a smoldering fire, exchanged a look. Miss Lou turned her attention to the elderly couple seated on the sofa opposite her husband, Dora and Harold, who looked equal parts fatigued and ill-at-ease. ''You poor dears. Look at the time! Please, I'll never forgive myself if you both don't take each other home this instant.''

''Harold, I'm going to call my caretaker and have him come get me. You go on now,'' the judge insisted.

Though both Eckleses looked relieved, they made it plain they were honor-bound to stay when their friends needed them, but Miss Lou finally persuaded them and watched as India's maid led them from the room.

As they left, Bennett slammed down the phone. ''God in heaven, India!'' he yelled. ''Why didn't you let me talk to Katie Smiths when she called earlier?''

''We were leading our guests in to dinner when she called, and it simply wouldn't do to interrupt the committee on a night like this!''

''When someone is accosted by a nutcase in my hospital, it takes precedence over any dinner guest! Didn't you even ask why she was calling?''

''No, I didn't. You spend way too much time there as it is. And with tonight being such an important night for me, I couldn't see how it would matter. If I had known it involved one of the electees I would have driven over to the hospital myself!''

The doctor set his jaw and turned to Judge Monette. ''Forgive me, Baylor. It seems that someone did attack Elizabeth while she was in one of the hospital rooms, but she's fine. A policeman took her into something like protective custody until Chief Foley could get to the bottom of things. He's a good man, McCall. Retired last year after taking a bullet in the back during a robbery. Very good man,'' he added, glaring at his wife, obviously still angry that she had not informed him about the call earlier.

What little color India possessed had gone out of her face as she listened to her husband's description of what had happened at the hospital. She slumped onto the sofa and twisted her pearls. ''The evening is being ruined. I'm sorry, but everyone is blowing this out of proportion. We should all be thinking of the coronation, not some idiot criminal.'' She shook her head and buried it in her hands.

Miss Lou nodded toward the desk. It was obvious that India was at a breaking point, and she didn't need spectators to see it. ''Why don't you call Clay, Baylor? See if he'll come get us?''

Baylor marched to the phone. After several rings, he punched in the code for remote message retrieval and listened, swore under his breath, then returned the phone. ''I'm not getting an answer, Lou. Elizabeth called. Sounds fine. Said she'll call us first thing in the morning. But the damn thing broke off before she could leave her number.'' He bowed to his hosts. ''Bennett, India, thanks for everything. You folks go on to bed, we'll call a cab.''

India snapped to attention and attempted to regain her composure. ''No. I won't hear of it. Jones!'' she yelled, and a second later an elderly black man arrived at the study door. ''Jones, please get the car and bring it around. I need you to take the judge and Miss Lou over to Fairbreeze.''

"Certainly. But I'll have to use your daughter's car. She took the Cadillac to take her young man home. He wasn't feeling too steady."

"That worthless little—"

"Bennett!" India cried out, her eyes huge. "Please, our guests have been through enough, here."

Dr. Heywood looked sheepish, and hastily ordered Jones to get the car. The servant disappeared, leaving an awkward silence and tension thick as summer fog.

"Can I offer you some tea, or a brandy, Miss Lou?" Bennett finally said.

"No, thank you. How about you, India?" she said, aggravated that Bennett seemed oblivious to his wife's fragile state. "It was a perfectly gorgeous dinner party, but I bet you didn't eat a bite."

India stared at the picture hanging over the fireplace. It was Bennett's mother. She had been a Queen of Midnight, and was wearing a formal blue gown with her Queen pin proudly displayed on the bodice. "I didn't eat a bite at any of the parties the year I was an electee. Mama made us diet. She was sure I was going to win, you know. Then Daddy had to kill that man." India shook her head and tears began to run down her face.

Bennett Heywood went ashen with embarrassment at his wife's behavior. Miss Lou and the judge averted their eyes. The scandal involving India's father and his mistress, Elaine Gibbs, had ruined India's chances for election to Queen of Midnight. But it was an old scandal, and seldom mentioned now.

Miss Lou felt a shiver of fear for India's sanity. "India, darling, why don't you let me get you some tea or something."

India bolted upright and stared at Bennett, as if she

hadn't heard Miss Lou's voice at all. "I think I'll go up and check on Rosellen's gown. She never hangs things up, you know," she replied, then astounded them all by leaving the room without another word.

"Baylor, Miss Lou, my wife has put herself under so much stress," Bennett began.

Miss Lou touched his arm. "Please. It's a dreadful end to a perfect evening. Go up to her, Bennett. I think she needs to hear some kind words."

"Thank you," he said. He shook hands with the judge and left the room.

"Damn stupid contest, anyway," the judge muttered.

Miss Lou stared at the painting of Bennett's mother, a beautiful woman who had not, despite her night of glory as Queen of Midnight, led a very happy life. She looked intently at her husband, glad to see the news about Elizabeth had not upset him to an extent that was more than his regular medication could handle. "Let's go home, darling."

"You okay, Lou?" he asked, giving her a tender squeeze.

"Yes, I'm fine." Which was more than she could say for the family who lived in the grand home they were leaving.

Chapter Six

Petey Connor and Ray Robinson waited for Cracker inside Petey's van. It was parked in an alley on River Place, behind an abandoned restaurant just four blocks from Knights Landing Road.

"When is she coming?" Petey asked, slurring the words. He had been drinking since early afternoon. He was very, very drunk and even more frightened. Ray had told him about the fiasco at the hospital and Petey knew Cracker wasn't going to be pleased.

Ray glanced at the luminous green dial of his watch. His breath was a plume of gray in the van's frigid interior. "She told Cracker she would meet us in an hour. That was at two-fifteen. It's three-ten now."

A sound like a shot tore through the air.

Petey yelped and struggled to open the van's rear door to admit Cracker Jackson, whose knuckles rapping angrily against the metal door had made the startling noise.

Cracker pulled the door shut with a vicious snap, and settled onto the bench Petey had installed. "Start at the beginning, Ray, and tell me how you managed to screw things up so royally."

"I was doing fine until that cop showed up."

"You were not doing fine. You acted like a third-rate amateur. And you're damn lucky you got out of the hospital. I hear Chief Foley has put a very good description of you out on the street, Ray."

"I didn't even hurt that girl," he began.

"You assaulted a damn debutante. And you got yourself looked at by Tommy Lee McCall. Some cowboy like McCall makes you, you're made until they got your sorry hide behind bars. As of now, you're out of this deal." He reached into his heavy leather jacket and grinned when Petey and Ray both flinched. "You think I'm going to shoot you, Ray?" Cracker pulled out a roll of bills and counted off two hundred dollars, then tossed the money at Ray. "Take that and buy yourself a train ticket. I'd suggest you go back to Galveston—and don't call us. We'll get back to you when it's safe."

Ray snatched up the bills and stuffed them into his sweatshirt. "You going to drive me to the train station?"

"Yeah, we'll drive you. As soon as we meet with our employer. Hey, Petey," Cracker suddenly shouted at the third man, kicking his leg with his steel-tipped boot. "Are you awake?"

Petey nodded once.

Suddenly, headlights crossed the front windshield of the van and a dark sedan pulled up a few feet away. The three men inside the van waited, but the woman they had come to meet with made no move to get out of her car.

"I guess she wants me to pay her a house call," Cracker snarled. "You stay here," he said to Petey, then turned his glare onto Ray. "You come with me. You got the gun I gave you?"

"Why do I need the gun, man? You think something's wrong?"

"I want you to be armed, just in case. Never can tell what an angry female's planning to do, especially one as nutty as that one." Cracker laughed—an ugly, rasping sound—then threw open the van's rear door and jumped out.

He glanced over at the sedan and tried to see inside, but the tinted windows were too dark. Ray jumped down after him, fell to the ground and struggled clumsily to get up. He followed behind Cracker, and felt his chest pocket several times, fearful of the hard shape of the gun and the thought that he might have to use it.

Cracker stopped at the passenger side of the sedan and grasped the chrome handle. The door was locked.

"Hey, open the door!" he bellowed, his words echoing hollow in the thin, cold air.

Ray glanced back at the van, and saw Petey jump to the ground, motioning "What's up?" with his hands.

Ray shrugged and turned back to Cracker, just as the sedan's passenger window opened with a whine. Ray saw the flames from the shotgun at the same instant it extended its deadly bite into Cracker Jackson, killing the ex-cop before the sound of the explosion was over.

Ray screamed and fell to his knees beside Cracker's dead body, which saved him from the full force of the second blast, which singed his scalp and filled his hair with blue smoke and gunpowder. The sedan skidded off with squealing tires and racing engine, but not before sending a third volley of shots at Petey, who had the good sense to throw his wounded body into a rolling dive under the van.

Ray bolted from the scene, away from Cracker's bleeding, broken body, and from Petey screaming in pain. He was a block away when he realized a car was coming—her car was coming, fast behind him. He turned and screamed a curse in Spanish at the headlights, but the pathetic sound didn't stop the driver. The car knocked Ray Robinson fourteen feet into the air with the impact of its heavy, American-made front bumper.

He was dead when he landed on the frost-covered asphalt, in the street in front of the Belle Fleur Elementary School.

The man in the gray pickup truck, parked silently across the street, watched for a moment as the sedan raced off. He knew who was driving it, and it made him sick. He blinked and looked at the guy on the ground. He had seen plenty of dead men, and he knew this guy was beyond any help he or anyone else could offer.

He put on his parking lights and rolled off down the street, in the opposite direction from the sedan, wondering how the horror of the night was going to come together. His lights slid over the school's nativity scene, which stood right next to a poster hawking tickets to the Queen of Midnight Ball.

THE MORNING WAS NOT going well, Elizabeth decided. She scolded herself for thinking there was any way it could have gone well, what with the judge, her mother, and the charming Mr. Tommy Lee McCall all intent on running the show.

Especially since the "show" in this case was herself, whom they were all treating like she wasn't even there. "Excuse me, Daddy, but—"

"Hang on, Elizabeth," the judge ordered, his hand held up for silence. He turned his attention back to Tommy Lee, whom he had been questioning for the better part of the past twenty minutes. "Now let me get this straight. You are telling me that if I call someone at the FBI, my word isn't enough to get them looking into these piece-of-trash letters someone sent Elizabeth?"

"I'm just saying, Judge Monette, that since the letters weren't sent through the mail—"

"I don't give a great goddamn about that. Those sons of b—"

"Daddy, please listen for a minute and stop swearing," Elizabeth interrupted. She frowned right back at her father, who was glaring at her with the same degree of frustrated animosity he'd been aiming at Tommy Lee.

"Elizabeth, darling, come sit down," Miss Lou interjected, patting the kitchen chair next to her. "You and your daddy both need to calm down a little. We're all on the same side here, right, Mr. McCall?"

"Yes, ma'am," Tommy Lee agreed, smiling first at the judge, then at Elizabeth.

They both stood their ground.

"Just don't go off calling in the militia, Daddy. That's all I want. When Chief Foley gets here, you can discuss things with him. Mr. McCall told you twice he has retired from the force and can't act in any official capacity."

The judge sat and beckoned to Elizabeth to take the empty seat beside him. "I'm sorry, sugar. But I can't believe you didn't come to us with this nonsense about the letters, as soon as it happened. And why in the hell you didn't call me about the car..."

Elizabeth held her hands in the air to stop his scolding. "I know. I know. But I thought I could handle it, that it wasn't any big deal."

"It *is* a big deal," Tommy Lee countered. He was leaning against the counter, a cup of coffee in his hands. His eyes were bright and he looked none the worse for his roll on Government Boulevard yesterday.

Unlike her, she thought, who was black-and-blue and bleary-eyed. Elizabeth pulled the sweater her mother had brought around her and winced as her knees protested her walking over to the table to join her parents. She picked up the mug Sissy Lane had poured full of steaming coffee and brought it to her lips. The aroma revived her and she met her father's stare. "Mr. McCall is right, Daddy. It's a big deal, if it was intentional. I'm just not so sure that it was."

"Do you think Elizabeth was attacked because she is an electee, Mr. McCall?" Miss Lou queried, her eyes wide. "I mean, do you think someone would want to hurt her just because of that?"

Tommy Lee joined them at the table, turning a chair around backward and resting his arms on the curved back. "Could be. It could also be because of the other matter."

"What other matter?" the judge barked.

Elizabeth sighed. She had really planned to run this conversation in a smoother, less sensational manner, but everyone else had their own agenda and kept getting off track. She had hoped to find a good time to tell her parents that she had met Tommy Lee because she'd wanted to hire his sister, the private detective, but her parents had burst in demanding all the details about her accident and the hospital attack, and now things were a jumble.

So much for her famous organizational skills. "My adoption."

Miss Lou gasped and met her husband's gaze. "I thought you were going to keep that a private family matter, Elizabeth."

"Not that we're ashamed of anything like that," Judge Monette added hastily.

"Look, I know it's hard to discuss this openly after keeping it hidden so long, but I decided to find out more about my—" her voice caught as she wrestled with her conflicting feelings of wanting to be frank but also afraid of hurting the two people she loved more than anyone else on earth "—birth parents. You know how I've struggled with those images—'night terrors,' you used to call them—I've had since I was little. I thought it was time to try and solve the whole mystery, not just the part you two knew about."

"But, you mean you think those dreams mean something?" Miss Lou asked, her voice trembling.

"Yes, I think they are memories, not nightmares." Her voice was low and clear, like that of a child put on the spot but unwilling to take the easy way out and lie. "I think I saw my mother killed."

Miss Lou gasped, then covered her mouth. Tears filled her eyes. The judge looked away, and his hands shook as he laced them together.

"So she hired me to help," Tommy Lee explained. His voice was calm but he was moved by Elizabeth's handling of a most delicate situation. The banged-up beauty sitting across from him was certainly much more than just a debutante.

"My sister's a private investigator. Specializing in paternity cases, adoption information, stuff like that. Elizabeth came to her but got me instead. We're going to try and track down what happened to her parents."

"Well, all I've got to say about that is she nearly got herself killed, twice, since she met up with you," Judge Monette said, grabbing his cup like it was a life preserver.

"Daddy," Elizabeth began, "don't start—"

"Baylor," Miss Lou interrupted in a hoarse voice. "Don't blame Mr. McCall for that. We owe him a lot for saving Elizabeth—not once but twice. I think you owe him an apology."

The old man made a sound in his throat but put the mug down slowly. "Thank you for saving our girl, Mr. McCall. But am I to understand that what Elizabeth thinks she's remembering is the real reason behind those attacks on her?"

"In my opinion, it can't be ruled out."

"But that's crazy," Miss Lou sputtered. "She's been ours for twenty years, for heaven's sake! Surely no one would worry about what a child might remember!"

"But I was someone else's before then, Mama," Elizabeth countered. "I'm sure there was a terrible tragedy involved. I need to find out what it was. Now, more than ever."

"She's right," Tommy Lee agreed. "Because if the attacks are related to her looking into her adoption, then even if she stopped looking, she wouldn't be safe. None of you would. Someone doesn't want her to find out something."

"But who?" Judge Monette asked. He ran his gnarled hand through his thick gray hair. "We never knew the names of her parents. The attorney who handled the case, and the judge, said we would never be able to find out. I don't know much about adoption law, but I do know that sealed records are sealed records. I couldn't get a look at the ones closed by another judge.''

"The lawyer who contacted you was Emmett Peach. Right, sir?''

"Yes.''

"Do you know if he's still around?'' Elizabeth questioned.

"No, I don't. He's my age or older, though. So he's probably retired if he's not dead.''

"Baylor!'' Miss Lou admonished. "Honestly.''

The judge relaxed for the first time that morning and winked at his daughter. "Your mama doesn't like to admit she's married to an old man.''

Elizabeth grinned. "Tommy Lee thought we might start with Mr. Peach. See if he remembers anything he can tell us.''

"Who was the judge on the case, Mr. Monette?'' Tommy Lee asked. "He might be able to tell us something, too.''

"Dead men tell no lies,'' Baylor replied, all seriousness again. "That gentleman was Mr. Harrison Goughis III. He's long dead. His sister, Tela, was a good friend of Lou's. When did old Harrison meet his Maker?''

"In 1992, I think,'' Miss Lou answered. "A year later we lost Tela. Remember we flew in during that hurricane for her funeral in Belle Fleur.''

"Tela?'' Tommy Lee asked, the hairs on the back of his neck rising. "What was Tela's last name?''

"She was born Tela Goughis, but married Brett

Rose. Her daughter Tammy Rose is an electee this year," Miss Lou told them. She patted her daughter's arm. "I bet you are sick of me relating everything to that Pageant. But that's how I met Tela. She and I were electees the same year."

Tommy Lee met Elizabeth's wide-eyed glance. "So the judge who handled Elizabeth's adoption was Tammy and Luvey's uncle?"

"Yes," Miss Lou replied. "But you're not suggesting that young woman has anything to do with what happened to Elizabeth, are you? Why, she's the most timid little thing."

"Do you know her sister?" Elizabeth added quietly, noticing the look of discomfort on Tommy Lee's face.

"Who's her sister?" the judge asked.

"Luvey Rose, darling," Miss Lou said with a twinkle. "The beautiful redhead who helped us when you were last at the hospital."

"Oh. Her." The judge grinned.

"She's Tommy Lee's ex-wife," Elizabeth deadpanned.

"Oh. Oh, my," the judge said, looking confused.

Tommy Lee shook his head. "God, sometimes I really hate small towns."

The four of them sat in a silent circle for a moment, each wondering over the tangle of relationships involved.

"Chief Foley's just pulling in," Sissy Lane suddenly hollered, returning to the kitchen carrying a platter of sliced ham retrieved from the pantry. She was tall and tawny-skinned, blue-eyed and beautiful, her front teeth capped with gold. "I'm going to get you a decent breakfast, *chére*," she said to Elizabeth. "And you folks, too. Can I get you more coffee, Judge?"

"Oh, please don't bother, Mrs. Lane."

"I told you to call me Sissy, Judge." She turned her bright gaze to Tommy Lee. "And you'd better get some more chairs. Chief Frank's got three big old boys with him, and if I know cops, they're not going to turn down breakfast."

"Three guys?" Tommy Lee turned and headed for the door, opening it to admit a grim-faced Frank Foley. Two patrolmen stood leaning against a second car, and Foley's day sergeant, John Bulow, was standing behind the chief.

"Frank, come on in. What the hell you doing with such an escort?"

"Is Miss Monette still here, Tommy Lee?"

"Yes, she is," he answered, his voice wary. "As is her daddy, Judge Baylor Monette, and his wife. Why don't you boys come on in. I think the judge has some questions."

Frank Foley's face darkened and he muttered an oath under his breath. He stomped in and removed his hat, his sergeant on his heels. "Hey, Sissy," he said to the housekeeper.

"Chief, I'm cooking right now. My biscuits and gravy. Big plate for you. Come in."

"Don't make nothing for us, Sissy, we're leaving right away."

The chief continued over to the table, his hat pressed against his chest. He and Tommy Lee exchanged a look, but the chief directed his remarks to the table. "Good morning, everyone. I'm sorry to bust in on you all so early. Miss Monette, Mrs. Monette," he added, nodding a greeting to Miss Lou. He extended his hand, "Judge Monette, how are you, sir?"

"Chief. Good to see you again. Have a seat, if you will. I have several questions I'd like to ask."

"I'm sure you do," the chief replied. "But I'm afraid they're going to have to wait. I need to take Elizabeth and Tommy Lee with me back to Belle Fleur."

"What for?" Tommy Lee demanded. He was standing behind Elizabeth's chair, gripping it with both hands. He knew Frank Foley as well as anyone, as well as cop procedures. He didn't like what he was hearing because it could only mean one thing: something worse had happened.

"Two men were murdered in town early this morning," the chief announced. "We think they might have been involved in the attack on Elizabeth yesterday. I want you two to take a look at them."

"Murdered!" Judge Monette barked.

"Oh, my God!" Miss Lou added.

"I don't like this," the judge continued. "What in the hell happened to them?"

"Shotgunned. Out by Belle Fleur Elementary." Chief Foley kept his eyes on Elizabeth. "Can we ask you to come along now, Miss Monette? I've got to get an investigation under way."

Elizabeth felt her ears ringing. The smell of the frying ham made her feel dizzy. In her mind she heard a far-off echo of a woman screaming, and the sound of glass breaking. She wanted to run and hide and not think. Her arms began to tremble and she grabbed the edge of the table, willing the memory to recede.

Suddenly Tommy Lee's hand was on her shoulder. He squeezed it gently.

"Why don't you go get dressed?"

She stood. "Mom and Daddy, you go on home. I'll

be there later. There's no reason for you to come along, Daddy," she told him, reading the stubborn set of his jaw. "Go home and rest. I'll call as soon as we're done." Elizabeth hurried from the room, glad to escape, though followed by the memory of Tommy Lee's telling her that the past was often best left buried.

Chapter Seven

Elizabeth and Tommy Lee found themselves back inside Dottie Betts's office, exactly twenty-four hours after they had met there.

Tommy Lee crossed to the window, which was still wide-open, then turned and hung up the phone, which was listlessly beeping "busy." He moved up the thermostat, since the air temperature was only about forty degrees, and motioned to Elizabeth to sit down.

"Let me call over to Lester's Café and get some lunch and some coffee."

Elizabeth, shivering inside her sweater and Tommy Lee's borrowed coat, nodded her agreement. She sat with her arms wrapped around herself while Tommy Lee ordered soup and sandwiches. He hung up the phone and stared at her.

She stared back. "Now what?" she asked, pulling off her gloves and blowing on her fingers to keep them warm.

"We look in your file. Dottie said on the phone that she'd left a call for Emmett Peach. She must have come up with his number before she got benched by her obstetrician."

Elizabeth nodded. She looked behind Tommy Lee at the magnolia-tree limbs, frost-covered in midafternoon. Tears stung her eyes and she brushed them away. Suddenly she didn't want to be in this office, in this town, in this state. She didn't want to be who she was, or whoever the hell she might be. And she didn't want to have seen with her own two eyes two dead men she didn't know lying naked and bullet-ridden in the Belle Fleur morgue.

"When did Chief Foley think they would have a confirmed identity on the two men?"

Tommy Lee jerked his head around and stared hard at Elizabeth. "He thought by tomorrow. Stop thinking about those men, Elizabeth. You didn't even know them."

"I didn't know them, and they didn't know me, but they tried to kill me yesterday. I heard Sergeant Bulow tell Chief Foley that they found New York license plates in the parking lot."

Tommy Lee didn't respond. He didn't like the feverish, tight look of Elizabeth Monette's face. He should take her back home, right now, and put all this investigation crap on hold. He slapped the folder he was looking in closed and stood. "Put your gloves on again. We're going."

"Are you nuts? You just ordered lunch," Elizabeth retorted, her voice full of tears. "I'm fine," she said angrily, then louder, "tSop staring at me like that. I'm fine."

Tommy Lee went to her and pulled her out of the chair, folding her stiff and frightened body into his arms. Immediately she began to cry—huge, lung-filled sobs. She clung to him, burrowed her face into his chest, collapsed against him. He held her as tightly as he could and still let her breathe.

For five minutes she cried and he held her. A knock sounded on the glass door, and a male voice called out, "Delivery!"

Tommy Lee still held her and yelled, "Charge it to the account and leave it."

A few seconds later Elizabeth took a deep, shuddering breath and looked up at him. "I'm sorry," she said.

He brushed her soft hair out of her eyes and gently touched the tiny, zigzag line of stitches at her hairline. "Don't be, Elizabeth. Looking at dead people is a shock for anyone."

He was acutely aware of her body, of its curves and warmth. Without thinking anymore, he bent his head down and covered her mouth with his own.

He had meant to be tender and calm and comforting. But his passion flared the moment his lips touched hers, and he put aside his good intentions and was greedy, and demanding and thorough in his kiss. And Elizabeth Monette, electee of the Queen of Midnight Pageant, kissed him back like anything but a debutante.

Tommy Lee broke away from her while he still could and took a step back. His hands, and if he wasn't mistaken, his knees, were shaking. He ran into the desk, knocked over Dottie's lamp, bent to pick it up and knocked over the chair.

Elizabeth started to laugh—discreetly at first, then with full-throated mirth. He glared at her, then broke up himself. Laughter was good; it let off steam as readily as a fistfight. The two of them sat on the desk, their arms wrapped around each other, for a full twenty seconds, laughing like kids. Then he squeezed her shoulder and glanced at the office door where a bag of food sat waiting. "Hungry?"

Elizabeth's blue eyes looked into his and her mouth, puffy from his demanding kisses, pursed into a smile. She raised her left brow. "Starving. How about you?"

Tommy Lee felt the heat emanate from the center of his body outward. He wanted her. Badly. It was insane, he told himself.

Elizabeth turned to him and took his face in her hands. "You know, I never thanked you properly for jumping out of that window over there for me."

Tommy Lee circled her waist with his hands and pulled her close. "I was thinking about reminding you of that last night when you were lying half-naked in my guest room."

"I wasn't half-naked...."

"You weren't nearly naked enough for my taste," he replied. He kissed her, openmouthed and passionate, hiding none of his intention. When they broke free from each other, Elizabeth's eyes were shining.

"So why didn't you?"

"Why didn't I what?"

"Remind me to thank you. Properly."

Her teasing was womanly and self-confident. His heart raced. "You were pretty beat-up last night. The way I was feeling, I didn't want to start anything that would cause you any more pain."

"I'm pretty tough, Tommy Lee." With that she pulled him closer.

His body responded to her in what Tommy Lee feared was an inappropriate client-detective manner.

But he didn't care. He moved his left hand to her neck, then down to her waist and under her sweater, and finally, inside her bra. Her nipples were hard and silky. He laid her gently down and kissed her neck and breasts and belly, feeling light-headed and as hungry as a wolf.

The phone ringing two inches from his ear stopped him at the last possible moment. Elizabeth reached to push it away but Tommy Lee intervened. "Wait, it might be Chief Foley." He picked up the receiver and watched hungrily as Elizabeth pulled her sweater down over her incredible body.

"Betts Investigation. This is McCall."

"Tommy Lee?" Chief Foley said. "You okay?"

"Fine, Chief, what's up?" Tommy Lee smiled at Elizabeth, who was tucking her sweater back into her pants and trying not to limp. He'd forgotten how banged up her knees were, and felt a moment's remorse that perhaps he'd hurt her.

"And the second guy was Ray Robinson. Drifter. Ex-con. Cracker must have met up with him in prison."

"Who?"

"Aren't you listening, man? I told you, Henry Jackson, Cracker Jackson, was positively ID'ed as the guy with the shotgun blast to the face. Robinson is the other corpse the unit picked up by the school. You knew Jackson, right?"

"Yeah. I ran into him a couple of times, but he was bounced off the force when I was a rookie."

"Well, anyway, got something really interesting on the bullets we dug out of the body. Hand cast and antique. Bulow remembers some old case that had the same bullets, he thinks. We've sent them to New Orleans, FBI, for a match against anything on file.''

"What about the witnesses?" Tommy Lee asked, forcing himself to stop looking at Elizabeth so he could concentrate. "Did the woman who called in get a look at anything?"

"Naw. But we talked to an old guy who lives over on Kings Landing Lane, in a shotgun cottage behind the big houses. He was walking his dog and thinks he saw a gray pickup truck parked across from the school, with a guy in it."

"Did he get the plate?"

"Right," the chief drawled sarcastically. "You been watching too many cop shows, Tommy Lee. But he did remember the bumper was tied on with some kind of wire or rope. So we'll be looking."

"I'd appreciate being informed of any developments, Chief."

"You aren't a cop anymore, Tommy Lee," Foley said. "Don't you remember you're a private eye?"

Tommy Lee smiled and swore at his friend, low enough so Elizabeth couldn't hear. "Thanks, Chief."

"Yeah, well, I'll expect the same in return, McCall. Did you get Miss Monette back home safe?"

"Not yet," he replied, accepting the coffee cup she handed him. "But I'll do that soon."

"You'd better. She looked like hell," the chief said. "And I've already had fifteen messages this morning from executive board members of the Queen of Midnight Committee chewing my ass about security. Plus that damn pantywaist Mayor Prince. So I don't want any more close calls for Miss Monette. Word I'm hearing is she's the new Queen."

"You don't say," Tommy Lee answered, suddenly picturing Elizabeth—who was eating a ham-and-Swiss sub sandwich like she'd never seen food before—wearing a crown and little else. He tugged at the corner of his mustache. "Okay, Chief. I'll talk to you." He hung up.

"How are things going?" Elizabeth asked, handing him an unwrapped sandwich.

He accepted it and nodded. "Good. The two dead guys are ex-cons, one an ex-cop named Jackson. Robinson was the phony doctor. Foley has a couple of leads about a third guy they're sure was at the scene." Briefly he recounted the information about the rare bullets and the pickup truck. "I expect we'll know more pretty soon."

"Good." Elizabeth dusted crumbs from her mouth and walked around the desk. She retrieved her file folder and began reading from the two pages of handwritten notes.

She hoped she seemed nonchalant to him, but her heart was still racing from what had transpired. She was no stranger to romance, had had her share of boyfriends and gone through two serious relationships, both of which she had broken off when the men involved wanted something more permanent.

But she had never been kissed like Tommy Lee had kissed her. Had never wanted someone like the way she wanted him. Had never considered ripping the clothes off a man she had known for only twenty-four hours with the intention of making love with him until he could no longer walk straight. Despite her intentions to be cool, she flushed and found herself grinning.

"Something funny in the file?" Tommy Lee asked.

"No. Just a private thought," she said, risking a direct look into his brown eyes. A tremor went through her as she watched him bite down on the sandwich. "There's a number in here by Peach's name. Why don't I call it?"

He took another bite and nodded. "Why don't you. We'll go out and see him."

Great, she thought. *Then we'll go to the first place that has a bed so I can feel your naked body on me.* Elizabeth flushed and knocked the phone off the desk. She picked it up, realizing he was enjoying her awkwardness as much as she had his.

"Don't laugh at me, Tommy Lee. I'm a little weak-kneed."

"Why's that?" he challenged, his hand once again on her waist.

"Why do you think?"

Tommy Lee stared hard at her. She wasn't being coy. She was vulnerable, open, wanting to know how he felt. "I want to kiss you again, Elizabeth. A lot."

She licked her lips. "You want 'a lot,' as in 'much,' to kiss me? Or you want to kiss me a lot, as in several times?"

"Both," he said. He dropped the sandwich on the desk and pulled her against him. His hands explored her body while she watched him, her eyes heavy-lidded with desire.

"I want to make love to you, Elizabeth. In a proper room, with a proper bed. And a fire. And a lot of time, as in hours."

"When?" she breathed.

He inhaled and brought his hands to her face, kissing her on the nose. "As soon as I'm sure you're safe from whoever the hell hired those two thugs."

"No mixing business with pleasure, Mr. McCall?" Elizabeth countered, but her brain told her Tommy Lee was right. First things first. Everything in her life was a jumble now. Adding a relationship with this passionate, complicated man wouldn't do anything to solve the mysteries swirling around her.

Worry clouded his eyes. "Don't misunderstand me, Elizabeth,"

"Shhh," she replied, her fingers on his lips. "We'll slow this freight train down, Mr. McCall. But only for a little while." Elizabeth took a step back and gave him an up-and-down scrutiny. "Though it looks like you might need a cold shower to completely cooperate in this decision."

Before he could reply, Elizabeth picked up the phone. "Okay, on to business. I'll call Mr. Peach."

He looked a little dazed, but raked his hair back with his hand and picked up the discarded sandwich. "Do that."

Elizabeth dialed and was startled when a woman answered.

"Baptist Haven, this is Lucille."

"Ah, may I speak to Emmett Peach?" Elizabeth asked.

"Mr. Peach is resting now, ma'am. Would you like to leave a message or call back later?"

"Ah, yes. But may I ask, what is 'Baptist Haven'?"

"We're a full-care-facility retirement home, ma'am."

"And Mr. Peach lives there?"

The woman's pleasant Southern voice took on a suspicious tone. "May I ask who's calling, please?"

Elizabeth looked at Tommy Lee, wondering if she should leave her name, then decided to go ahead. She didn't need his okay, Elizabeth told herself. "Elizabeth Monette. My father, Judge Monette, is a friend of Mr. Peach's. I wanted to check and see how Mr. Peach is doing, since we haven't heard from him for a while."

Tommy Lee started choking and shaking his head violently, waving his hand to indicate she shouldn't say anything more. His actions so surprised Elizabeth that she didn't hear what the woman said.

"I'm sorry, what did you say?"

"I said, he's doing much better than he was. His doctors expect him to make a full recovery."

"Was he ill?" Elizabeth pressed.

"Well, I guess I can tell you, hon," the woman said, her voice dropping into gossip mode. "The poor old coot got knocked over the head last week. Someone, Dr. Heywood thinks it was probably some kid, broke into his room and then hit the poor old dear upside the head with his Bible, of all things! Don't know what the world's coming too. Probably looking for drugs or something."

"My goodness," Elizabeth said, her voice tight. "Well, thank you. Can you give me the address? Daddy and I would like to send some flowers." She scribbled down the information. Tommy Lee had crossed the room and was staring down at what she was writing, his face suffused with anger.

Elizabeth said goodbye and hung up, then crossed

her arms and challenged the glowering man she had minutes before been kissing. "What?"

"Are you crazy?" he exclaimed. "Don't go leaving your real name with people! For God's sake, Elizabeth, someone's trying to kill you!"

"But those men are dead," she retorted. "We just saw them."

He sighed, trying to calm himself. He leaned against the desk, his big hands smoothing down his rumpled jeans as he shook his head in disbelief. "Yes. Yes, we did see two dead men who were most likely involved in that near miss out on the street yesterday. But someone killed them, Elizabeth. Brutally and in cold blood. Someone we don't know. Someone who hired them. Someone who hired them to hurt you."

Elizabeth felt sick. She took a deep breath of air and collapsed into the chair beside the desk. "I'm sorry. I guess I didn't think all this through."

He crossed his arms over his chest. "No, you didn't. So why not let me make the calls. What did you find out about Peach?"

She didn't like the look on his face when he yelled at her, but the look of disbelief when she told him what had befallen Peach was even worse. By the time she'd finished her story, he was pulling his leather coat back on. "Let's go."

Grabbing her bag, she flipped off the light and tossed the remnants of lunch into the trash can. "Where to? Baptist Haven?"

"No. You're going home."

She whirled around and stared at him. "Why?"

"Because I'm not dragging you around with me. I've got some checking to do. You'd better get some rest. Your mama said you've got a party to go to tonight, anyway, and Chief Foley tells me the committee to pick the Queen is all over his butt. Besides, don't you need to do your hair, or something?''

Despite herself, Elizabeth reached for her hair. ''What's wrong with my hair?''

''It looks like you've been letting someone run his grubby hands through it. ''

She glared at him, but the playful look on his face calmed her down.

''Look, I'd rather go with you.''

''And I'd rather you didn't.''

''I hired you—''

''If you're going to pull that crap, I'll quit.''

They stood inches apart. ''After what just happened in there,'' Elizabeth began, ''I'm surprised you can act so damn arrogant.''

Tommy Lee opened his mouth to shout back at her, but closed it. Gently he lifted an errant hair from her cheek, felt her tense at his touch and wanted more than his next breath to kiss her. ''We don't have time for fighting.''

''Really? I thought detectives always had time to romance the women who paid them.''

He didn't want to respond to that, but snapped, ''Yeah, well, I thought the women who hired detectives knew when to shut up and listen to the experts.''

Elizabeth moved away from him with a scowl, but she stopped arguing.

Tommy Lee pulled the office door closed, locked it and took Elizabeth's arm as he walked her toward the elevator. She didn't look one bit happy, which was fine with him.

But she was going home.

And he was going to see Emmett Peach and find out what the man knew about a twenty-year-old adoption, and why the hounds of hell were sniffing around anyone who asked about it.

Chapter Eight

Petey Connor woke with a start, shivering with fever, his body as stiff as the bloodstains dried on the collar of his flannel shirt. He was huddled in the corner of his van, covered with a sleeping bag that smelled of gasoline and cooking oil.

He had parked in an abandoned boat shed out by the marina. He figured he would be safe there for a couple of days, and he had enough food and water to make it until he could clean up.

As long as he didn't get an infection and die. The first-aid kit was primitive—alcohol and gauze, some bandages and aspirin and a nearly empty tube of antibiotic cream. But he had made use of it, and had managed to stop the bleeding from the worst of his injuries.

He was one lucky SOB compared to old Ray and Cracker. He didn't mind either of them being dead, but he sure was angry that they had been stupid enough to get themselves killed by a woman.

Well, he'd be sure and pay her back, three times over. "Whoever said there ain't no honor among thieves," he rasped, his voice echoing eerily in the van. Exhausted from the effort of thinking and being awake, Petey wrapped the sleeping bag tighter around him. He was loaded with cash, thanks to having the presence of mind to rob Jackson's dead body of the roll of bills before driving off. He wished he'd had time to find Ray and get his gun, but with the seventeen hundred dollars he did have he could drive over to Mobile and get himself as many guns as he needed.

With his hands shaking furiously, Petey downed five aspirin and reached for the half-full bottle of tequila and took a swig.

His body stopped shaking, and as consciousness started to seep away, he spent a couple of moments enjoying his thoughts of revenge. And of collecting even bigger from the woman who had nearly killed him. He had no idea who she was, since Cracker had been too uptight to share her name with him. But Petey knew how to find her.

He had the two phone numbers he'd fished out of Cracker Jackson's pocket, one of which was certain to be hers. And, as soon as he was stronger, he was going have what the woman who had killed his two cohorts wanted most—Elizabeth Monette.

He was going to ask the woman for twenty-five thousand dollars to kill the Monette broad and keep quiet about her earlier nonsense. Then, when the murderous bitch brought him the money, he was going to shoot her right between the eyes. *That one's for you, Cracker,* he thought.

Petey's mouth stretched in a parody of a smile as his mind clouded over and floated above the cold floor of the van.

TOMMY LEE SAT BESIDE the old man's bedside and stared down at a face that looked a hundred years old.

Emmett Peach was tall and frail, his head completely bald. The only visible hair on the man was his eyebrows, which were as black as caterpillars and just as bushy.

He was sleeping peacefully in a nearly upright position, against two fresh pillows, his plaid pajamas snugly buttoned at his neck. The only sign of his recent brush with lawlessness was a faint, greenish bruise above his right ear.

The nurse on duty had told Tommy Lee he could stay fifteen minutes, then he would have to leave. He glanced at his watch and pulled on the corner of his mustache. It had been ten. He cleared his throat and grinned when Mr. Peach turned and looked at him with a toothless smile.

"How are you, son? Your daddy here?"

Obviously Mr. Peach had mistaken him for someone. "My name is Tommy Lee McCall, Mr. Peach. How do you do?" He held out his hand for what would probably be an awkward shake, and was pleasantly surprised when the old man grabbed it and pumped it vigorously .

"Tommy Lee. Your daddy here?"

"No, sir, my daddy died several years ago. Stephen McCall, crab fisherman by trade. Did you know him sir?"

Emmett Peach looked confused, but calmly folded his hands over his chest. "My daddy must not be coming, either."

Tommy Lee realized the futility of his trying to discuss an incident that had happened twenty years ago with Emmett Peach, but felt he owed it to Elizabeth to give it one try. "Mr. Peach, I'm trying to find out some information on an adoption you handled about twenty years ago. A little girl, five years old, who had lost her mama in a violent incident. Don't know about her daddy. Maybe was a family in Alabama?''

Emmett Peach looked over at Tommy Lee. His blue eyes had faded to the pale, pale gray reflection of a winter sky in a street puddle after a storm. "Why?"

He took a breath. "The little girl is all grown up. But she may be in danger, for some reason connected to the adoption. If there is anything you can tell us, we would really appreciate it."

Mr. Peach looked across the room toward the TV, mounted on a shelf on the wall opposite his bed. He seemed to be staring at a picture only he could see. "I remember that case. Interesting one it was, too. The mother was dead. Murdered. Can't say anything about the father." He raised his frail fingers to his bloodless lips and made a motion like a key closing a lock.

A surge of excitement shot through Tommy Lee's blood and he understood in a flash his sister's enjoyment of her job. "I understand, and I won't press you about him, sir. But could you tell me anything about the mother? She is dead, after all. Do you recall her name?"

Several moments of silence passed. "The little girl was called Marylynn. Pretty name, pretty little child. Tall for a girl. Blue eyes that would break your heart." He leaned closer, grasping the metal railing of his hospital bed to support himself. "She looked a lot like her grandmama. I bet she's a beauty now."

It pained him to think the Monettes had changed her name. She'd lost everything as it was. It would have been cruel to take her name, too. But he didn't stop to sort that out now. His pulse pounded in his head. This man knew Elizabeth's grandmother!

"She is a beauty, sir. In fact, you can judge for yourself, if you will. I'd like to bring her for a visit. Can I have her do that? I'm sure she would like to hear about her grandmama."

Emmett looked interested, but hesitant. "I knew her other grandmama, too." The buggy eyebrows danced up and down. "Quite a naughty one, that."

"May I ask her name, Mr. Peach? I'm sure my friend would be very interested in knowing any of her kin, especially if they're still around."

"Some are, some are. But they're not in 'Bama. Gracious." Mr. Peach laughed, a tinkly, clear sound that hinted at the personality inside the frail exterior. "Goodness, the doctor wouldn't like hearing someone thought his mama was from Alabama!"

Suddenly Mr. Peach began to cough. Tommy Lee leaned forward to pat the man on the back, but he shook his head and pointed to the glass of water on his bedside table.

Tommy Lee handed it to him, then set it down again. He waited for a moment, hardly able to keep from asking the next question. *Dr. Who?* he wanted to shout. The sound of quick footsteps and a loud, "Well, Mr. Peach, you're awake!" stopped Tommy Lee. He looked toward the door where a frizzy-haired woman, dressed in hospital whites and ridiculously high-heeled pumps, stood surveying the scene.

"Hey, there," the woman said to Tommy Lee, hurrying into the room, her thin, metal-tapped heels making nicking sounds like nails dropping on glass. "I'm Lucille Thompkins."

Tommy Lee stood. "Tommy Lee McCall, Miss Thompkins."

Lucille crossed over to the bed and shook her finger

at Mr. Peach. "I hear you didn't eat your lunch today, Mr. Peach. Am I going to have to come feed you myself?"

Emmett Peach made a face and folded his hands again on his chest. He shut his eyes.

Lucille walked a few feet around the bed and tapped Tommy Lee on the arm. When he came closer, she linked her arm in his and in a little-girl whisper said, "We'll let him get some sleep now. So nice of you to come see him, hon. He don't have many visitors."

Tommy Lee cast a last look over his shoulder. Mr. Peach still had his eyes closed, but Tommy Lee felt sure he was wide-awake.

"Of course. I'll come see him again. Tomorrow, around noon," he said in a loud voice, sure Mr. Peach was listening to every word.

"That'd be wonderful, Mr. McCall. You can have lunch with the old dear in the cafeteria. He'd like that."

She escorted him to the door, and Tommy Lee realized he was being asked to leave. He glanced back at the room where Emmett Peach lay pretending to sleep. "Who is Mr. Peach's attending physician, Miss Thompkins?"

"Dr. Katherine Smiths is his admitting doctor, Mr. McCall. But he sees whoever is on call. Most of the physicians from Belle Fleur General are over here. Why do you ask?"

"Has any progress been made in finding out who attacked Mr. Peach?" Tommy Lee returned, falling easily into his cop stance.

Lucille Thompkins took a step back. Her tiny green eyes narrowed. "You know, I don't rightly know. Why don't you give the police a call, hon. I'm sure, since that's their job, they might be able to help you with that."

Tommy Lee felt like handcuffing her to a car bumper, but instead he smiled. "Thank you, Miss Thompkins. I'll do that. Good day."

"Good day, Mr. McCall. Tomorrow is chicken nuggets and fresh applesauce. Won't that be nice? We'll see you at noon!"

Tommy Lee kept walking, wondering how soon he could get Elizabeth out here, and if they had a snowball's chance in hell of getting in to see Mr. Peach without having to go through the way-too-nosy Miss Lucille Thompkins.

LUVEY ROSE WAS entertaining. Since last evening's role as the bearer of bad-but-oh-so-interesting news, her popularity with the Queen of Midnight electees had grown dramatically.

She and Tammy sat in her cozy sitting room, hosting a late-afternoon cocktail party for the group, while the drinks and gossip flowed like the Mississippi after a thunderstorm. Mayor Prince was, as always, his witty self. Holding forth from the center of Luvey's silk-covered settee, he was focusing his remarks on Luvey's ex-husband.

"Why don't you get his little cop behind over here and we can hear about his Schwarzeneggeresque rescue of Little Miss Monette, right from the horse's mouth?"

"Tommy Lee and I don't speak much. Though making conversation was never his strong suit."

Several guests tittered and Tammy blushed. "Luvey, you shouldn't go on like that about Tommy Lee."

"Yes, I should, darling," her big sister teased. She

was draped in an electric-blue jumpsuit, the neckline of which was cut down to her navel. "Some day you'll understand what I mean when I tell our friends here Mr. McCall's best asset was his mouth, but not when he used it for talking."

The giggles went up a notch, but not high enough to cover the sound of the phone ringing. Luvey's maid came to the living-room entrance.

"Phone, Miz Rose."

"Take a message, please. I'm entertaining."

The maid crossed the room and said something privately to Luvey. The smile fled her perfect features and she stood abruptly, oblivious to the appreciative stares of all her male guests. "Paris, darling, tell a naughty true story about a scandal involving a past Queen of Midnight. It will teach the girls who won't be Queen that winning isn't everything."

"I've got just the one," the mayor purred, putting his arm around Tammy's shoulder. "Since Rosellen isn't here, maybe we can revisit a certain bon mot about her grandfather's fascination with white trash!"

The tittering increased as the crowd smelled blood and Luvey could make her escape. "I'll take it in the study," she called out in the hallway, then waited to hear the click of her maid hanging the extension up in the kitchen.

"I told you not to call me here," Luvey hissed into the phone. But before she could say more, her caller began to explain why he was interrupting the party.

Luvey remained silent, slumping into the chair, her red hair flying around her head as she shook it in frustration. "I don't believe this could have happened. What are we going to do now?"

She listened, then shook her head even more vehemently. "If she finds out, it's all over, darling. Neither of us are any match for that kind of fight."

The caller argued, then asked for a meeting. "Okay. I can't tonight because of the dinner party. And tomorrow Tammy has her final fitting. Friday is the Parade of Lights on the river. We'll do it there. At the marina. Meet me at slip 25C."

Luvey stood, her body taut with anger and the energy of fear. "Look, I can't see you before Friday. If she confronts you before then, well, you'll have to wing it."

With a grim smile, Luvey nodded at the words spoken so truly in her ear. "Yeah, I know we're in this together, lover. That's the problem." She slammed down the phone and stomped back in to her guests, her festive mood ruined, but her urge to hurt someone in full bloom.

ELIZABETH SAT BOLT upright in bed. In the dark she felt her heart racing and a scream dying in her throat. Clutching at her chest, she listened for the sound of footsteps, a sign she had once again scared the devil out of her sleeping parents, but the old house was quiet.

The clock beside her read 3:38 a.m. She took several deep breaths and tried to forget the worst nightmare she had ever had.

But she couldn't. It was as vivid as the sound of her heartbeat in her ears. She was young, a tiny girl. Swinging on a homemade plank hanging from a huge magnolia tree. It was summer. Someone—she couldn't see who—was pushing her with gentle hands. When she turned to look at him, she saw a monster dressed in white.

She jumped from the swing and instead of landing on the soft, squashy grass of the field, she fell through a plate-glass window. The crash was like dying, loud and clear and unchangeable. She screamed for her mother as blood streamed down her face and arms, but her mother didn't come.

For her mother was lying dead in the broken glass of the window, cut to pieces, eyes open and staring.

Shivering, Elizabeth slipped out of bed, pulled on her robe and crept down the stairs to the kitchen. She poured milk into a pan and put it on the stove, then restlessly walked around the small kitchen and breakfast room, stopping to look at and touch the hundred familiar objects her mother had brought with her from their home in Baltimore. Photographs of herself as a Girl Scout, her dad and mom at the Grand Canyon; cushions she had helped her mother embroider, the summer she was sixteen and caught the mumps; the "special" turkey platter her mother had painted in one of her self-improvement classes and which they used faithfully every Thanksgiving and Christmas.

But nothing comforted her or erased the images from her mind. Even with her eyes open she could see her real mother, blond hair, slim fingers, lying on her back on a linoleum floor covered with glass, dead and silent as the night.

Elizabeth poured the milk into a mug and stood sipping it, looking out the back windows. She saw the dark lawn and acreage beyond her mother's garden, the shape of the caretaker's cottage, the outline of her father's car. She wanted to cry but instead rested her head against the wall, reaching out to touch the cold plastic of the phone.

She wanted to talk to Tommy Lee. He had dropped

her off at two-thirty this afternoon, and had called when she was at a party with her parents, leaving a message that he would pick her up tomorrow morning at eleven. Suddenly Elizabeth wanted him to come over and hold her like he had today in his sister's office. She wanted to kiss him the way she had on the desk, as she had in her mind a hundred times since then. She lifted the receiver, then laughed at her own stupidity. She didn't even have his phone number. And now it was four in the morning.

Elizabeth hung up the phone and poured out the rest of the milk. She turned the lights back down and started up the stairway. Had she turned off the pan of milk? She walked to the stove and saw that she had, then her eye caught a shadow on the wall. A shadow that slowly moved.

Her heart pounding, Elizabeth turned in the dark toward the window across the small kitchen. There, outlined by the light from the quarter moon, was the silhouette of a man. He was still, watchful. Tall, with big shoulders, the man wore a hat with a bit of a brim, like a Greek fisherman. He was holding something long and cylindrical in his hand.

A gun. A shotgun.

A scream crept up her throat and she bit down on her knuckle to keep from crying out. The shadow moved away from the center of the window, along the back of the house. Toward the door. Elizabeth bent down and peered over the counter toward the back door, which had only a flimsy piece of lace covering it. He would see her. She ducked lower, her mind a blank. Should she cry out? Would he shoot her, come in and kill the judge and Miss Lou in their beds?

Elizabeth heard the knob turn back and forth

quickly, while the man checked the lock. She would have to make a run for it, she decided. Cross the kitchen and go upstairs. There was one door to lock, and she would have time to rouse her parents and call the police from the upstairs phone.

Her ears straining for the least sound, she held her breath, poised to run. And heard footsteps, hollow on the cement steps outside, moving away from the house.

He was leaving. Or was he going around to the front? Elizabeth stood upright, and screamed when the light went on behind her.

"Elizabeth, I'm sorry child!" Judge Monette cried out.

"Daddy! I'm sorry," she said, racing across the slippery floor to give him a hug.'

"Why on earth did you yell like that? Why are you up at all?"

"Baylor?" Miss Lou's voice called from the stairway. "What's going on?"

"Nothing, Lou. Go back to bed, darling. I just scared the daylights out of Elizabeth."

"Elizabeth? Is she up? I'll be right down, you two," she called out.

The judge hugged Elizabeth to him. "Now you've done it. Neither of us gets to eat cookies now."

"Daddy," Elizabeth countered, "I think I saw someone outside."

"What? Where?" He brushed by her and headed for the back door.

"Out on the back lawn, in front of the windows."

Her father leaned down and peered into the darkness. "Don't see anything. Although there's a light on at Clay's. Maybe he was up looking around."

Relief flooded through her veins. But what about the gun? Of course, her father had several old guns he used for hunting ducks. Surely he would have given one of them to his caretaker to hoist around while he checked locks. "What a jerk I am, Daddy. I'm going to go back upstairs. Night." She kissed him, then hugged her mother as she entered the room. "See you in a few hours."

Then she was gone.

"What's going on?" Miss Lou asked.

The judge shook his head. "I think she had a nightmare. So bad she thought she saw someone outside."

Miss Lou collapsed into a chair. "That poor, poor girl. We should never have told her—"

The judge grabbed a bag of cookies and slapped them onto the table in front of his wife of forty years. "Stop it. You were everything a mother should be and could be to that child since the day we set eyes on her. She knows it. You know it. You're still the best thing that's ever happened to either one of us. We did the best we could. We'll get her through this. So have a cookie. Eat."

Miss Lou squeezed Baylor's hand and kissed him. But when she picked up a cookie and nibbled it, her eyes glancing toward the stairs, she could taste nothing but fear.

Chapter Nine

Tommy Lee pressed down on the gas pedal, not liking one bit the way the brief exchange with the woman next to him had gone. All he said to her when she had walked into the kitchen where he was waiting was, "Hey, Queen of Midnight," and she had snapped his head off.

"Don't call me that."

"Hey, I didn't mean any disrespect. But the word I hear on the streets is that you're it."

"Well, you've been traveling on the wrong streets, Tommy Lee. Now, let's go, I've got a lot of things for us to do if we're going to make any progress on what you've been hired for."

He had wanted to grab her and kiss her like he had yesterday, but Elizabeth was emitting enough "Don't touch me" vibes to stop a tank. She was dressed in a pleated skirt and heavy wool hose, little black boots, and a vivid blue sweater that showed off her curves and brought out the color of her eyes. He was letting himself feel bowled over by how beautiful she was, but managed to act nonchalant in the face of her mood. With a grin he had said goodbye to Miss Lou—who had sat quietly through her daughter's ill-mannered welcome—and followed Elizabeth out to the truck.

He hadn't tried to open the door for her, which was just as well, because he didn't trust himself to stand that close to her and not take her in his arms. And he hadn't spoken to her at all during the last fifteen minutes, which was also just as well since he found himself feeling so stirred up and mistreated. He didn't want to talk for fear he would open his mouth and whine like a high-school boy.

Which was how he felt, he suddenly realized. Like a damned high-school kid, head over heels in love with the prom queen, too tongue-tied to speak what was in his heart.

Which was probably the first smart thing he had done in the past thirty-six hours, he realized. With a cold blast of reason Tommy Lee told himself he must have read this whole thing with Elizabeth the wrong way.

She had not been attracted to him.

She had only been looking for some comfort after two horrendous attempts on her life. She had no feelings for him—a washed-up cop with an uncertain future. Hadn't she just told him she thought of him as only an employee? Hadn't she?

He felt a flush creeping up his chest to his neck and gripped the steering wheel with both hands to keep from punching it. What a jackass he had been.

"Where are we going?" Elizabeth suddenly asked.

"You talking to me?"

She pursed her lips in a way that made his gut twist. "Doing your Robert De Niro impression this morning, Mr. McCall?"

"You playing your Cruella deVil role, Miss Monette? Maybe I can find some puppies for you to skin and get you in a better frame of mind.''

That backed her down a bit, he was happy to see. She lowered her eyes to her hands, which had twisted up the blue woolen scarf hanging from her coat as if it were a hankie. She jutted out her chin and stared straight out the window, but he knew she was trying to keep from crying.

Suddenly Tommy Lee had a terrible feeling he had judged everything wrong this morning. He might not have known the woman long, but he knew her well enough to know she wasn't a snob, or mean as a snake, despite her testiness earlier. Elizabeth Monette was the real thing.

''What happened since I saw you last?'' he asked quietly, willing to take another hit to get to the bottom of her troubles.

''What are you talking about?''

''Something is wrong with you, woman. It doesn't take a damn detective to tell that.'' His eyes bore into hers. ''Why don't you tell me about it. Since I'm working for you, and all. Hell, I'll just add another charge to your bill if I can fix it.''

Elizabeth blinked quickly, and he watched as two tears tumbled down her wind-pinked cheeks and fell onto her sweater. She dug her hand around in the pocket of her jacket and pulled out a folded piece of paper, which she threw onto the seat beside her.

Steadying the truck's wheel with his left hand, Tommy Lee picked up the coarse sheet of paper and stared at the cutout letters pasted onto it. ''The next time, you are dead, Elizabeth. Long live the Queen.''

He cursed and looked at her. ''When did you get this?''

"I found it this morning when I went out to get the newspaper. It was stuck in the back door."

He cursed again, realizing his prints and hers had probably obliterated any pertinent evidence of the sender. "Did you call Chief Foley?"

Her eyes were round, the thick lashes wet. "No. I thought I would talk it over with you first."

"Dammit, Elizabeth! This lunatic was on your property yesterday sometime. You should have had the cops out there dusting for prints, looking for footprints and such."

"I didn't want to scare my parents to death—" she began.

"Oh, so you'll hide it and act like this is nothing?"

"We're good at hiding things in my family," she said, her voice touched with bitterness.

"Don't go feeling sorry for yourself about that," he retorted. "Your parents are people, which means they are not perfect. I'm sure they thought they were doing the best thing for you by not telling you about the adoption."

"I know that, but..." Her voice trailed off, then she said rapidly, "It's just so damn frustrating, Tommy Lee. To think your whole life you are a certain person, then to find out at twenty-five, that you're not that person at all."

"Why aren't you? Being related by blood to a couple of other people doesn't change how you act, what you've done, who you love. Does it?"

Elizabeth started to smile at him, that million-dollar-beam-of-sunlight smile, but she quickly swallowed it. "I'm sorry I was so short with you this morning. You are right. But let's stop indulging my personal problems and talk about what we're going to do next."

He glanced at his watch and frowned. He really wanted to talk with Chief Foley about these letters. He had made a mistake not mentioning them to him earlier. "Okay. We're almost at Baptist Haven. I'm taking you to see Emmett Peach." As she sucked in her breath in surprise, Tommy Lee filled her in on his visit the day before with the elderly lawyer.

"He knows who my grandmother is?"

"Evidently he knew both grandmothers," Tommy Lee replied, pleased that her eyes had brightened a bit at his news. "He wasn't completely lucid, but I think once he meets you, he'll share some information that should make finding your parents' identities fairly simple. And as soon as we're done there, we'll go over to the police station and bring Foley up to speed on all this. Maybe he can post a guard at night, or something."

"The judge would never stand for that."

"I'm sure the judge would stand for anything that would make you a little safer."

"Do you really think I'm still in danger? I thought with those men dead…"

He pulled on his mustache. "The morgue has two dead men, Elizabeth. And someone still on the loose who is brazen enough to come onto your property in the middle of the night sounds pretty dangerous to me."

"Okay," she agreed, her voice tight. "But then we have to go to the deAngelis law firm."

"Where?"

"Down on Market Street. DeAngelis used to practice with Mr. Peach. They've operated out of the same building for forty years, so I'm hoping they may have some files on my adoption. Maybe Mr. Peach will call them for us, pave the way.''

''How'd you find out about that?''

Elizabeth explained she had spent her evening with her parents going over all the documents the judge and Miss Lou had regarding her adoption. ''Anyway, with what we've both found out already, we're on our way!'' Despite her optimism, she suddenly felt a stab of regret that her formal association with the handsome ex-cop was going to be terminated so quickly. Of course, after yesterday, she would have thought they would still have quite a personal relationship, but could she be sure?

Brushing aside the thought, Elizabeth picked up the letter again. ''By the way, I think I saw the guy who left this.''

Tommy Lee jerked his head around to her so fast that the truck swerved. ''What? When?''

Elizabeth told him about the shadow on the window. ''But when the judge came downstairs and saw the light on at the caretaker's house, we just assumed—''

''Assumed! God in heaven, Elizabeth. Don't ever assume. When you assume, all you do is make an ass of you and me. Haven't you ever heard that little expression?''

''Tommy Lee, I really don't appreciate these paternal little lectures. Honestly, you're never going to make it as a detective if you don't get control of yourself.''

''I don't know what you're talking about.'' And he didn't, or at least, he hoped he didn't. His ego spoke next, ignoring the warning from his brain. ''Unless you're referring to yesterday in Dottie's office. And if you are, Miss Monette, let me apologize for kissing you. It won't happen again, I'll make damn sure of that.''

She looked miserable, and shocked over what he had said. "I wasn't talking about that. But thank you for bringing it up. And if that's the way you want it, that's fine by me."

The way he wanted it, he thought to himself in frustration. Of course, he didn't want it that way. But how the hell did *she* want it? He turned into the parking lot of Baptist Haven too fast, and the rear wheels fishtailed on the salted asphalt. "Fine by me, too."

He was glad she looked upset. He stared out the front windshield, then gasped. His pettiness with Elizabeth, which he was already feeling bad about, flew out of his mind like a bat from a barn as the scene before him flashed a big red stop sign in his brain.

There were four Belle Fleur city police cars parked in the retirement-home parking lot, three with lights flashing. The fourth, the chief's new Buick, sat at the entrance. A uniformed cop was leaning against the hood, talking on the phone. The driver's door was open, as if the chief intended to come running out and jump in. Since the town only had nine units, whatever had brought out this many cops had to be major-league. Tommy Lee spotted Mayor Prince's yellow Mercedes-Benz in the front row of the visitors' section and let out a low whistle.

"What's happened?" Elizabeth asked in a dazed voice.

"Something big." He stopped the truck and jumped down, reflexively reaching for his gun. It wasn't there and his hand moved nervously away from his leg.

"Stay here, Elizabeth. Let me find out what's going on."

For once, she did what he said without any argument.

Sergeant Bulow flipped off the cell phone he was carrying and nodded at Tommy Lee. "Hey, man, I was just tracking you down. Chief wants to see you."

Tommy Lee glanced toward Elizabeth. The hair on the back of his neck was tingling, and he had the odd notion he should run, and take the woman waiting along with him. "What happened in there, Bulow?"

The ruddy-faced sergeant shook his head. "An old man got hisself dead last night, shot up with enough drugs to kill a bull. Same old gent someone hit upside the head with a Bible last week."

"Emmett Peach." Tommy Lee's voice felt strained. He didn't like the way Bulow's head snapped back at hearing the victim's name coming from his mouth.

"How did you know that?"

"A guess. Where's Foley?"

"Around back. He said I'm supposed to take you to the station when I find you, but since you're here, maybe I should tell him."

The tense feeling in Tommy Lee's neck crawled down his back and grabbed onto his spine. He glanced over at his truck just as Elizabeth Monette slammed the door and began walking toward them. So much for listening to him.

Bulow looked toward the pickup and frowned. "Isn't that the Monette woman?"

Tommy Lee ignored the question. "What's going on out back, Bulow?"

The cop turned again to Tommy Lee. "We got a double on our hands here, Tommy Lee. Asides from

Mr. Peach, a woman by the name of Lucille Thompkins got her head near blowed off with a shotgun." He shook his head. "Four murders in two days. Belle Fleur ain't had but five other murders the whole twenty years I been on this job. What the hell you got yourself involved in, son?"

THIRTY MINUTES LATER Chief Foley joined Tommy Lee and Elizabeth in the hospital administrator's empty conference room. The chief was obviously unhappy, and he directed the brunt of his anger at his ex-favorite cop.

"I'm not liking things around here at all, Tommy Lee," Chief Foley began, settling at the head of the small, overly waxed table. His sunglasses slid a couple of inches when he laid them down and he covered them with his callused hand. "For some reason, you are personally acquainted with four-out-of-four dead bodies Dr. Willis at the morgue is going be preparing for the ground. Care to explain why you're suddenly on such close terms with the about-to-dies?"

Tommy Lee leaned back in his chair and crossed one boot-clad leg over the other. "I wasn't 'personally acquainted' with those two chumps that got themselves killed night before last, nor did I know Mr. Peach. I stopped by to see him yesterday about a business matter, which is also the first time I laid eyes on Miss Thompkins. I'd say it's coincidence. Case closed."

The chief laughed a mirthless chuckle and pointed his finger at Tommy Lee. "I'll say case closed, Tommy Lee, if and when that be the case. Now what kinda business did you have with a man who'd been retired from his profession for fifteen years?"

Tommy Lee didn't look at Elizabeth, but he felt her tense in the chair beside him. "I can't discuss that."

Foley stared at him, his face blotchy with anger. "Can't or won't?"

Tommy Lee shrugged.

The chief turned to Elizabeth. "Can you discuss it, Miss Monette?"

"Mr. McCall is in my employ for a personal matter, Chief. That's all I want to say, other than I didn't know those two men who were killed, but the smaller man, Robinson, might have been the person standing across the street when the car tried to run me down."

"Which you already know about, Chief. So it's just saying it again." Tommy Lee slammed his chair down on the floor again and stood. "And all of us are too busy to sit here talking about something we already covered. Miss Monette and I have business to attend to, so if you need any more questions answered, let me know."

"Sit down, Tommy Lee," the chief ordered.

Elizabeth sucked in her breath, watching Tommy Lee. He crossed his arms and smiled, but made no move to sit. "I don't work for you anymore, Frank. So you get a warrant if you want to ask me anything more about Mr. Peach."

She watched the chief and read several feelings flashing across his narrow face—what looked like regret, anger and frustration, mixed with confusion. Tommy Lee seemed to be able to elicit those things easily from people, she thought.

"Tommy Lee," Elizabeth began, remembering his conviction that she should tell Chief Foley about the hate mail and the visitor last night, "maybe we should mention…"

His brown eyes silenced her. "Let's go, Miss Monette."

She stood, feeling the chief watch her. But even if she didn't know anything about police matters, she knew enough about Tommy Lee McCall to know this wasn't the time to get between him and his old boss.

They hurried down the hallway and out to the hospital lobby. Sergeant Bulow was standing with a young woman wearing a badge identifying her as a reporter for the Belle Fleur *Press Register.* The cop had a plastic bag full of what looked like trash. Elizabeth looked closer and saw they were neatly cut-up pieces of magazine headlines. *The letter!* Elizabeth thought. *But who...?*

She whispered to Tommy Lee, "Look at those scraps in the—"

"I see them, darlin'. Don't say a word. Just keep walking."

They hit the parking lot and didn't stop when the young reporter yelled, "Can I have a word with you, Tommy Lee?"

He smiled and waved. "Good to see you, hon. Tell Duval he's getting fat." He hoped reference to her brother, the cop who had taken their statements at the accident scene two days ago, would stop her questions. It did.

Elizabeth thought they had escaped when she settled in the cab and Tommy Lee slammed the door of the truck, but before he crossed around the back and got in, the yellow Mercedes pulled in front of them and Mayor Prince bounded out. In the gray daylight his hair looked even more unnaturally red than usual.

Tommy Lee slammed his door and started the engine, but not before Prince stepped up on the pickup's fender and knocked on Elizabeth's window.

"Damn his hide," Tommy Lee started. "Hang on, Elizabeth, I'm going to back up."

She put her hand on his arm and squeezed. "It's okay. It'll be worse if we run." Elizabeth cranked down the truck window and smiled. "Hey, Mr. Mayor. How are you?"

"Darling girl!" the mayor exclaimed. "The question is, how are you? We're all just quaking in our boots about your horrible experiences. Hello, Mr. McCall," he said with a wave. "How's your sweet sister?"

"Doing as well as can be expected."

"Bless her heart! Twins, she's carrying. I hear you are taking on her business. Are you in the employ of our Elizabeth, now? Trying to track down the fiends who have made her return to our fair city such a nightmare?"

"Elizabeth and I are just friends, Mayor. But we really have to be going—"

Prince grasped Elizabeth's arm. "But what are you doing out here, Elizabeth? Did the police tell you what a horrible thing happened? First those criminals out by the school and now more murder!"

"I don't think you should be discussing police business with us, Mr. Mayor," Tommy Lee interrupted, gunning the engine in the hopes the fumes would chase the weaselly city official off the side of his truck. "I'm retired, you might remember," he added with more bite than he would have liked.

"Of course, you are right, Mr. McCall. How are you feeling, by the way? That bullet staying put, is it?"

"Bullet?" Elizabeth stammered, turning away from Prince to stare at the man next to her.

"It's fine. Not going anywhere, Mr. Mayor. But we are, so if you'll step back and let Elizabeth roll up that window before she catches her death, I'd appreciate it."

"Surely, of course. And I'm glad you are feeling well. You certainly look the picture of health. I was just saying that to your ex, you know. Luvey was bragging on about you a bit, by the way. Don't quite know how that girl is settling for that old coot she's seeing now, when she had a nice young turk, like yourself." The mayor winked at Elizabeth. "But you know some girls. They'll trade in a hunk for a fat bank account anytime."

"Goodbye, Mr. Mayor," Tommy Lee intoned, no goodwill at all left in his voice. Suddenly a new fear bloomed in his mind.

Had his ex-wife something to do with the attacks on Elizabeth? She was ruthless, and had been at the hospital at the same time the phony doctor showed up. But why? She didn't really care that much whether or not Tammy was named Queen, did she? He pulled on his mustache and nodded at the mayor, "If you'll just step away, I don't want you to get hurt."

"Just one more moment," the mayor replied, turning his attention back to Elizabeth. "I'll see you at the Parade of Lights dinner on the river, won't I? You look absolutely no worse the wear for your accident." He put his spidery little paw on Elizabeth's hair, brushing the bangs to the side. "Those stitches don't even show with your hair brushed over, honey. You'll be the prettiest thing there."

"Thank you, Mr. Mayor. Yes, I'll see you Friday

night. Goodbye.'' She cranked up the window and he finally stepped off the truck.

Tommy Lee threw the car into Reverse, spraying gravel and rock salt all over the luxury sedan. Elizabeth saw a brief smile on his face when he checked his rearview mirror for the mayor's reaction, but the two of them had more important things to talk over than his vendetta against Mayor Prince.

She crossed her arms over her chest and stared at Tommy Lee. A tiny little piece of her mind was trying not to think of Tommy Lee in bed with Luvey, and the rest of her was battling the thought of how it had felt to kiss him. ''So, why the change of heart about telling the police about the letters?''

''You saw that scrap bag full of cut-up magazines. If they got that from that Thompkins woman's trash can, which is what I'd bet, then they would be a little too interested in the fact that you got some hate mail she glued together.''

''Why?''

He shifted gears and the truck sped up. ''Because they might think you had a reason to kill her.''

Elizabeth threw her head back and laughed. It was such a preposterous conclusion, she couldn't help it. ''Me? Kill two people I don't even know? Surely you don't think the chief pictures me a murderess?''

''Maybe not.'' His next words were clipped and as cold as steel. ''But maybe he thinks you hired someone to do it.''

''Oh, my God,'' she breathed, overwhelmed by the logic of what Tommy Lee was saying. ''Well, then, maybe that's even more reason to show them the letters. Convince them I'm the target, not the shooter.''

He grinned at her attempt at cop lingo. ''I don't

know if that is what he would think. Cops think in straight lines, Elizabeth. Connect-the-dot mentality is the way we work. Frank might think you're working the sympathy angle to get elected Queen. Besides, do you want to open the whole kettle of fish about your birth mother being killed, and how the deaths of all these people in Belle Fleur might be linked to your looking into who she was?''

Elizabeth swallowed hard. ''Do you really think all these deaths are connected to my trying to find out about my identity?''

''What other answer can you come up with? You get letters, someone cuts your brake line, then tries to run you down with a car. All this happens after you start inquiring about your past and my sister made a couple of calls looking into your adoption. Then, when it's clear you might be elected Queen of Midnight, some nutcase sends a phony doctor after you to do who-knows-what and people start ending up dead. It's looking to me like there has to be a link in all these events, and unfortunately, the link looks like you.''

''But why?''

''Someone is jealous. Or afraid of having brought the past up. Or both.''

Elizabeth felt cold and hot all at once. She leaned her head against the seat, taking comfort in the hum of the engine. Outside, the day was dreary and damp. No sign of Christmas cheer; only winter's grim reduction of the landscape to gray and lifeless brown. She closed her eyes as a piece of a dream—or a memory?—took shape inside her head. She saw a doctor—not the man with the dirty fingernails, but another man. A tall man with a kind voice. She couldn't see his face, but she could hear him. He was reading a fairy tale to her. *Cinderella?*

Could that kind man be trying to kill her now? Had he killed her mother?

Could he be her biological father?

"No," she whispered aloud, shutting her eyes against the horror of murder of one parent by another. Her hands trembled and suddenly she wanted to talk about anything but herself. She reached out and touched Tommy Lee's arm. "So tell me about the bullet."

He swore under his breath. "That's ancient history, Elizabeth."

"Hey, that's what I'm interested in, remember?" She had the urge to touch his face, but knew it would have been too intrusive, for his eyes were naked of defense.

"Please tell me. I really want to know."

Grudgingly Tommy Lee began to relate the reason one of Belle Fleur's finest was retired. It was a gruesome, terrifying story. He did not pretend any heroism. "I didn't want to die. I was more afraid of dying than of anything I had ever experienced in my life when I hit the asphalt on the garage floor. I saw cigarette butts and oil drips, and thought how much I wanted to see the sky again. When I lost consciousness, I remember praying. Not a prayer with words, just thinking that if there was a God, would He please help me now.

"When I came to, Katie Smiths was standing over me, crying. I've known Katie since we were kids in school, and I'd never seen her cry, so it scared me more than I was before. A priest was in the hospital emergency room. It made me so damn mad, I decided to fight a little bit harder. She told me later I had stopped breathing when they tried to remove the bullet, so they left it there.''

"Did they ever catch the man?"

"Not yet." Tommy Lee blinked, then turned and met her gaze. "But I will."

Elizabeth sat quietly, then realized she was holding her breath. "So the city made you retire?"

"Right. Your friend Mayor Prince told the chief he didn't want me to keel over when I was giving out a ticket and scare some citizen to death," he joked, his voice raw. "But anyway, that's why I'm baby-sitting Dottie's business for a while."

"What are you going to do when she comes back?"

"Maybe I'll go back to oystering. I don't know."

His voice told her he didn't want to discuss it further. She stared out the window of his truck. They were downtown. The Bonaparte Hotel was in the distance. In a moment they would be near his office. She flashed back to being held in his arms yesterday, and felt her cheeks warm. "Are we going to Dottie's office?"

"Yeah. I'm going to make a few calls and cash in a couple of favors—try and see if there is any information yet on the gun used to blow away those two guys. Then we need to sit down and talk about where we're going, here."

Elizabeth nodded, unwilling to speak. The last thing she wanted to do was repeat yesterday's faux pas and mistake a remark about their professional relationship for one about something personal. She felt the distance between them expand, and an ache in her stomach she couldn't explain.

Chapter Ten

Three hours later, Elizabeth and Tommy Lee walked into the lobby of deAngelis & Willis, Attorneys at Law. The pre-Civil War building, built in 1855, was gracious and reeked of old money and current connections.

Visitors to the firm were presented with a tableau of freshly painted crown moldings, harlequin black-and-white marble floors, and a thousand-dollar custom Christmas tree covered with antique ornaments.

Tommy Lee squinted at the purple, silver and black color scheme on the fourteen-foot spruce, then realized they were the Queen of Midnight Committee colors, and he snorted. Damn crap even mucked up the holidays, he thought.

A plaque naming the past and present partners of the firm hung beside the tree, and Tommy Lee noted Dr. Bennett Heywood's name, along with Mayor Prince's.

That group really stayed together. Like cops, they liked their own kind. Elizabeth beckoned him to follow her to the elevators. They climbed in and she pressed the button for the fourth floor. "Mr. deAngelis isn't in, but his secretary said she would be glad to have a chat with me. She recognized my name as one of the electees and couldn't have been nicer. We'll see if she has any idea where Mr. Peach's old files are stored."

"Being a debutante is finally paying off," he muttered.

"Yes. Especially since Philip deAngelis is the Caretaker on the Queen of Midnight Committee this year." She smiled at him, hoping her little piece of gossip would impress him.

It did. The "Caretaker" was the person on the nine-member committee who counted the votes for Queen. Supposedly, he was the only one who knew her identity until the night of the ball. Theoretically, no one was to know who the Caretaker was, as the position was awarded based on a drawing of straws, and kept a secret until New Year's Eve.

He whistled. "Nice work. How'd you find that out?"

"Miss Lou found out. I think her dressmaker told her."

"And how did the dressmaker find out?"

Elizabeth shrugged as the elevator doors opened. "Mrs. deAngelis told the dressmaker, on the q.t. But Miss Hattie, that's the lady who sews, has worked for my mother much longer than for Mrs. deAngelis. Anyway, strip a woman down and come at her with pins and she'll give up most anything." She found herself blushing at the double entendre.

"I'll remember that," he said softly, taking her arm as they stepped out of the elevator and approached the elegant black woman seated at the reception desk.

In the last couple of hours Elizabeth and Tommy Lee had formulated a cover story to explain why she wanted some old records of Mr. Peach's. She was going to say she was working on a book for Judge Monette, who had requested she look up some cases of Mr. Peach's to cite in various chapters. Tommy Lee, as a representative of D. Betts, Investigations, a firm well-known to local lawyers, was her assistant.

To the amazement of both of them, the ruse worked like a charm. Five minutes later they were walking toward the elevator, Elizabeth clutching a note from Beverly Woods, personal assistant to Philip deAngelis, authorizing the clerk in the adjacent office building where the "files" were kept to allow them to examine Mr. Peach's papers.

"You tell Judge Monette Bev Beaulois says hello," the secretary called from behind them in a cheery voice. "He won't know me by my married name. Fine man, your daddy."

"I certainly will, ma'am." Elizabeth raised her eyebrows at Tommy Lee, a grin of triumph on her face.

Before they could complete their mission, however, the elevator doors opened and a young man stepped out, with India and Rosellen Heywood in tow.

"Elizabeth!" Rosellen said in surprise. "How are you? We were just talking about you."

"I'm fine, Rosellen. Hello, India." Elizabeth nodded, noting that India Heywood looked anything but happy to see her. Rosellen, on the other hand, grabbed her by the arm and hugged her, despite the fact that she only knew her from the few social events over the last couple of weeks.

"Dear Elizabeth! My God, we were all so worried about you! Have you recovered from your accident? And Daddy told us that someone attacked you in the hospital! Do you know who it was?"

"No, I—"

"Of course, she doesn't know him, Rosellen! Goodness," India interrupted. She stared at Tommy Lee, openly dismayed at his leather jacket and blue jeans.

"Oh, sorry, every one. This is my friend, Tommy Lee McCall. Tommy Lee, this is India Heywood, her daughter Rosellen, and Rosellen's friend." Elizabeth smiled. "I'm sorry, I don't know your name."

"DeAngelis," the young man said proudly. "Paul deAngelis. My father is Philip deAngelis. Are you here to see my father professionally, Elizabeth?"

"Ah, I'm—"

"She's working on a project for her father," the receptionist suddenly announced from behind them. She had walked up so quietly, Elizabeth hadn't heard her.

"Her father?" India Heywood asked nervously.

"Judge Monette. Baylor Monette," the woman replied.

"You know Elizabeth's family, Mother," Rosellen said hurriedly, taken aback by her mother's rudeness.

Elizabeth wondered suddenly if India Heywood might be drunk; she looked flushed and sounded so tipsy. "Well, we really have to go," Elizabeth said. "Thanks for your help," she added to the receptionist as she and Tommy Lee entered the elevator.

"Of course," the woman said. "What brings you here, Paul?"

"I'm looking for my dad. Mrs. Heywood wants to discuss something with him about the ball."

"He's at Luvey Rose's. For cocktails," the woman replied.

"He's where?" the young man asked. "You must

be mistaken, Bev. He was to meet Rosellen and her mother and me at the Saint James for a drink.''

"Sorry, Paul. He told me he was going over at 3:00 p.m."

As the elevator doors closed, Elizabeth and Tommy Lee exchanged a glance. From his tone, it was clear Paul deAngelis didn't like the fact that his father was at Tommy Lee's ex-wife's house. "We can't seem to get away from your ex today," she said softly.

Tommy Lee sighed and stared at his boots. He had been thinking the same thing, and trying unsuccessfully not to jump to conclusions about why that was.

ELIZABETH WAS STILL feeling a bit guilty about misleading Paul deAngelis's secretary when Tommy Lee passed the last half of the last stack of dusty manila folders across to her.

"Here you go," he offered. Then sneezed.

"Bless you," she replied, taking the folders and placing them on her lap. They had gone through three years of cases, but not come across anything to reward their efforts. Elizabeth felt gritty and sweaty and cold all at once. "Do you think Beverly Woods is going to mention to Mr. deAngelis that we came in?"

"Yes."

"What do you think will happen then?"

Tommy Lee shrugged, which caused the file folder he was looking at to slide off his knees and dump all its contents onto the concrete floor. He leaned over to retrieve the papers and felt a pain in the muscle under his shoulder blade. Carefully he sat up. "He might call the judge."

"Or the cops?"

"Why us? Them, I mean," he corrected.

Elizabeth glanced through the small pane in the upper part of the door. Stenciled on the frosted glass was Research Carrel 2. "What we're doing here now is probably against the law, don't you think? Both the clerk at the courthouse, when I picked up my birth certificate, and your sister, explained there are strict confidentiality laws protecting the people who put children up for adoption."

"If your birth mother is dead, I don't think she has any rights."

"But what about my father?"

Tommy Lee piled the folders and rested his elbows on the small table. "We're just looking around for information. Don't worry about any laws being broken. Let's just try to get to the bottom of one piece of this puzzle."

"Nice way for a cop to talk," Elizabeth joked.

"Accent on the 'ex,'" he retorted, but smiled.

She turned to the file at hand, full, like the rest, of correspondence and documents. Most had cover letters and billing records stapled inside the front cover. All had Mr. Peach's robust, rounded handwritten signature and were neatly typed with the initials EAP/emg at the bottom. Suddenly Elizabeth stopped and stared at the letter stapled to the next-to-last folder in her lap.

It bore a handwritten note that read, "Mr. Peach, I'll never be able to thank you enough for handling the probate and insurance reports for me. My daughter, Marylynn, and I will be forever in your debt, and I will always remember the years I worked for you with fondness. Very truly yours, Elaine Gibbs."

So "emg" was Elaine Gibbs. Another thought struck Elizabeth and she gasped.

"What did you find?" Tommy Lee asked, coming to stand behind her.

She motioned toward the file. "Didn't you say Mr. Peach mentioned the name 'Marylynn'?"

He looked at her, his forehead wrinkled. He hadn't told her that 'Marylynn' might be her name, but he had to bring it up now. "Actually, I wasn't sure if he was talking about your mother, or you, frankly. Did the judge or Miss Lou ever mention that they had changed your name?"

She looked shocked. "They specifically said they had not, that I was presented to them as Elizabeth 'Doc.' And they gave me the middle name Anne for Miss Lou's mother."

"What's it say on your birth certificate?" Tommy Lee asked softly.

"That my name is Elizabeth Anne Monette, my parents are Luisa and Baylor, my date of birth is May 4, 1972. Which proves nothing, by the way."

"What?"

"When you're adopted, the government issues you phony paper. It's like you are in the witness protection program, or in the Orwellian future where no written document is trustworthy."

"Wow, I didn't realize they actually changed your birth certificate." He stood and stretched, then looked at his watch. "I need to call New Orleans. My contact in Firearms Tracing said I should call back at five-thirty tonight and he might have more info on whether that gun that killed those two men matches any past crime."

"Go ahead. I'll just look through the rest of this. Marylynn is kind of an unusual name. Maybe I'm on to something here."

"Hey, Newt Gingrich and Strom Thurmond are unusual names, but this is the South, honey, where weird is the norm."

"You're right, there." She met his gaze and wondered if it was her imagination or if Tommy Lee looked paler. He seemed to be moving slower today than yesterday. Which might be typical of some injuries. "If you're going to make a call, I'd try the lobby. I think I saw a pay phone." Elizabeth waved a folder at him. "I've only got a couple more after this one."

"I'll be back," Tommy Lee said, and left her amid the crisis mementos of a hundred people's lives.

Elizabeth thumbed through the file that was labeled "Gibbs, H. and Gibbs, E." There were two news clippings, faded brown-yellow and curling around the edges, describing a grand-jury investigation into one Jefferson Randolph's part in the death of a local man, Harold Gibbs. She scanned them quickly.

The story was common—and tragic. Jefferson Randolph had evidently been having an affair with Mrs. Elaine Gibbs; or her husband, Mr. Harold Gibbs, *thought* they were having one, at least. Harold confronted the two in a Belle Fleur parking lot one night, drunk and waving a gun. Jefferson Randolph subdued him, and in the struggle, Harold Gibbs was killed.

The grand jury issued a "no indictment" verdict, the smaller article reported, then noted that Jefferson Randolph and his family wished no further inquiries from the press.

The rest of the file consisted of an insurance policy in the amount of six thousand dollars on the life of Harold Gibbs, a photocopy of a canceled check in that amount from American Banner Insurance, and an "In Memoriam" folder.

The letter was from Sacred Heart Chapel, for a service held thirty years before for Harold Gibbs. "Beloved husband of Elaine, father of Marylynn, son of Edith and Clayton." Burial was at Cedar Pines, a small cemetery on the other side Fairbreeze, not far from the Monette home.

Elizabeth stared at the name Marylynn. This Marylynn couldn't be her, then, for Marylynn Gibbs was a teenager, alive at her father's funeral thirty years ago.

She frowned and made a last note of the name Jefferson Randolph. It sounded familiar, but she didn't know from where. Miss Lou would know, however, she was sure. Though Miss Lou seldom gossiped, she seemed to know everyone's family tree in the area, back a hundred years.

Elizabeth opened the last file, labeled "Gibbs, M./minor child." She was expecting it to be linked to the case she had just examined, assuming it would be the child of E. and H. Gibbs.

It was, but it was not connected with the inheritance or wrongful death of a father, though a death certificate was inside. It was for a white female, one Marylynn Elaine Gibbs, age twenty-five. Cause of death was clearly delineated on the Belle Fleur city police report as a homicide.

With her heart racing, Elizabeth read the report. Police had been called to a small home near the marina in the early hours of the morning and found "victim, white female, approximately twenty-five years old, dead from two shotgun blasts at close proximity."

One witness was found on the scene the night of December 19, twenty years ago. It was a five-year-old girl, identified as the woman's child. "Child appears traumatized and unable to talk. Will interview at later date," a policeman had written, but no other report was attached.

Elizabeth's mouth was hot and dry. Angry tears filled her eyes. She picked up the last piece of documentation in the file. It was addressed to Emmett Peach from someone named Nan, written on a pink While You Were Out phone-message form dated February 19, 1978. It read, "Elaine Gibbs called re: adoption. Have you interviewed the couple? Please call. Urgent!" It was dated two months to the day after the death of Elaine's daughter, Marylynn.

Elizabeth returned all the documents to the file and hugged the folder to her chest. Her brain felt empty of all thought. She rocked back and forth in the chair, a ringing sound in her ears. At that moment Tommy Lee came through the door.

"Hey, I've got news about the gun and—" He stopped in his tracks and pulled the door shut behind him. "What's wrong, kid? You look like you've seen a ghost."

"I haven't yet," she said, her voice shaking like a leaf. "But I'd like you to take me out to Cedar Pines Cemetery. Do you know where that is?"

"Yeah. But why?"

Two beats of silence passed. "I want to introduce you to my mother, Marylynn Gibbs."

PETEY CONNOR WAS QUITE pleased with how he was looking. Twenty-four hours ago he wouldn't have given himself better than a fifty-fifty chance of living till the weekend, but now he was feeling pretty good. He had broken into a Cal 33 sailboat in dry dock about fifty feet from where his van was hidden, and had found some great clothes, blankets, enough bottled water to bathe in, as well as several tins of tuna fish and other goodies. Now, cleaned up and shaven, sporting the absent captain's navy blue cashmere turtleneck and slacks, he was looking pretty natty.

The sweater hid the wound on his neck, and the food quieted the ache in his gut. He jumped down from the boat, looked around, and headed for the restaurant at the end of the marina.

The telephone inside the men's room was a step-in model with a door. Petey settled himself and pulled out the two pieces of paper he'd fished out of Cracker Jackson's pocket. The first was a disappointment.

"Belle Fleur Hospital. Surgery department," a young female voice answered. Damned if he was going back there after that mess Ray got into, no matter what, he thought. Petey hung up and dialed the next. Bingo. The maid announced that he had reached one of the ritzier households in Belle Fleur.

Petey asked to speak to a member of the family and chuckled when the voice explained that the lady in question was out. "Tell her a friend of Cracker's called," he said, hardly able to control his mirth, "and ask her to give me a call at his number." He sauntered out of the booth, deciding he would celebrate with a couple of beers. He would bet with his little message, she'd call the cell-phone he had taken from Cracker Jackson's dead body, pronto. And if not, he'd just pop around for a visit, he decided, stepping into the restaurant where he could see the rich man's boat he had just plundered. That was what he'd do. He would just cab it over to Kings Landing Road and make his pitch face-to-face. Petey grinned and followed the smell of food into the dining room, liking the way the evening was going just fine.

TOMMY LEE STOOD a few feet away from Elizabeth as she stared at the neat row of tombstones.

He couldn't imagine her thoughts. She looked stricken, as if a bolt of lightning had whacked her and left her bereft of hope or breath or spirit.

She just stood silent and pale, her gray coat loose around her, her hair matted and blowing in the wet wind while she stared down at the granite markers. There were three.

Harold Gibbs, dead thirty years, husband of Elaine, beloved father of Marylynn.

In the cruelest act of fate, the daughter lay beside the father, gone after only twenty-five years on earth. A weeping angel was carved into the tombstone, hands folded, eyes to God. The words Mom and Dad Will See Our Little Angel In Heaven were carved into the stone.

Six months after the death of the daughter, the mother joined her family. Died Of A Broken Heart was etched on Elaine Gibbs's headstone in script, above a biblical verse about suffering on earth and the rewards waiting in heaven.

Elizabeth had found her mother, grandmother, and grandfather, Tommy Lee realized. Two died violent deaths, the third followed from grief. He wanted to take her into his arms and crush her against his heart and tell her it was okay, but he couldn't imagine that it was.

During the last few months he had felt adrift, without a future, the past only a painful memory. So he understood having no place to turn, feeling a part of nothing.

He ached for Elizabeth and knew that nothing he could say would help.

"Elizabeth," he murmured minutes later, the fog turning to rain all around them. "Let's go get dinner. Then I'll take you home. You've got a lot to tell the judge and Miss Lou about all this."

She didn't move, and for a moment Tommy Lee had the insane thought that she, too, had turned to granite and joined the rest of the ill-fated Gibbs clan.

But then she moved.

Slowly she turned to face him, giving him the saddest look he'd ever seen. "I'll buy you some soup," Elizabeth said as she walked by him to the truck, her back straight, her eyes focused on something he couldn't see.

He didn't reach out to stop her.

THEY DIDN'T STOP TO EAT, after all. They drove in silence across the bridge. When Elizabeth saw the turnoff for her home, she touched his arm with a cold hand and said, "I'd like a rain check on the dinner, Tommy Lee. Can you just drop me off?"

"Of course."

He didn't go in with her. "I'll call you in the morning," he offered, holding the truck's door open for her.

"Fine." She hesitated for a moment, inches from him, but totally alone. "I need to ask you a favor."

"Anything," he said, fully aware that he had never said a single word that he meant more than that one.

"Would you be my date tomorrow at the Parade of Lights dinner? I'm sure there will be a lot of questions about the past few days, and now the murders...."

Elizabeth looked away, toward the window where Miss Lou was standing and watching them from her kitchen. "I know you hate all this Queen of Midnight stuff, but I'd really appreciate it. Maybe we can do a little sleuthing."

"Such as?"

"I told you I recognized the name Jefferson Randolph. A couple of minutes ago, I remembered who he is." Her blue eyes were cool and direct, as if lit by a faraway light. "He was India Heywood's father."

Tommy Lee blinked and shook his head, trying to fit that fact into the scattershot chunks of information swirling around them. "India Heywood's father, Bennett Heywood's father-in-law, killed your..." He couldn't finish it; felt embarrassed for some reason.

"Yes, if Marylynn Gibbs was my mother, then India's father killed my grandfather."

"What does that tell us, Elizabeth?" Tommy Lee asked, his voice almost a whisper.

"It tells us two current electees for Queen of Midnight have some very bitter shared history."

"You and Rosellen Heywood."

"Exactly."

Tommy Lee whistled. "Wow, I don't know what this all means." He shook his head. His thoughts were humming like a telegraph line in an old Western, but the signals were garbled. He couldn't see a conclusion. "Why would the Heywoods hate you, though? Their family member killed yours, not vice versa."

"Mayor Prince told me at the luncheon the other day that India was everyone's choice to be Queen of Midnight when she was eighteen, but some nasty business with her father came up. He didn't elaborate, because I had to leave to meet you, but I'm sure that with a little prompting, he'll explain the scandal in all its gory detail. I'm sure if it was because her father was having an affair with my grandmother, and because her father killed my grandfather, she would have plenty of reasons to hate me."

Elizabeth blinked. "If I think like a cop, your dot-to-dot logic points to India Heywood as someone who might want me dead."

"Well, with that as an incentive, of course I'll escort you to the dinner party. I'd be honored," he added, hoping his tone was light.

Elizabeth smiled wanly, her mouth beautiful though it was wind-chapped and naked of lipstick. "Thank you, Tommy Lee. I think we might be able to dig up some information, now that we have my mother's name—though what we really need now is one thing."

He leaned closer, fighting himself to keep from touching her. "What's that?"

"To find out who my father was. That's the key, Tommy Lee."

His cop instincts told him she was right. "Okay, it's a good plan." He glanced down at his boots. "Is this thing black-tie?"

"I'm afraid so."

"No problem. I used to have one of those monkey suits. It's at my sister's. This will give me an excuse to check in on Dottie's family, make sure they are all holding up, with her in the hospital."

"Thank you," she said, then kissed him lightly on the cheek.

He didn't touch his face where her cold lips had left an icy burning against his skin. He drove back down the gravel road toward the highway, thinking way too much about that kiss.

When Tommy Lee got near the highway, he saw a slim, gaunt man behind the wheel of an old pickup turn onto the road to the Monette property.

The man nodded and kept driving on. Tommy Lee watched in the rearview mirror as the man parked the truck, its rear bumper wired on with some rope and chains, behind the caretaker's cottage. The fellow came around to the main house and knocked. He must be Clay Willow. Tommy Lee had the thought to go back and question the man, see if he had seen anything the night before, warn him to keep an eye peeled, but decided against it. Willow had already entered the house.

Elizabeth had more than enough to talk through with the judge and Miss Lou. He would give her some space.

He wheeled his pickup out onto the open highway. His face twitched and he resisted the urge to put his hand on his cheek to see if he could feel the shape of her lips.

You're losing it, man, a voice inside his brain warned. Tommy Lee pressed down on the gas and sped away, wishing with his whole heart that he could stay.

INDIA AND BENNETT Heywood, along with their daughter Rosellen and Paul deAngelis, arrived at Luvey Rose's house well after the bloom had worn off Luvey and Tammy's party.

Which was par for the course, India thought. Paul and Rosellen had been fighting over something for two days. She hadn't heard them, but her daughter had been walking around with the pinched look of someone who is about to withdraw into a sulk. To make things worse, Paul acted like he was ready to hit someone all through dinner, while her husband insisted on talking of nothing but "the sad state of affairs in Belle Fleur."

Honestly, she concluded. With all the pressure of waiting to hear confirmation that Rosellen would be crowned Queen, one would think Bennett would refocus his attention on what really mattered. Such as getting Philip deAngelis to confirm what she knew in her heart had to be true.

Standing next to Bennett, she grabbed and downed in one gulp the champagne cocktail proffered to her by Luvey's servant. "Four murders in two days, it's a disgrace, Mayor," the doctor intoned.

"It's a real mess, Bennett. Though interest in the Pageant is at an all-time high!" Paris was rocking on his heels, nodding in agreement, but seemed to be listening as intently as he could to the conversation taking place right behind him, between Luvey and Paul deAngelis.

India snagged another glass of champagne and remembered someone had told her that the mayor had noted with glee at the luncheon a few days ago that Rosellen Heywood was looking anything but regal these days.

That was Paris for you, she thought, letting her own ears tune in to the twosome on the settee. Scratch whatever back was closest and hope they would return the favor. The little cow-pie.

"I understand my father was here earlier," Paul was saying, downing his third shot of whiskey from the bottle on the coffee table. "Why didn't you tell me you invited him?"

"Honestly, Paul," Rosellen interrupted, "Luvey doesn't have to clear her guest list with you."

"Stay out of this, Rosellen," he snarled. He stared hard at the redhead lounging across from him. "I want to talk to you about the dinner party tomorrow. You never told me for sure if you're riding on my boat during the Parade of Lights party. I need to know right now."

Luvey smiled brightly. "Let's not bore everyone with your insecurities, darling. Call me later. I'll be here." She turned her green eyes toward Rosellen. "I saw a painting of your daddy's mama, when she was queen. She was wearing the most gorgeous brooch. A big old diamond crown, with rubies pink-red as cherries in it. Do you ever wear that, darling? It would go so nice with your coloring. You brunettes always look great in red."

"That pin was stolen years ago, Luvey." Rosellen's eyes were glassy and her face looked feverish. She kept staring at Paul, who ignored her.

"Talking about jewelry reminds me, has your mamma got her tiara all polished up, Rosellen?" Luvey asked.

India couldn't play the silent observer anymore. Rosellen was like a baby mouse up against that she-cat. India walked to stand behind her daughter. India laid her hand on the girl's shoulder. "Yes, yes, I have, Luvey, dear. Thank you for asking. I only wish the tiara was as gorgeous as the one your grandmother Antoine wore. It's a shame that beautiful thing is locked up down at the bank these past thirty-odd years. No one has been able to fill her shoes and wear it again for your family. It's such a shame!"

Luvey rose to the insult like a shark to chum.

"Well, hopefully Tammy, here, will get to give you all a glimpse of it in a couple of weeks." She smiled wickedly. "Although, of course, we all know she's not the favorite this year. Rosellen, have you seen Elizabeth Monette since her terrible attack? I'm hearing from a very well-placed source that she is the odds-on bet. Probably just a sympathy vote for being chased after by that riffraff, wouldn't you say, India?"

India had the urge to crush her champagne flute into Luvey's large, scarlet-colored mouth, but smiled sweetly. "Well, darling Luvey, if that's the only pillow talk you're getting from Philip deAngelis, I guess you'll just have to be as surprised as everyone else on New Year's Eve!"

"Mother, please," Rosellen pleaded.

"So, you're bedding my old man, too?" Paul demanded in a dead voice.

"Well, well," India chortled. "Such a messy little end to your evening, isn't it, dear?"

Paul continued to ignore Rosellen while turning a look of hatred on Luvey.

Luvey had the good grace to blush. "Paul, darling, this is so silly. Why don't you take poor Rosellen home. I'm afraid her mama has upset her."

Paul's face went white while Rosellen looked like she couldn't take a breath or she'd set off a trip wire. Tammy simply looked drunk.

Before India could reply with a coup de grace, Luvey's maid rushed up to the sofa and announced, "That man's on the phone again."

Luvey gave India a smile full of daggers, then snapped at her servant, "What man?"

"That man what called before. I thought Louise told you."

"Louise didn't tell me anything, but I can't talk to anyone now," Luvey said sternly, waving her hand. "I still have guests."

"Okay," the maid said, but her mouth looked worried. "I'll tell him, then."

"A secret caller?" Paris asked.

"I don't know who it is—" Luvey began.

The maid took that as her cue to speak up. "He won't say his name, but he told me to tell you he's a friend of Cracker's."

The silence was as thick as summer mist on the bayou, and just as sticky.

One woman inhaled sharply, while another felt as if she might faint.

"Tell him he has the wrong number," Luvey ordered, her voice unsteady.

"Okay," the maid murmured, walking from the room. She picked up the phone in the hallway and spoke into the receiver. "Sir, Miss Rose said you've got the wrong number. You want to leave a message?"

Silence.

"Sir?" the woman repeated.

But the line was dead.

Chapter Eleven

Tommy Lee had not slept well. His back was giving him fits and he kept dreaming stuff about graveyards and shotguns and women in white with their faces blown off.

To make matters worse, he was as stiff and tender as if he had been in a bar fight with two gorillas. He hoped it was only the aftereffect of his dive into the asphalt on Government Boulevard, but his mind offered up a worrisome doubt. The ounce of metal that was embedded in his back was something he didn't like to think about.

But maybe he should, because whenever he turned a certain bit too much to the left, he got a jolt like an electrified snake bite down his spine.

Turning his head slowly, he read the clock beside his bed. Five thirty-five in the morning. He should go into the hospital and tell Katie Smiths about the pain, but she'd probably just make jokes about getting her funeral dress ready. Besides, he didn't have time. When he'd arrived home last night at nine, there had been a message for him to call his FBI friend in New Orleans.

The guy had made an astounding discovery. The

gun that had been used to kill Cracker Jackson and Lucille Thompkins had been involved in another murder.

The murder of a young woman, twenty years ago, in sleepy little Farquier County. The dead woman's name was one Tommy Lee had just grown familiar with.

Marylynn Gibbs, Elizabeth's mother.

He had debated going to Chief Foley right then with the news, but had decided that Elizabeth had been right last night when she'd said she needed to find out who her biological father was.

He was the key, Tommy Lee knew.

The devil of it was, he might also be a murderer.

The cop in New Orleans had promised to fax over the information to Dottie's office by 10:00 a.m. So that left four hours and change to try and piece together a good plan to keep Elizabeth off the front page, ferret out the killer and track down her old man. He wasn't looking forward to telling Elizabeth the news that her mother had been killed by someone who still owned the murder weapon and had no compunction about using it.

She was too smart not to jump to the same conclusion he had—that the guy she once called Daddy might be willing to kill her just to keep her quiet about the past.

Tommy Lee reached for the phone on the floor. He would call the station and see if Sergeant Bulow was on early watch. He was hoping to barter on their past friendship and find out any info Frank Foley might have gathered, but before he could pick up the receiver, the thing rang.

"Hello?" he answered.

"Tommy Lee, it's Luvey. How are you, darling?"

His glamorous ex-wife was a notorious late riser. Breakfast before noon was not in Luvey's known rituals. Which meant she had not been to bed.

Which could mean anything; none of it good. "What do you need, Luvey?" he answered.

"Now that's something you learned a long time ago," Luvey replied in a voice that could dry paint on a wall in a deep well. He grinned, liking the fact that nothing stirred in his mind or body even when she turned on the charm.

"I'm on my way out the door, Luvey."

"At this hour? Come on, Tommy Lee. Are you afraid of dealing with little old me in the middle of the night? Worried you might be a little too vulnerable to some wonderful memories?"

"I could go a month without sleep and not be that vulnerable," he said with a wolfish grin, enjoying the conversation more and more.

"Honestly," Luvey whined, "I think the police force trains you boys to be rude."

"Not rude. Direct. Saves all you taxpayers a lot of money. So there's no need for you to pretend to want to seduce me. Now, this is my last time asking, but what do you want?"

"It's not me, Tommy Lee. It's a friend of mine. Philip deAngelis. He needs you."

"Cops need lawyers sometimes, Luvey, but I've never heard of a lawyer needing a cop, unless one of his clients wanted to dispute a bill."

"This is serious, Tommy Lee. And very, very sensitive. Can you be discreet?"

He made a face. That damn virtue was evidently a

requirement now that he was off the force. "Talk, Luvey."

"Well, Philip and I are good friends, so he turned to me for help. You see, he knows you and I used to be married, so he wanted me to ask if you could meet with him and advise him on a personal matter he wants to tell you about."

"Take a shortcut, darlin'. You tell me exactly what the man's 'personal matter' is. But I can't fix parking tickets anymore."

She blew her breath out in an effort to keep from losing her temper. "Tommy Lee, someone is threatening Philip's life. They told him they would kill him if he didn't change the votes for Queen of Midnight and announce a certain person as Queen."

He sat up quickly—too quickly—in bed. The muscles in his shoulder were on fire. He moved the phone to his right hand and flexed his left shoulder again hesitantly. The pain got worse. "Who threatened him?"

"We don't know that. Some man!"

"How did they threaten him?"

"Over the phone. They left a gruesome message on his private answering machine he got for me to call him at, well, and of course, some other friends. Anyway, they also left a letter," she added hurriedly. "They left it inside his locked car!"

To Tommy Lee's astonishment, Luvey appeared to be genuinely worried about someone other than herself. "Who did they want to be named Queen?" he asked, looking through the darkness for his service revolver. He found it under the bed. He slid it across the carpet and tucked it into his jeans.

She sucked in her breath. "This is the insane part.

Philip said the girl the man demanded he change the votes to already won!''

"Who is it?''

Luvey gasped. "Philip would never tell me that!''

He grinned again. "The old man is cheating on his wife and sleeping with you, but he'd never break a promise to the Queen of Midnight Committee? Give me a break, Luvey. If the girl already won, what's Philip's problem?''

"Tommy Lee, don't be thick. How would it look if someone thought they had pulled off a dirty trick like this? Poor Philip can't be a part of anything that even looks like a rigged election. But he doesn't know if he should just tell the man his choice already won, which of course is against his code of silence. He knows he should report all this to the police. But if he does that, there will be a huge investigation and then that girl probably won't even get to be Queen because of the scan—''

Luvey's voice was cut off with a tiny click.

"Luvey?'' Tommy Lee said, standing and squinting into the darkness outside his window. It looked like snow; the sky was colorless where the sun was rising, as if painted with gray chalk.

He hung up the phone, then dialed Luvey's home number from memory. He got a disconnect recording.

Savagely he hung up and pulled on his jeans. If he called 911, where would he send them? He didn't know if Luvey was at home, or with Philip deAngelis in some cozy hideaway. And if he sent the cops to the attorney's house, he would probably only find the old bastard's wife.

Who would sue him.

"Damn it!'' he said in frustration, stepping into his

boots. If he called the station and had them call the phone company to trace Luvey's new number, he still wouldn't know if that was where she was calling from.

Gingerly he pulled a heavy woolen sweater over his sore shoulder and headed for the front door. He shoved his gun into the front of his jeans, then grabbed his jacket from the back of the couch where he'd thrown it. He walked softly so as to not wake up Sissy Lane, and reached for the doorknob.

The front bell rang and he jumped back as if he'd been stung by a wet bumblebee. Before he even took the time to check through the window to see who his unexpected visitor might be, he threw open the door.

Elizabeth was standing on his porch. Her eyes were red-rimmed and swollen. "I'm sorry I'm here so early, Tommy Lee, but I need to talk to you."

"What is it? Are you okay?" Instinctively he reached out and took her arm, scanning her head-to-toe for signs of a new injury.

"No, no. Nothing more like that has happened. I've just been up all night thinking this over, and I've come to the conclusion my father must be a doctor. Which means he probably still works in medicine, maybe even at—"

His mind ran ahead of her words. Could it be? Was her very own father right there in plain sight at Belle Fleur General? He put his arm around her shoulders, shut the door behind him and steered her toward the truck. "Let's talk this over while I'm driving, Elizabeth. Something real serious has happened."

"Where are we going?"

"To try and find Luvey and whoever she is with!"

"Luvey? Who do you think she is with?"

Tommy Lee inhaled and tugged on his mustache. "The killer."

THE DRIVE BACK ACROSS the river to Belle Fleur took seventeen minutes.

Elizabeth listened in shocked silence to Tommy Lee's summary of the events since she had last seen him. It was bad enough to hear the news about Luvey's sudden end to the phone conversation as well as the attempted blackmail of Philip deAngelis, but his quiet recounting of his discovery that the gun that had killed Cracker Jackson and the woman at Baptist Haven had also taken her mother's life was nearly too much to bear.

Even worse was the thought that immediately came into her mind—that the only probable link between her mother and the other victims was herself.

"Do you think the murderer is my father?" Elizabeth asked in a small voice as the buildings of Belle Fleur's business district came into view. The Christmas lights were shining, and seemed a world away in their gaiety.

"It entered my mind, darlin'. If he knew you were coming back to Belle Fleur and knew you were looking into your family history, he might have gotten scared you'd press for an investigation into your mother's unsolved death. But I can't work out a good reason why he would have hired Cracker and his cohorts."

"To scare me off, I guess." She turned and put her hand on his arm, wanting to touch him to make herself feel some warmth. She felt as if she were frozen solid. "He *must* still be here in Belle Fleur, Tommy Lee. He must be working somewhere to have heard that your sister was looking into things for me. She only called the courthouse and the hospital, right?''

"That's what she said. But I think there was another message in her file on you." He shook his head to clear it as the truck barreled down the off-ramp, two miles from Luvey Rose's home. "Remember that slip I showed you? There was a phone number written down and the words 'Check this' penciled by it. We'll call Dottie later and find out what that was all about."

Elizabeth didn't appear to be listening to him. "If he had wanted them to kill me, they could have when I was still back in Maryland. Instead, he killed them after that guy attacked me in the hospital."

Tommy Lee blew out a long breath and shook his head. "We're making too many jumps here, Elizabeth. I agree he might be around here if he's behind this, but I think we're missing the obvious. Cracker Jackson and Ray Robinson were working together, probably with a third man. An unidentified bloodstain was found out at the scene by the school. Whoever the guy is might have killed the other two after some kind of fight."

"But who hired them if it wasn't my father?" she asked, unable to keep an edge of hope out of her voice.

"Your mother's killer. Whoever it is—your father or anyone else—wouldn't want you finding out about your mother for the same reason we just discussed. Your dad may be long gone, and the killer still lives here."

Elizabeth frowned as Tommy Lee slowed down and quietly started up the alley behind the stately homes on Kings Landing. "What we're forgetting is the Queen of Midnight tie-in, Tommy Lee. The murderer could have scared me off without dragging the Pageant into his threats. And now that we know Philip de-Angelis is being threatened, it seems to me there's a whole motive connected to that damn beauty contest that we're missing.''

Tommy Lee parked the truck and sat staring down the alley. He felt like a schizophrenic. He was checking out the position of the cars parked along the road, noting the rusty van pulled up behind the Heywoods' garage. It seemed sinister, but when he flashed the lights toward it, it was empty.

He called on all his intuition to search the shadows for suspicious movements, wondering with one side of his brain how best to approach Luvey's house, while Elizabeth's words were sparking all kinds of thoughts in the other half.

"Someone got away with murdering Marylynn Gibbs," he said in a whisper. "Who would have wanted to kill your mother, and why, is the only motive that would explain this resurrected mayhem going on twenty years later.''

Elizabeth nodded. "If we could only find someone who knew my mother. Someone who can tell us who she was romantically involved with. Miss Lou was no help at all when we discussed all this last night. She'd never heard of Marylynn Gibbs. The only thing she could offer was that it was common knowledge India Heywood has always blamed Elaine Gibbs for India's mother's suicide."

"Well, maybe Mrs. Heywood's vendetta got transferred over to Marylynn." Tommy Lee turned his brooding stare on Elizabeth. "And then maybe India found out about you—Marylynn's child. If she's a real psycho, just hearing you're running against her daughter for Queen of Midnight could make her snap."

Elizabeth pictured the sweet face of Rosellen Heywood, who struck her as lonesome and sad despite her pretty exterior, then flashed on the tense, outwardly cool India Heywood. Was the poor girl living with a lunatic for a mother? "Yes, Rosellen Heywood is an electee, Tommy Lee. But why would India Heywood kill my mother for something Elaine Gibbs did? My God, she was already married to the most prominent physician in town—what could she have been so afraid of?"

"That's the big missing piece of the puzzle, kiddo. Motive. What could your mother have done to make India Heywood angry enough to have her risk everything?"

An answer nagged at Elizabeth's mind, but she couldn't focus on it. "This sounds like the Hatfields and McCoys," she said in disgust. "A feud like this is completely crazy!"

"Yeah, well, think about Othello. When jealousy masquerades as love, people kill and pretend they are justified. I saw it on the job too many times to deny it, Elizabeth. We always hurt the ones we love, I think the song goes."

"That's true," she agreed softly, touching his face with her hand. She knew withdrawing from him last night at the cemetery had hurt him, but she wasn't ready to explain to him how she felt. "But if you are right, then 'love' hasn't got anything to do with it, to paraphrase another tune."

Tommy Lee moved close and looked into Elizabeth's face. He pressed her hand against his mouth, wanting nothing more than to ask her how she was handling everything. But it wasn't the time. He truly was worried about what his dingbat ex-wife might have gotten herself involved in. "Wise and beautiful. You're something, Elizabeth. But we're going to have to put this brainstorming on hold for a little bit. I've got to check this thing out with Luvey." Quietly he cracked open the truck's door. "Stay here and wait. I'm going to find out if Luvey is even home."

"Can't I come with you?"

"No." he closed the door and moved around the pickup to stand by her window. "If I'm not back out in five minutes, or if you see anything the least bit strange, you drive the truck directly to the police station and tell Chief Foley the whole thing."

"The whole thing about Luvey calling you?"

He leaned forward, letting himself touch her lips with a quick, hard kiss. He pulled away instantly, not willing to test her reception to him while all these traumas were weighing on her heart. Besides, he knew if he wasn't back to her in five minutes, he might well be dead. "The whole thing about everything, Elizabeth. Now lock the doors and time me." He looked at his wristwatch, then back into her huge blue eyes. "It's 6:08. I want your butt out of here at 6:13. Got that?"

"Be careful," she whispered.

He winked, and turned and slipped from sight.

Elizabeth craned her neck to the left as far as she could, but Tommy Lee's tall figure had melted into the shrubbery around Luvey Rose's garage. She saw no sign of anyone, but stared at the shadows, forcing herself to breathe shallow and slow.

She glanced at her watch. It was 6:09 a.m. exactly. A car engine echoed in the distance, then quieted. Elizabeth looked out the truck's back window, but no vehicle had pulled into the alley, which ran the full five hundred yards behind the four houses on Kings Landing Road.

With a sigh, she pulled her coat tight around her and watched. A hollow tapping sound, like leather boots running on pavement, made her turn once again behind her, but she saw no one. As she strained to hear, the noise died out.

For a full minute she stared, thinking of Tommy Lee. She pictured him, with his leather jacket, scuffed cowboy boots, and impossibly handsome face. She willed him to reappear, to walk toward the truck and slide onto the seat beside her. She wanted to feel the warmth from his hard thigh against her fingertips. Wanted to kiss him again. Just wanted him.

She stared down at her watch. It read 6:12 a.m. One minute to go. But she couldn't leave Tommy Lee. Without another thought, she slipped out of the truck and ran across the expanse of asphalt like a cat, congratulating herself for wearing sneakers, which made her steps silent. Flattening herself against the closed garage door, she walked slowly toward the bushes where she had last seen Tommy Lee. There was a gate behind them, standing ajar.

On tiptoe, Elizabeth slipped through the gate and found herself in a small courtyard behind Luvey's house. The two-story house was designed like a small French chateau. It had a wrought-iron balcony on the second floor, and lovely tall windows. The courtyard was paved with antique brick and dotted with huge pots of shrubs, which were covered with tarps against the freezing December nights. At the edge of the courtyard, Elizabeth spied French doors. One was open, and a filmy ivory lace curtain drooped onto the brick.

Elizabeth glanced at the watch. It was 6:13 a.m. Where the devil was Tommy Lee? Her heart rate increased with each breath. Was she endangering Tommy Lee and his ex-wife by staying a second longer? Or did he need her help?

Her questions without answers spurred her to action. She dashed across the courtyard and paused. No noises came from the inside of Luvey's house, save for the ticking of a huge clock on her mantel. Elizabeth stepped inside.

The living room was gracious and beautifully decorated in shades of green and mauve. The smell of evergreen was everywhere, and a dozen pots of poinsettias were huddled around the fireplace. She could picture the red-haired Luvey draped across the sofa, and an alarming image of Tommy Lee beside her popped into her brain. She chewed on her bottom lip and crossed the room. It led to a center hallway with a kitchen at one end, a small staircase at the other. Two rooms, both with walnut doors closed against her prying eyes, stood across from her.

If Luvey had household help, their quarters would most likely be on the other side of the kitchen. Should she go in there and try to rouse someone? Elizabeth pictured herself scaring the maid out of her wits and wondered how big a crime breaking and entering and scaring household help senseless was.

She stood straining to hear any sound of talking, but heard nothing. Elizabeth glanced at her wrist. It was 6:15 a.m.

A shot, fired in a room upstairs, ripped through the morning silence like thunder. Instinctively Elizabeth crouched down in the doorway, wildly looking behind her for a phone. She ran across the room and pulled it off the table.

No dial tone.

And it was then she saw the body. A man. He was dark-haired and small. His clothes were too big and he smelled like salt water and lemons. She felt the bile burning up her throat and she stepped back away from him. He was covered in blood, as was the side of the sofa he was slumped against, hidden from her initial view of the room.

Without a moment's pause, Elizabeth was back on her feet and running upstairs. The door to the first room she came to was ajar.

Philip deAngelis was slumped in a chair, his eyes open, his breathing shallow. Luvey Rose lay on the floor at his feet, the pink nightgown she wore spattered with her own blood. Elizabeth kneeled beside her and pressed on the woman's wrist with her fingers.

There was no pulse, and Elizabeth knew without a doubt that she was dead.

"Tommy Lee!" Elizabeth called out, her voice aching with fear. "Tommy Lee!"

Across the room the balcony door was ajar. Elizabeth walked toward it, feeling both numb and alert, and more scared than she had ever imagined a person might feel and still breathe.

She knew he was there. And he was. Tommy Lee was sprawled on his back, his eyes closed, a tiny rivulet of blood running from his scalp onto his forehead where he had been struck by something heavy enough to knock him out.

"Oh, my God," she whispered, falling to her knees. She grabbed his hand, but he didn't wrap his fingers around her wrist as she prayed that he would. She reached frantically for his neck. There was no pulse. She called upon the three years of elementary CPR training she had taken as a teacher, tilted his head back, made sure there was no obstruction and began to blow. With each breath, she knew in her heart that she had fallen in love with Tommy Lee McCall, and would not let him die.

"Elizabeth!" a male voice called from the door, nearly scaring her out of what wits she had remaining.

She moved her hands to Tommy Lee's chest, placing one on top of the other for her compressions. Clay Willow, the handyman, stood in the doorway. His face was ashen and he looked ill with fright.

"Do you know CPR?"

"Yes, I do. Are you hurt?" the man rasped. He'd been running and was panting.

She had no time to explain, or ask him how he came to be where he was. "I'm fine. Come help me."

Clay hurried to her. "How long has he not been breathing?" the handyman asked, his voice oddly calm, his question precise.

"I don't know. Probably only two or three minutes." Elizabeth was crying. Her arms were shaking. She felt like she wanted to scream. "Wake up, Tommy Lee," she cried as Clay blew into the silent lungs and she pushed with every ounce of strength she had. "Damn it, you can't die!"

Tommy Lee took a shallow breath, then groaned. "Oh, thank you," Elizabeth cried out, hugging her face against his chest. He took another breath and moved, groaning again as if he were in the midst of a terrible nightmare.

"Elizabeth, run down the street and get Dr. Heywood. And have them call for an ambulance and the police.''

She pulled herself into a sitting position and stared at the man who had appeared like a ghost. ''What are you doing here, Clay?''

''I followed you when you left this morning,'' he said simply, his pale blue eyes full of concern. ''Now go, hurry. I'll stay with Mr. McCall.'' He turned from her and took Tommy Lee's pulse, throwing a blanket over the ex-cop's long legs.

Nodding, she struggled to her feet and raced from the room. She chose the front door and ran down the steep incline of Luvey's driveway to the street, past Paris Prince's mansion and up the walkway to the Heywoods'. Breathless, she pounded on the front door and rang the bell ten times frantically, calling out, ''Please, Dr. Heywood. Someone open the door, we need help!''

India's maid threw open the door. Behind her, Rosellen Heywood stood with a look of abject fright on her face. Her hair was dripping from the shower. Both women were dressed in nightclothes.

''Please call the police, Rosellen. But first get your father. Luvey Rose has been murdered and Philip deAngelis attacked!''

''God in heaven!'' the maid shouted, then ran off screaming toward the kitchen, ''Dr. Heywood, Dr. Heywood! Come quick!''

Rosellen began to cry. ''But what are you doing here, Elizabeth? I don't understand. Were you just at Luvey's?''

''Rosellen! What in the world—'' India Heywood's voice floated down to Elizabeth and she looked up. India was standing on the stairway. She was fully dressed in black pants and sweater, black boots and gloves, as if she were going out.

Or had just come in. Elizabeth thought back to the sound of leather boots on the pavement. Had India just come from that brutal scene at Luvey's?

Elizabeth began to tremble harder now, and felt herself shrinking back from the woman. India's hair was mussed, and her eyes were wild. "Elizabeth, what's happened?" she demanded.

"Mother, please, it's too terrible," Rosellen cried out, her anguished voice bouncing off the walls and echoing in Elizabeth's ears. Inside her head, she heard a woman screaming, saw a woman lying in a pool of blood, heard footsteps and breaking glass and a child crying in terror. A door slammed at the back of the house and Elizabeth could not have said if it was in her mind or in the actual present. She wondered if her memories had finally driven her mad.

"Tommy Lee McCall is hurt. Luvey was killed. Philip deAngelis is unconscious. We need an ambulance. The police..." Elizabeth said in a wavering voice. The room was spinning around her as she fought to remain conscious. She had to get back to Tommy Lee, but she suddenly felt her legs go out from under her as she sagged onto the black-and-white marble floor.

"Philip deAngelis is seriously hurt?" India questioned. "We'll have to have another tally of the Queen of Midnight votes!"

Chapter Twelve

"The operation is a very tricky one," Dr. Bennett Heywood continued. "The bullet fragment has worked out of the muscle, and is dangerously close to penetrating Mr. McCall's left lung. We have waited several hours, and we can't leave it there any longer."

Elizabeth was numb with worry. She had not seen Tommy Lee, except through the window of his room, since they had ridden to the hospital in the back of an ambulance.

She cleared her throat. "Is there any sign of permanent damage from the blow he received, Dr. Heywood?"

"None that we can see, Miss Monette. He's responded to our brief questions, shows no brain swelling, and the fracture has no interior bleeding." He squeezed her shoulder. "You did an excellent job with your CPR."

"I had help. I hope you told Mr. Willow the same thing."

"Who?" the doctor asked, a quizzical look on his face.

"Clay Willow. He works for my parents. Wasn't he with Tommy Lee when you got there?"

"No. No, but the paramedics were already on the scene when I arrived." Dr. Heywood glanced at his watch, then nodded to Dr. Katherine Smiths. "Well, now, if any of you have any more questions, I'm sure Dr. Smiths can help. I'm due in surgery. My daughter is running that office for me, so I best not destroy her schedule. Keep a good thought, everyone," he ordered, then rushed down the hall.

"Miss Monette, can you come with me?" Dr. Smiths asked, motioning for Elizabeth to follow her into Tommy Lee's hospital room.

Elizabeth gave Miss Lou's hand a squeeze and hugged the judge. She smiled at Frank Foley. The four of them had kept vigil outside Tommy Lee's hospital room for the past day. Twenty hours of hell.

She followed the doctor into the dark isolation ward, her heartbeat pounding in her head. Dr. Smiths held out scrubs, gloves and a mask for Elizabeth, and helped her pull them on.

On the opposite side of the room, Tommy Lee lay on his side, propped up with pillows, tubes in his arm and taped over his nose. Part of his head was shaved and bandaged, giving his handsome profile a dangerous look. Elizabeth's eyes filled with tears but she straightened her back and gently took his hand in both of hers.

"He's awake," Dr. Smiths said in a hushed voice. "They've given him his meds, but he'll be awake for a few more minutes." She winked and gave Elizabeth's arm a pat. "He asked for you a hundred times even though we told him he couldn't see anyone before we operate because of the risk of infection. He just kept asking, though. Stubborn mule."

"Thank you," Elizabeth replied.

Dr. Smiths patted her shoulder and left them alone. Elizabeth squeezed Tommy Lee's hand. "Hey, mister. How you feeling?"

"Like day-old roadkill," he said, struggling to open his eyes. He squinted at her getup. "Is that you under all that, Elizabeth?"

"It's me. They don't want me breathing on you and making you sick before they operate. How do I look?"

He squeezed her fingers and smiled. "Like a Queen. I hear you saved my life after that bastard took my head off with that shotgun butt."

"Right. And now I own you. Isn't that how it goes in some cultures?" She flushed at her own bold remark, but just hearing his voice had a druglike effect on her. It was all she could do not to lie down beside him and hug him, she was so glad to see him alive.

"Look, I need to talk to you. I don't want you to argue with me, I want you to answer my questions and listen. Okay?"

"I really don't think you should be thinking about anything stressful, Tommy Lee. Wait until after the operation."

"I've got a lot of things to say. And I might not be around to say them after the operation, Elizabeth." He squeezed her hand more tightly.

His words frightened her witless, but she had no right to let her fears silence him. "All right, but then I've got a few things to say, too." And she did. She was going to tell him she loved him. He couldn't die on her, then; he would feel too guilty.

"Fine." Tommy Lee seemed to relax. He closed his eyes and cleared his throat, then met her eyes. "I know Luvey's dead, and that Petey Connor. I wish I had gotten him before Luvey did. Did deAngelis make it?''

''He's expected to, but he's still in a coma.''

''What's Foley's take on the whole thing?''

''He thinks Luvey hired those three men to harass me and make me drop out of the contest so Tammy could be Queen.''

''Connor's the son-of-a-dog that shot me,'' Tommy Lee rasped. ''Did Foley tell you that?''

''Yes, and he said he wished he'd gotten him before Luvey did, too.''

Tommy Lee's mouth contorted like he wanted to smile, but couldn't.

Elizabeth knew he was fading into sleep, so she kept talking. ''The chief thinks Jackson and his guys pressured Luvey for more money after they screwed up at the hospital with me, so she arranged to meet them but panicked and shot them. Petey Connor got away, broke into her house and killed her.''

''It doesn't make much sense, though,'' Tommy Lee said in a remarkably lucid voice. ''He shot deAngelis, Luvey shot him, he shot her, then whacked me over the head with a shotgun before falling dead downstairs?''

''I don't think they have it all worked out yet, Tommy Lee. Especially since I'm sure he was lying by the sofa right after I heard the shots. I don't see how he could have gotten downstairs and across the room before I came in through the French doors.''

''Why does Chief Foley think Luvey called me then?'' Tommy Lee squeaked. His eyes were closing, but he seemed to be listening.

''He thinks she made up the story about deAngelis being blackmailed to get you over to her house and find out what we knew about Emmett Peach. Frank feels Luvey got deAngelis to name Tammy the winner, but she had to be sure you were not on to her about the other stuff before she could relax."

"Did they find the gun?"

"Yes. They found the gun that shot them both upstairs under Luvey's body. There were three guns recovered in all." Elizabeth shuddered, the remembered scene surreal.

"All that murder just so her little sister could be Queen. I don't believe it, Elizabeth. Even if she did all that, why did she kill Peach and Lucille Thompkins?" His voice was weaker, but determined.

"Foley found out Lucille had worked under Luvey's direction in the volunteer program for a couple of years. They think she recruited her to find out information on me when Luvey heard a rumor that Dottie was looking into my adoption. Probably thought she could blackmail me into backing out to protect the judge and Miss Lou. She didn't know I couldn't care less about winning. But she never got far enough along in her scheme to do that."

He struggled to open his eyes. "This doesn't fly, Elizabeth. Does Foley know about the gun—that it killed your mother twenty years ago?"

"Yes, I told him to go to your sister's office and get the fax from your friend in New Orleans."

His eyes rolled open. "Does he think Luvey killed your mother? What was she—ten years old at the time?"

"He thinks it's a coincidence that the gun was used in both cases. Feels Luvey probably bought the gun from a pawnshop, or got it from Cracker Jackson. That the person who murdered my mother sold it and it sat around. He said guns sit for years around here. And there's no telling when she bought it.''

He sighed and squeezed her hand tightly. ''That's bull.''

''I think it is, too. But for now, let's leave it there.''

He closed his eyes again. Despite gaping doubts that the cops had solved the case, he felt pretty sure that Elizabeth was out of danger for now—reassured enough that he could go through with the operation. ''Okay, enough cops and robbers. I want to tell you something about how I feel, Elizabeth.''

''About what?'' she whispered, moving closer to him, gently brushing his hair off his forehead.

''About us. I want you to know I don't think you have made any kind of commitment to me.''

Stunned, she drew her hand away and met his gaze. ''I—I don't know what you mean.''

''I don't want you to think I'm expecting anything from you, Elizabeth.'' He was fighting to order his thoughts, but the fuzziness in his brain was drizzling down to his mouth. But he had to tell her, before he went into surgery, how he felt. She had suffered enough loss and trauma in her life. He didn't want to leave her with regrets if he died. His soul would never rest.

But he wasn't a saint. He loved this woman, and he wanted her to know it. He didn't want to leave her; he wanted them to have a life together. Despite the crossroads he found himself at, he wasn't going to be so noble as to not tell her the truth about how he felt while he had the chance.

''Elizabeth,'' he whispered, fighting against the blackness calling to him.

Despite her aching heart, Elizabeth put her lips on

his cheek and kissed him, kissed his mouth, her warm tears dripping onto the gauze mask. "Don't talk. Rest, darling. You're going to be fine, Tommy Lee."

"I don't…" He took a deep breath, knowing he was blacking out. He had to tell her those two things. Not to leave. And that he loved her. "I don't, I don't—" he began again, then managed two more words "—love you."

Elizabeth covered her mouth with one hand and stared at Tommy Lee. She watched silently as his breathing deepened and the tension in his fingers slackened. Gently she laid his hand on the bed. He was sleeping peacefully, like a man who had unburdened his soul.

A sob rose in her chest and she turned and ran from the room, down the hallway, away from the judge and Miss Lou and Chief Foley, out the door into a gray, stinging rain. She knew it was impossible, but thought she felt her heart breaking into a million pieces, like a fairy-tale slipper in a little girl's dream.

THE EMERGENCY MEETING of the Queen of Midnight Committee was being held at Bennett and India Heywood's home.

Despite the fact that it was a week before Christmas, no one seemed full of holiday cheer. Most of the women assembled in India's den wore black and very sedate jewelry. The men were in dark suits and ties, except for Paris Prince, whose tie sported loony-looking reindeer cavorting with red-suited elves.

He, as first alternate to the committee, was taking the place of Philip deAngelis, who lay in a coma in a private hospital in Baton Rouge.

In a highly irregular move, but necessary in the

minds of the nine committee members, eight of the electees and their dates were also present in the Heywood mansion. After all, Paris Prince had argued in a closed, members-only meeting that morning at the Monettes', since the girls had invested so much time in the event, they should be part of the decision to cancel or postpone it.

"Attention, please," Dr. Heywood called out to the group assembled in his ornate, 19th-century ballroom. His voice echoed off the polished mirrors. "As we all know, Philip deAngelis is not with us tonight, but our hearts and best wishes are with him. I've talked with his son, Paul, and with Philip's doctors in Baton Rouge, and I'm confident that he will make a full recovery. However, we are all well aware of the enormous amount of negative publicity, as well as the tragic circumstances surrounding the death of Luvey Rose. Tammy has gone into seclusion with family in Mobile, and has told me personally that she will not be participating in the Pageant."

A low hum of whispered exchanges vibrated through the room. Elizabeth sat staring straight ahead, feeling nothing. She had been like this for a week. But it was better than the bone-rattling pain she had endured the day Tommy Lee had revealed his feelings, or rather, his lack of feelings, to her in the hospital.

Despite his rejection of her, she had kept tabs on him and knew he had pulled through completely. She had sent a card, with a short note, care of Dr. Smiths. It had taken her hours to write and rewrite it. It had sounded formal and cold, but she had sent it. "I can't tell you how glad I am you are recovering, or how relieved I am that all this is over," she had written.

"Please bill me for your services. I am no longer interested in finding out more about the past."

He had called three times this week, but she had no intention of speaking to him. She didn't want a casual relationship with the man. She would not have been able to bear it.

Elizabeth had settled on letting her ego rule the day. She didn't want him to think her pathetic, or needy. Even though she loved him and cried in her room nightly, as inconsolable as a schoolgirl. Even though she knew she would never be able to shake the gloom or the pain of losing him from her life.

Forcing herself to pay attention, Elizabeth blinked several times and listened as Dr. Heywood droned on.

"Under the circumstances," he continued, "I'm sure we would all agree that Tammy has made the right choice. Therefore, on behalf of the planning sub-committee, I would like to make some recommendations on how to proceed. We will then have a short period of discussion, then the full committee will retire and vote on the final decision on staging our Pageant this year."

He beckoned India to the front of the room. "In the service of expediency, my dear wife, India, will sum up the position for keeping to our original plans. India."

"Thank you, Bennett." India nodded. Her navy blue silk taffeta dress rustled, and her ever-present pearls gleamed in the glow of the room's twin chandeliers. "Ladies and gentlemen, I propose that we continue our Pageant as originally scheduled, on the same day, in the same place. We should not let these hoodlums or the sordid scandals of certain individuals sway us from our course of traditional celebration of Farquier County's crowning glory.''

Elizabeth felt India's eyes resting on her. She began to blush, but did not turn her eyes away from the woman's steely gaze. She had thought her a murderer a few days ago, and though it was another woman who had committed the crimes, Elizabeth remained convinced that India Heywood was unbalanced. Her speech tonight proved it.

"Thank you, ladies and gentlemen.'' India stepped to the left of Dr. Bennett and the murmur of conversation notched up a degree.

"That woman's a shark,'' the judge said to Miss Lou, loudly enough for Elizabeth and several others to hear.

"Shhh, Baylor. Let's hear everyone out.''

"We should *throw* her out, uppity old hag,'' he replied. "Like she has any business looking down on someone because of a family scandal.''

Elizabeth exchanged a look with Miss Lou, who rolled her eyes. But Elizabeth was glad the judge was no more cowed by India's dig at the Monette household than Miss Lou was.

The next speaker was Paris Prince. The diminutive mayor, his own brush with the law pretty much forgotten in the wake of the current dramatic events, bowed to the assembled group. "I just want to offer an alternative to our little group. I, and I think many others, feel that it's unseemly for us to have our usual big shebang, what with Philip lying in a coma and poor Luvey gone to her Maker. I would suggest we present a news release to the *Press Register* and hold a small dinner party for the girls, then postpone all the hoopla until next year.''

"And what about the electees?" India interrupted, ignoring Bennett's hand on her arm. "Are you suggesting we freeze the contest and renominate the same group?"

Paris frowned and ran his skinny hands through his hair. "No, no, I don't think we can do that. We have a whole new group of young ladies coming up."

"But what about the girl who should be Queen this year?" India demanded, taking two steps toward Paris, then turning to her guests. "Shouldn't the girl who won as Queen get her rightful chance at glory?"

"But we'll have to hold another election!" Paris argued back. "Unless Philip wakes up in the next six days—which isn't likely—no one knows who won."

"He wrote the Queen's name down and it's locked in the chest, Mayor. Everyone knows that—"

"As does everyone know it's not official until the Caretaker certifies it on New Year's Eve!"

"Well, everyone should just vote the same way as before," India countered. "Then the outcome will be the same."

"But what if Tammy won?" a voice from the crowd questioned.

The mayor wagged a finger at the elderly man who had interrupted the proceedings. "Now, you all just keep quiet. No one knows who won, and swearing folks to vote the same way might work. But I think it would be best if we just didn't have a Queen this year."

"That's unacceptable," India retorted, but Bennett grabbed her arm and whispered furiously to her. Rosellen was sitting in the front row of chairs, and Elizabeth felt a pang of sympathy for the young woman. The poor girl looked sick over the spectacle India was making of herself. Elizabeth had heard that her boyfriend, Paul deAngelis, had left Belle Fleur for good to care for his father and return to school. It was also common knowledge that Philip deAngelis was not the only member of the deAngelis household to have had an affair with the dead redhead.

The old saying, "You can't choose your relatives," flashed through Elizabeth's mind. It was true, she realized. She glanced over at the judge and Miss Lou. They sat, shoulders touching, holding hands. No one could have chosen better parents.

No one should have tried, a voice inside her head chided.

Elizabeth sat up straighter. The urge to find out the name of her biological father had faded to a dull question in the depths of her heart. It didn't seem to matter who he was now, even though she, like Tommy Lee, was not convinced Luvey Rose had orchestrated the terrible tragedies that had consumed the gossips throughout the entire state for the past few days.

Yesterday she had pursued the investigation, checking out yearbooks at the library, finding a picture of Marylynn Gibbs in her high-school yearbook. So she could go to the library if she ever wanted a look at her biological mother.

Elizabeth frowned, aware of the heated arguments going on all around her but not really caring what the outcome would be. She rose and walked to the back of the room for a glass of punch. Paris Prince came up behind her, his monkey-like hand patting her on the arm. "Darling girl, how are you holding up?"

"I'm pretty good, Mayor. Thank you."

"I am so glad to hear that. It was such a terrible, terrible shock to me. I mean, I was right next door, asleep, when poor little Luvey died.'' Tears sprang to the mayor's eyes and he dabbed them with the end of his tie. ''You know, I thought I heard a gunshot earlier that night, and someone running. I couldn't believe it, though. I looked out the window, but saw only the newspaper lying there. To think I might have seen the horrible man who killed all these good folks…''

Elizabeth sighed and looked beyond the mayor. She didn't know what, but something was wrong with the growing public opinion that this murder case was closed. Maybe she'd better call Chief Foley and make sure he knew that Paris Prince had heard someone running past his house, toward the Heywoods? It might be important. Elizabeth spotted Miss Lou and the judge exiting the door at the other end of the ballroom. ''Excuse me, Mr. Mayor, but my mother is calling to me. I'll see you later.''

''Of course, darling. Of course. But there's one more thing I've been meaning to talk to you about.'' He grasped Elizabeth's arm. ''I don't mean to be a gossip, but I've heard about you discovering who your mama was. I just wanted to tell you not to pay any mind to anyone who says she wasn't a fine woman. I knew Marylynn when her mama Elaine worked for old Emmett Peach. I was his clerk, and she and I were good friends after her daddy, your grandpappy, got himself killed.''

Goose bumps rose up and down Elizabeth's arm and her mouth fell open. ''You knew Marylynn Gibbs?''

''Yes, ma'am, I did. And she was a beautiful, smart little girl. Suffered over not having a daddy after that terrible shooting, but a real spunky little thing. I think, if she would have lived, that you would have been real happy to call her Mama, Elizabeth.''

Inside her head she heard a woman scream, shots, and crying, but she pushed them away and grabbed Paris's arm. "Do you know who my father was?"

A look of fear passed over his eyes. He moved his lips as if to speak, but then pursed them together. He was staring at the assembled group in the room, and seemed to exchange a glance with someone.

Elizabeth looked over her shoulder. India, Rosellen and Bennett Heywood were standing three feet away from them. They all stared at her impassively, though India seemed agitated.

"We need you in the study, Paris," India said in a silky voice. "Right now. Elizabeth, dear, why don't you go inside and get something to eat with Rosellen. Both of you girls are going to be skin and bones inside your ball gowns if you're not careful."

Paris bowed his head to India. "Of course. I'll see you later, Elizabeth. Don't you worry about the Pageant. We old folks will fix things up." He walked off with the senior Heywoods while Elizabeth and Rosellen watched.

"Go on in without me," Elizabeth said to Rosellen. "I really don't feel like eating."

"Suit yourself," the young woman answered, then walked off as if in a trance.

Elizabeth remembered snatches of gossip she'd heard that Rosellen took a few too many prescription sedatives because of her nerves, but she was feeling too excited by what Paris had said to dwell on it.

For two long moments she stood thinking, staring into space. Then suddenly a memory so clear, so irrefutable, materialized inside her head that she gasped. She saw her father, dressed in a doctor's white coat, leaning over her bed to kiss her good-night. He had a

A One-Woman Man

slim face, and blue eyes. He was very tall and had a tiny mole just below his right eye.

It was the face of a young Bennett Heywood.

Elizabeth covered her mouth with her hand and blinked several times to keep from fainting. Forcing herself to breathe deeply, she looked around the room. She had to get to a phone, she decided. Rejection or not, she needed to talk to someone. Someone who could give her a no-bull opinion on what she should do next.

Let him think she was pathetic.

She needed to talk with Tommy Lee.

Chapter Thirteen

Tommy Lee's housekeeper, Sissy Lane, answered Elizabeth's knock. She did not seem the least bit surprised to see the young woman standing, unannounced, on the porch at eleven-fifteen at night.

"Miss Monette," she said with her flashing, gold-accented smile. "Please, come in."

"Thank you," Elizabeth said, trying to keep her teeth from chattering, from the cold and her nerves. "I need to wake Tommy Lee up for a few minutes. I know he's probably still recovering, but—"

Her speech was cut short by Tommy Lee throwing the door fully open and staring at her as if she had come all the way from Venus instead of across the bridge from Belle Fleur. "Elizabeth," he stammered, tucking in his shirttail. "You're here."

She pulled her coat around her tighter, hoping he couldn't see how the blood was speeding through her veins at the sound of his voice. "Yes. May I talk to you for a few minutes?"

"Yes, of course, please come in," he urged, taking her arm while he closed the door.

He was moving slowly. Elizabeth saw gauze peeking above the open collar of his shirt. He looked thinner, and the patch of hair they had shaved off in the hospital was odd looking, but her heart told her she had never seen a more wonderful sight than Tommy Lee McCall walking, talking, and breathing on his own.

"You look great," they both said in unison, then compounded the awkwardness by replying, "Thank you!" at exactly the same moment. Their voices were shaded through with tension.

"I'll make some cocoa, Miss Monette," Sissy yelled over her shoulder as she disappeared toward the kitchen. "It'll be a few minutes."

"Let me try this again," Tommy Lee said, offering Elizabeth a seat on the couch. She sat down, then he realized she still had her coat on.

"Let me hang up your jacket for you first." Elizabeth popped up like a jack-in-the-box and nervously let him help her out of it, then sat down and smoothed her hair.

Tommy Lee crossed in front of her and sat down on the other end of the sofa. He winced a bit when he draped his arm across the back of the couch, but smiled as if he were sincerely glad to see her.

They sat in silence for a moment. "I got your card. I tried to call you a couple of times, but…" he finally said.

Suddenly Elizabeth regretted her decision to come and see him. She wasn't sure she could bear him saying aloud what his inaction had so clearly communicated. "Let's not discuss all that," she said. "I'm really glad everything went well with the operation. But the reason I'm here tonight is because I wanted to get your advice, your ex-policeman's view on it—"

"Soon-to-be-reinstated policeman," he interjected.

"Really?"

"Yes." Tommy Lee grinned. "Another month and I'll be back where I belong."

"I'm happy for you," Elizabeth replied. Hurriedly she moved on. "Anyway. I spoke with Mayor Prince tonight, and he said something about the day Luvey was killed that I think is really important." The mention of Tommy Lee's deceased ex-wife brought a look of grief into his eyes, so she quickly related what Luvey's neighbor had heard the morning she was killed. "So it just seems to me that someone else had to have been in Luvey's house that morning, Tommy Lee."

He was staring at her with admiration. "You make an excellent point, Elizabeth. But why did you come to me?"

Why had she come? she asked herself. "Because I think I remembered my father," she blurted out. "And I think you may have been right to think he is the person behind all this mayhem."

Tommy Lee sucked in his breath and leaned forward. "Who is it?"

Elizabeth told him what Prince had said about Marylynn Gibbs and her suspicions that her father was none other than, "Dr. Bennett Heywood. Younger, thinner, with a small mole that was probably removed. But it was him."

"Wow," Tommy Lee responded.

"So what would you suggest now?" Elizabeth asked. "Should I confront Dr. Heywood?"

"Elizabeth, my God! Do you know how dangerous that could be if—"

"If he killed my mother," she finished. Elizabeth closed her eyes and let her head fall back on the couch. Her stomach was tied in knots. It was an unsolvable mess. She couldn't think why she had bothered to come here and hash it over with Tommy Lee.

She felt him move, and suddenly he was next to her, his arm around her shoulders. "I'm so sorry, Elizabeth. Maybe we should call Chief Foley now, let things fall where they may. It'll be painful for you, but if Heywood is behind this, then he must be punished."

"I know. Maybe it really is India who is behind it, though. She's so obsessed with this Queen of Midnight thing. If she had a grudge against my mother because of what *my* grandmother, Elaine Gibbs, did with India's father, then she could be behind the whole thing."

"Hell hath no fury like a woman scorned, eh?"

Elizabeth stiffened. He was so close she felt his breath on her skin, smelled the warm, spicy scent of his soap. Tears welled in her eyes but she blinked them away and moved from the couch and across the room. She raised her chin in the air. She wasn't sure she could stand that he didn't care for her.

"I'm going to let you get some sleep, Tommy Lee. Give me a call if you can tomorrow. I understand Chief Foley is in early. I think I'll go over and see him, just tell him everything and let the fur fly. The Queen of Midnight Committee voted tonight to go ahead with the Pageant, so I don't need to worry about keeping myself out of the rumor mills." She opened the closet and pulled out her coat, then hurried into it before he could help her.

"I can't believe they're going ahead with it," he said, his voice dark and unreadable.

"A matter of priorities. Tradition comes first. A few bullet-riddled corpses can't stop that."

Sissy Lane bustled into the room, two steaming mugs and a plate of cookies on a tray in her hands. "You two ready for some refreshments?"

"None for me, thank you," Elizabeth said. "Good night, Tommy Lee. Miss Lane. If I don't see you before then, have a happy Christmas."

"Elizabeth, wait—"

But she rushed out the door before he could say another word.

Tommy Lee stood at his window and watched her drive off. It was true. He had kidded himself that it wasn't, but it was. She didn't care for him. For whatever reasons, stress—uncertainty—Elizabeth wanted nothing more to do with him on a personal level.

The note she had sent had devastated him. But he told himself it was for the best; she needed her space. And he didn't care.

But he did. "Damn it," he said aloud to his empty room. He sure as hell wasn't going to let her slip away without an explanation. He limped across his living room and picked up the phone. The number he called was a familiar one. Chief Foley answered on the eighth ring.

"Chief, I need to talk with you. I'll be right over. It's about the murders. I may know who killed those people—"

"Tarnation, Tommy Lee!" the chief yelled. "I know it's hard to accept, but your ex-wife must have—"

"No," he interrupted. "Luvey didn't kill those people. But I think I can prove who did."

Chapter Fourteen

Christmas day was cold and icy; a cutting wind blew off the river. Tommy Lee stepped from his pickup truck and raised his arm to ward off the worst of the wind, hurrying around to the passenger side to hold the door open.

Katie Smiths jumped down, two shopping bags in her arms, and they both ran for the Monettes' front door.

Miss Lou welcomed them warmly, as Tommy Lee had hoped she would, and the judge gave him a bear hug when he entered the family room. A roaring fire was crackling, and the festive, skirted table in the kitchen groaned with the spread of traditional fare.

"Katie Smiths, I do say you are more beautiful every time I lay eyes on you," Baylor boomed. "Your mama, Miss Hattie, is a fine, fine-looking woman, but I do think you are even prettier."

Katie Smiths grinned and poked the judge in the ribs. "If I tell Mama that, she is going to make you pay, Your Honor."

"You better cool it, Baylor," Miss Lou admonished, handing Tommy Lee a mug of hot buttered rum. "Miss Hattie does not come cheap as it is. If she starts tacking on an insult charge, you are never going to get her bill paid down.''

The foursome exchanged small talk, and Miss Lou made them all sit before Tommy Lee got the nerve to ask where Elizabeth was. "She's out with Clay, Mr. McCall. Mr. Willow has been ill with a bad cold, and since he refused our invitation to join us, she took some food out to him and said she would sit awhile.''

Tommy Lee nodded toward the bungalow beyond the yard, visible from the back windows. "I see he's got a fire going, too. Which is great. You folks know how much he helped me last week, and I never really got a proper chance to thank him.'' He stood and shot Katie Smiths a pointed look. "Why don't you keep the judge and Miss Lou entertained for a few minutes, Katie, and I'll take the package I brought along for Mr. Willow out to him.''

"I'll do it. You go ahead,'' Katie wiggled her hands like she was shooing away a bad puppy.

"I'll be back soon,'' he said, not missing the look that passed between Miss Lou and Katie. He knew they would gossip about him, but Tommy Lee found he didn't care. Katie was a good friend—maybe his best friend—and he had spent at least a part of Christmas Day with her for the past twenty years. Katie knew his reasons for stopping by unannounced, both to thank Clay Willow and to see Elizabeth. Katie was all for him sharing his pain with Elizabeth. "She's the one who needs to know how you feel, Tommy Lee. I'm convinced the girl thinks you don't want her in your life.'' When he had protested that he did want just that, Katie had smiled. "Don't tell me, bubba. Tell *her*.''

Tommy Lee had convinced himself that fear had led

Elizabeth to her coolness. Fear. After losing both parents, and a chunk of her own identity, she was afraid to lose any more people in her life. Which was why he couldn't wait to tell her how he was doing.

That he was well. That he loved her. That she could depend on him.

Tommy Lee stopped, his fist in mid-knock at the small door of Clay Willow's home. He felt like a kid courting a beauty queen. Well, damn it, that was what he was. He knocked, forcefully. It wasn't like him to have pussyfooted around Elizabeth without telling her how he felt, and he was mad at himself for his hesitation.

Until Katie had told him, Tommy Lee didn't know Elizabeth had stopped by his hospital room for hours every night for the week after his operation; nor had he known that Clay Willow had assisted in the CPR at Luvey's home. It had been a blow to his ego to receive that card from Elizabeth. But her lack of attempts to see him, or to return the three calls he had left on her parents' answering machine, had been a bigger blow to his heart.

"Damn fool," he said aloud, knocking a second time. It was time to face the music. He was ready. He had a bottle of whiskey for Clay Willow and a small red box for Elizabeth. Which she might just throw at him, if the anger he had read in her eyes the last time he saw her was on the level. It wouldn't be the first time he'd made a beautiful woman mad. Or the last, he hoped.

At the sound of the lock turning, Tommy Lee pulled his coat up around his neck.

A moment later Elizabeth pulled open the door. She was dressed in a soft gray cashmere dress, with a silver and gray scarf knotted at her neck. He sucked in his breath when her eyes narrowed at the sight of him. He didn't give a damn that she was mad. Or standoffish. Or defensive.

"Merry Christmas, Elizabeth. You are the most beautiful thing I have ever seen in my life."

She moved back as if he had pushed her, her blue eyes full of wonder. "Merry Christmas to you, too. With a line like that, I guess you'd better come in." He brushed by her and his body felt as if he'd been too close to the fire.

Clay Willow was sitting in a rocking chair by the woodstove. He looked ill and pale, but content. Tommy Lee strode across the room in four steps and held out his hand. "Merry Christmas, Mr. Willow. I apologize for busting in on you like this, but I wanted to thank you."

He put the bottle down beside the small evergreen plant on the table, then gripped his hands together.

"You are very kind, Mr. McCall," Willow replied. "But I would have done the same for anyone."

"Yeah, well, this 'anyone' wants to thank you." Tommy Lee let his gaze roam around the neat little cottage, then rest on Elizabeth. "How are things going with the ball? Are you ready for next week?"

"Yes. All ready. Miss Hattie, my mother's dressmaker, was here yesterday fussing with the dress. I still think it's in poor taste, after Luvey's death, but this Queen of Midnight thing is really bigger than all of us. My father, who usually thinks its bunk, talked me into staying in the Pageant out of a need for civic solidarity."

"Sounds like you've decided to make Farquier

County your home on a permanent basis," Tommy Lee said.

"Actually, no, I haven't. I've accepted a job in Austin, Texas. It starts in February. Daddy's doing much better, and—" Elizabeth's voice became strained "—I think it's time for a change of scenery."

Tommy Lee felt like someone had once again thrown him from the second-floor window. "When are you leaving?"

"First week of January," she replied. "I need to find a place to live, settle in. I'm really looking forward to a new town."

Tommy Lee just stared. Finally Clay Willow cleared his throat. "Won't you sit down, Mr. McCall?"

He took a step back. "No, thanks, I'm going to run back to the house. My friend Katie Smiths and I usually do our visiting on Christmas Day. It was Katie's idea to come out, and she probably is ready to push on, and all...."

"Running off again, Tommy Lee," Elizabeth said curtly. "So anyway, Merry Christmas."

Tommy Lee turned. He didn't even kiss her. Before he got to the door, Clay called out, "Wait, you can escort Elizabeth back. She was just going."

Elizabeth frowned at Clay. "No. I thought we were going to play a game of cards and you were going to eat something from the plate Miss Lou fixed."

The two men standing at opposite ends of the small room looked uncertain. "Actually, Elizabeth, I think I'm going to take a nap," Clay replied.

"Oh. Of course. Please, rest," she added hurriedly. She squeezed Mr. Willow's arm. She felt an affection for the soft-spoken man, but she didn't want to impose. Besides, one last short walk to the house with Tommy Lee McCall couldn't be that painful.

"Thank you for taking time out for me, Elizabeth. It was really kind," Clay said. He cleared his throat, then added to Tommy Lee, "I see from the newspaper that Chief Foley feels his murder cases are all solved. Do you agree that Luvey Rose was behind all that went on, Mr. McCall?"

The question was so unexpected, Tommy Lee was speechless. He glanced at Elizabeth, who was standing like a statue. "No, Mr. Willow, I don't."

"Are you still working on that case?" Elizabeth demanded.

"Nothing official. I won't be a member of the Belle Fleur Police Department again until January, but I'm keeping my hand in."

"I see," Mr. Willow said. "Well, I was hoping that since your operation, you might be going back on the force. I'm sure they could use a good man like yourself."

The three stood silent for five seconds, then abruptly said their goodbyes, Clay Willow adamantly refusing to come meet Katie Smiths.

Tommy Lee and Elizabeth ran across the lawn and into the Monette kitchen. Except for a recording of *The Nutcracker* playing softly in the background, the family room was empty.

"Judge?" Elizabeth hollered up the stairs, more than aware of Tommy Lee's eyes on her body when she took off her coat.

"We'll be down in a few minutes, honey," Miss Lou called down. "You and Mr. McCall sit a bit and chat. I'm showing off Miss Hattie's work on your ball gown."

Tommy Lee watched her digest that unlikely bit of information. Her face didn't show much, but the straight line of her back and shoulders said she was not amused at being left alone with him.

"Are you hungry?" she asked him carefully.

"Starved," he replied against his better judgment. He crossed his arms and leaned against the kitchen counter. "How about you?"

"No. No, I'm fine," Elizabeth lied, crossing her arms and looking him directly in the eye. "So why don't we quit pretending. What are you doing here, Tommy Lee?"

He wanted to make a joke, but the rawness in her voice stopped him. "I wanted to see you."

"Why?"

"To thank you. To find out if you'd talked to Foley about your theory about Bennett Heywood, and if he was following it up. To thank Mr. Willow." His voice felt ragged. "To tell you how I feel…"

The sounds of voices drifted downstairs as Baylor and Miss Lou and Katie Smiths made their way toward the kitchen.

"You already told me how you feel," Elizabeth reminded, "that day in the hospital. I appreciate your honesty. I hope you appreciate mine. There's no need to say anything more."

He saw the emotion in her face, the tension in her stance. She was hurt. What had he done? "What are you talking about? What did I say to you—"

"Please, Tommy Lee, just go." Elizabeth turned away from him and hurried into the family room as Katie came in holding an envelope of pictures. They were of Baylor and two horses he kept at a farm nearby.

"Look at this, Tommy Lee," Katie said. "The judge has an old brood mare just like the one we had at—" She stopped and put her hand on his arm. "What's wrong? Are you hurting?"

He wanted to say yes, but he wouldn't admit to the pain shooting through him at that instant. "No, I'm fine. But I think I may have overdone it a bit today. We should be going."

Miss Lou and the judge looked at each other. Katie turned her head toward the family room and nodded. "Okay, sure thing." She looked down at the picture in her hand with a trace of a smile, then suddenly asked, "Who is that?"

The judge looked down at the snapshot. "That's my caretaker, Clay Willow. You know him?"

The doctor took a deep breath and handed the pictures back to Baylor. "No, I guess I don't. Well, good night you two. Merry Christmas."

Tommy Lee was civil, but he wasted no time getting back outside and on the road leading away from Elizabeth Monette.

After five miles of silence Katie Smiths asked, "Do you want to talk about it?"

"No" was all he said.

DESPITE HER reservations about the Queen of Midnight Pageant, despite her sadness over Tommy Lee's behavior, despite her own fruitless attempt to learn her father's identity, Elizabeth felt grand.

Outside it was the coldest New Year's Eve in anyone's memory, but inside her dressing room in the east wing of the Belle Fleur Municipal Auditorium, wearing her pale blue silk gown, with her hair done up in a cascade of ringlets that fell softly onto her neck,

Elizabeth felt like a little girl who had magically become a princess.

Miss Lou, usually a portrait of serenity and rational behavior, was sitting in the chair beside Elizabeth's dressing table, crying into her third hankie. Baylor seemed struck dumb, and kept shaking his head and smiling.

Elizabeth grinned and shook her finger at them. "Will you two please stop! You are both acting like you never saw me dressed up before." She put on Miss Lou's mother's drop earrings, sapphires surrounded by a circle of tiny diamonds, and took a step back. She tried to strike a sophisticated pose, but could not pull it off.

"Oh, Elizabeth," Miss Lou cried out, "you are just so lovely!"

She walked over to her mother and put her arms around her. Miss Lou seemed fragile suddenly, like a china doll. "Mom, stop it. Really, you're going to a party. Be happy!"

Miss Lou tried a smile, but dissolved into tears again. "I wish your own dear mother could see you," she sobbed, bringing tears to Elizabeth's eyes, as well.

"She can, darling, she can," Baylor comforted, wrapping his arms around both women. "Now, let's pull ourselves together. The music's started out there and I'm ready to do some dancing."

He did a brief two-step for them, his big body as graceful as a young boy's. Seeing her husband's foolishness seemed to finally calm Miss Lou enough that they rose to leave. "We'll be in the audience for the crowning, dear girl. But if I remember right, you can't see a thing because of the lights. So remember to smile."

A sharp rap at the door interrupted Elizabeth's reply. She opened the door and found one of the young men who served as pages standing there.

"A delivery for you, Miss Monette." He smiled a huge smile and handed her a black velvet box, about six inches by eight inches. "And if you don't mind me saying, you look fabulous."

"Thank you," Elizabeth told him, then shut the door and handed Miss Lou the package. "What's this, mother? Another surprise? You've given me too much already."

Miss Lou opened the small white card that was attached to the box. "Maybe it's from Mr. McCall," she whispered to Baylor, and they both looked at their daughter.

"Mr. McCall does not support the Queen of Midnight Committee's efforts. Besides, as I told you on Christmas Day, Mr. McCall wasn't a social acquaintance, he was a business acquaintance. And as of a couple of weeks ago, we had no more business together."

"Daddy and I think we saw him earlier. Out in the lobby with that nice Chief Foley. He's wearing a tux!"

"The chief?" Elizabeth deadpanned, unable to stop the sudden increase in her heart rate.

Miss Lou raised her eyebrow at Baylor. He was oblivious and still staring at Elizabeth as if she were a dream.

"Just open it for me, please."

"Are you sure, dear?"

"Yes, ma'am. It's probably a gift from the committee."

Miss Lou slid out a small white card and read the

message in an unfamiliar hand aloud: "'From an Admirer.'"

Elizabeth met the judge's eye in the mirror. "Did you send this, Daddy?"

"No. But I wish I had."

Miss Lou handed Elizabeth the package. "You open it."

She sat down and stared at the package as a sudden flood of anxiety pushed some of her gay feelings away. It was as if she had seen the box before. Carefully she felt for the tiny brass catch on the lid, and the top flew open. "Oh my, oh my," she said in a shocked voice.

Her parents rushed to her side, and they both gasped. "Will you look at that gorgeous hunk of shine," the judge said.

"But who sent it?" Miss Lou asked, turning to Elizabeth.

She shook her head and stared at the obviously very old brooch pinned against the red satin backing. It was a miniature tiara, set in platinum, with a band of five rubies outlined by hundreds of diamond chips.

Someone rapped three times on the door. "Hello, in there," Katie Smiths called out. The door opened and the lovely physician, stunning in gold silk, peeked around the door. "Miss Hattie is here for a final dress check." Her eyes widened when she caught sight of Elizabeth. "Oh, honey, I think Mama outdid herself this year!"

Miss Hattie, all ninety pounds of her, resplendent in black bugle-beaded silk, darted in. She looked at Elizabeth without smiling, then ordered her to stand, turn, and walk toward her. The elderly seamstress noted the brooch in her hand.

"What's that, child? I don't think this gown needs much dressing up!"

Elizabeth opened her hand and presented the brooch for Miss Hattie's inspection.

"Elizabeth! Where on earth did you get that?" Katie asked. "Is it yours, Miss Lou?"

"No, no, it's not—" she began, but was cut off by Miss Hattie.

"Let me see it here, Miss Elizabeth," Hattie commanded. Elizabeth handed her the brooch and watched as Hattie turned it over several times, then held it up to Elizabeth's dress. "Wear it, darling. It suits."

With a swish of skirts and a whiff of lavender, Miss Hattie was gone. Katie Smiths remained behind, an oddly serious look on her face. "You know, Elizabeth, I think I may recognize that jewelry."

"You do?" Miss Lou and Baylor said in unison.

"Where did you see it?" Elizabeth asked, nervousness growing in her like choke-weed.

"I think it's in a painting. A painting of a past Queen."

Elizabeth's heart raced. "Who was in the painting?" She knew the answer before Katie spoke.

"Bennett Heywood's mother."

There was a loud knock at the door, which immediately opened. Tommy Lee McCall, a dangerous look in his brown eyes, walked in. "Elizabeth, I have to talk to you before you go with the group to be introduced." He nodded a greeting at the judge and Miss Lou, but from his stance everyone could see he wasn't about to be put off.

"What's wrong, McCall?" Judge Monette demanded.

"Nothing. Yet. But I need to talk to Elizabeth in private for a moment, if you folks don't mind."

"I'm staying," Baylor started, but Miss Lou cut in.

"Now, Baylor, let's leave these two alone. You heard Elizabeth say their relationship was just professional. Haven't you always said 'Business is business'?"

"I'll see you after the coronation," Katie said, linking arms with Elizabeth's parents and leading them out before the judge could protest anymore.

Elizabeth stared at him, and Tommy Lee looked right back at her.

"Just business between you and me, huh?"

"Isn't that the way you want it?"

"Does what I want matter?" he countered. "It seems to me what you want is ruling the day."

"What do you mean?" she retorted. "You told me you didn't love me that night in the hospital, Tommy Lee." Elizabeth's voice cracked but she raised her chin. "What more is there to say?"

His jaw fell open and he took two steps toward her. Tommy Lee took Elizabeth in his arms, pain and incredulity clear in his face. "I said what?"

Despite the makeup and the excitement and her pact with herself that she wasn't going to go into this with him, she started to cry. Tommy Lee crushed her in an embrace, kissing her hair, her ears, her mouth.

"Elizabeth, you foolish girl. I never said that. I would never say that. I love you! You're the one that sent me the Dear John letter. I thought you wanted no part of any kind of relationship with a broken-down cop—"

"Shut up," she said, a smile beaming through the

tears, her hands on his dear face. "This is crazy, Tommy Lee. But I do love you."

Then came a quick rap on the door and the words, "Ten minutes, Miss Monette," broke their embrace. Elizabeth accepted the handkerchief Tommy Lee extended and glanced in the mirror. She might be a bit smudged, but she thought she looked happier than she ever had. "I'm so glad you're here. Walk down with me and you can watch the ceremony from the wings."

"Hold on. Now that you've made me the happiest guy I know, I can get back to what I needed to see you about. You're in danger here tonight, Elizabeth. I don't want you to go out there to the ceremony."

"What are you talking about?"

"I know who your father is. He's here. I saw him drive up, and everything fell into place. Remember the night Ray Robinson and Cracker Jackson were killed? The old woman who called the cops saw a pickup truck with a tailgate wired shut."

"Yes, but—"

"And Katie mentioned to me she saw those pictures your dad had of the horse—"

"Tommy Lee, I don't know where you're going with this!" Elizabeth finally shouted in frustration. She heard the ceremonial music outside and recognized the Queen's march. She was supposed to be lining up in the corridor, getting ready to walk in the candlelight procession onto the stage.

Tommy Lee draped his arms around her and held her close. Despite his certainty that disaster was about to strike, he was nearly undone by Elizabeth's beauty. "Clay Willow's fingerprints are all over the shotgun recovered at Luvey's house, Elizabeth. We don't know if they are from twenty years ago, when your mama was murdered, or from a few days ago when Luvey was, but he's obviously up to his neck in this."

"Clay?" she replied in a dazed tone. "But he's a handyman. He's my father's friend...."

"No, he's not, darlin'," Tommy Lee was forced to reply. "He's Bennett Heywood's younger brother, Tyler Heywood. And unless I'm mistaken, Tyler Heywood, who disappeared from Belle Fleur when you would have been just five years old, is your biological father."

ELIZABETH SEEMED TO Tommy Lee to be in a state of shock as they hurried through the maze of utility tunnels under the auditorium. She had listened to his summary of how he had worked during the past week piecing together the last bits of information they had, and all the reasons he believed she was in danger.

Despite all that had happened, though, she didn't seem willing to believe that her blood kin would really try to kill her.

"Are you sure he's here?" she asked as they ducked down the hallway behind the kitchen and raced, her high heels clattering, for the service elevator that would take them up to the parking garage.

"Yes. I saw him myself, but there was too much of a crowd between us and I couldn't catch up to him. I think he has a gun with him."

"What?" She stopped suddenly, and Tommy Lee had to pull her along with him. "You mean he came in here toting a gun in plain sight?"

"No, but I saw the outline of the holster against his tux. I don't know how he thinks he could get away with anything in front of all these people."

Tommy Lee pulled back the heavy door of the service elevator. "Go ahead. Jump in."

Elizabeth stared at him. "Stop being such a cop. All you've done tonight is give orders." She crossed her arms and refused to budge. "Tell me why, Tommy Lee. Tell me why you think my father killed my mother and those other people."

"Because he and your white-trash mama had a little baby that threatened to ruin the Heywood family, just like your white-trash grandma ruined my mama's family," said a female voice from the shadows.

Elizabeth and Tommy Lee whirled to face the young woman stepping into the light, her face frozen into a look of hatred and fear. "So I think old Uncle Tyler just killed that little tramp, Marylynn. She was going to sue him, make the whole story public. Ruin Daddy's career. It was bad enough she stole my grandmama's brooch, Elizabeth," the woman said, light glinting off the barrel of the gun she held pointed at them. "It didn't belong to her. And it sure doesn't belong to you."

Elizabeth cried, "Rosellen!"

Tommy Lee started to move and put himself between Rosellen Heywood and Elizabeth, but she shouted, "Stay still or I'll kill you, Mr. McCall! I just smacked you last time we met. This time, I'll let the business end of the gun do the work."

"You killed Luvey, and Petey Connor?" Elizabeth gasped. "But why, Rosellen, why?"

"Because I hired Cracker and his bum friends to make sure you were out of the competition. If my mama knew you were Marylynn's little girl, and you beat me out for Queen, it would kill her. Luvey was just in the wrong place at the wrong time the other night." She shrugged. "Course, the fact she was sleeping with my boyfriend and his daddy didn't help her case when she asked me not to shoot her."

Rosellen was a surreal figure to behold. Her green eyes glittered in the dim light of the corridor, her silver dress glowed as if it were lit from within. "You two just step back into the elevator and shut the door. I'll send you up to the parking lot."

Elizabeth followed Tommy Lee's upward glance and saw the frayed cable above the gears of the elevator mechanism. The Belle Fleur Civic Auditorium was the biggest in the state, outside of New Orleans. It had four stories below ground, six above. If Rosellen got them even five stories up, they wouldn't have a chance.

"I worked on that a little every day, the past week. Used my daddy's gardener's shears. They work real good. I wasn't sure if I was going to tell you all this or not, Elizabeth, us being blood relations and all, but when Miss Hattie told Mama she thought you had a brooch just like the one Dr. Heywood's mama wore in the painting, well, I knew I had to, darling. 'Cause, of course, my mama didn't raise no fool."

"But, if what you say is true about Tyler Heywood, why would he send me the brooch, Rosellen?" Elizabeth asked. She was trying desperately to think of a way to distract the young woman just long enough for Tommy Lee to make a grab for the gun.

"I don't know. It doesn't make too much sense, now that you ask. Maybe he was just trying to apologize for things."

A searing pain behind her eyes made Elizabeth gasp. She raised her hands to her face. "What?" Tommy Lee asked. "What is it?"

Suddenly Elizabeth could see it all.

She was five years old, waiting in her bed for her mama. She heard a loud popping noise, and a woman scream, and glass shatter. Even though she had promised her mother she wouldn't, Elizabeth went back downstairs. And saw...no, not her kind-faced father standing in the kitchen, a huge, smelly gun in hand. Not Tyler Heywood, whom she knew as Clay Willow. He had not killed her mother.

"Oh, my God!" Elizabeth cried out. "It was India Heywood. India killed my mother!"

Tommy Lee moved toward Rosellen, supporting Elizabeth with his shoulder. He heard applause above him. The orchestra was playing. "This is sick, Rosellen. Don't do this to your family. They covered up what India did, God knows how, but they can't cover up this. Put the gun down. There's still time for you—"

"Stop it!" Rosellen raised the gun toward Elizabeth. "All Mama ever wanted was to be Queen of Midnight. Your grandmama, Elaine Gibbs, snagged my grandpa. All the good it did her. Her lover killed her husband and she ended up with no one, and my mother ended up losing her chance. What was Mama supposed to do when Tyler came home saying he and Marylynn Gibbs were going to get married and that she had his child? Poor Mama." Rosellen shook her head, her glassy eyes shining even brighter with the movement.

"Your poor mama?" Elizabeth suddenly yelled back, lunging out of Tommy Lee's grasp. "What about mine? She was the one wronged, she was the one murdered! And your mother is a murderer, Rosellen. And now you're just like her!"

Rosellen began to laugh—a demented, animal sound. "And now you're going to be just like your mama, Elizabeth. Dead!"

Tommy Lee dived headlong at the woman. The gun went off in an earsplitting burst of fire and smoke while the ceiling plaster above them exploded like a grenade. Elizabeth screamed and Rosellen cursed.

He wrestled the gun away just as Chief Foley and Clay Willow came running down the hallway, followed by a small band of Belle Fleur cops. India and Bennett Heywood brought up the rear.

"Rosellen, baby girl, what have you done?" India cried, but Bennett held her arm. He was staring at his brother, Tyler, whom he hadn't seen since that night twenty years before when he had broken the news that India had killed Marylynn.

But Tyler Heywood was staring at Elizabeth. His face was white as the plaster floating like ashes in the air. The full grief of what he had lost, what he had agreed to cover up for the sake of his family, what it had cost him, showed in his eyes.

"Elizabeth, I'm so sorry. Please, forgive me."

Elizabeth looked at him and shook her head. She was shaking, and thought she might scream if she had to talk to him. When Tommy Lee's arm came up protectively, she buried her head against his shoulder. "Please, go away."

"I will. But just know, I had to put you up for adoption. There was no way we could let India go to jail for what she did to your mama. She was sick—"

"Stop it!" Elizabeth cried, holding her hand up as if she could deflect his words. "I don't want to hear any more. Not tonight. Not ever."

Tommy Lee hugged her closer. "Take me home,"

Elizabeth whispered. She had misunderstood him that night in the hospital. She had misunderstood many things. But she knew she had finally learned what her blessings were in this life. It was time to leave behind the feeling of incompleteness, the nightmares, the doubts about who she was.

She was Elizabeth Monette.

"Take me home, Tommy Lee."

So he did.

Epilogue

"Dottie Betts, that's Tommy Lee's sister, gave birth to twin boys, Raymond and Randall, on February 17. The following month, on March 25, Tommy Lee and Elizabeth were married.

"Miss Lou and Judge Monette held the wedding reception at their home in Fairbreeze, and it was beautiful, I can tell you that, although I was not invited." The mayor grinned and continued his news summary of the last few weeks, holding the rapt attention of the small gathering sitting in the sunshine on his porch. "India Heywood and her daughter were sent to a private medical facility for the mentally insane down in New Orleans. India will be tried for murdering poor little Marylynn Gibbs, but not Rosellen. She's much too ill. Dr. Bennett Heywood has sold the hospital to one of them health maintenance organizations and run off to Alabama."

Paris smiled at Binnie Duval, Patrolman Duval's sister who worked for the *Press Register*. "So Elizabeth solved that old mystery of what had happened to poor little Marylynn Gibbs. Enough of a shock to knock someone senseless, I tell you, but not that little gal. You know, when Aspen was named Queen that night, Elizabeth actually found the stamina to call her and wish her all the best.''

"What happened to Tyler Heywood?" Binnie asked.

"No one really knows that," the mayor had to admit. "But I suspect he went back to wherever it was that he'd been the last twenty years. He saw his baby girl again. Learned that she was safe, and raised well by people who loved her. Hard for him to ask for more, I'd say."

"He might have asked for Elizabeth to be Queen," Binnie said sarcastically. "After all, this was the last Pageant that's ever going to be held. I heard that from three separate sources very close to members of the executive committee. It's been ruined now forever."

Paris threw his head back and laughed at Binnie's naiveté. "Don't count on that darling, don't count on that. I think as long as there is a Farquier County, there will be a Queen of Midnight. They are all just going to have to work some to live up to this last ball for excitement."

As his laughter filled the air, his guests joined in, but most secretly hoped their host was right. For the Queen of Midnight Pageant *was* Farquier County.

And with things the way they were, who knew but that a child born to Tommy Lee McCall and Elizabeth Gibbs Monette McCall might be the very best thing that ever happened!

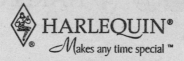

MEN at WORK

All work and no play?
Not these men!

July 1998
MACKENZIE'S LADY by Dallas Schulze

Undercover agent Mackenzie Donahue's
lazy smile and deep blue eyes were his best
weapons. But after rescuing—and kissing!—
damsel in distress Holly Reynolds, how could
he betray her by spying on her brother?

August 1998
MISS LIZ'S PASSION by Sherryl Woods

Todd Lewis could put up a building with ease,
but quailed at the sight of a classroom! Still,
Liz Gentry, his son's teacher, was no battle-ax,
and soon Todd started planning some
extracurricular activities of his own....

September 1998
A CLASSIC ENCOUNTER
by Emilie Richards

Doctor Chris Matthews was intelligent, sexy
and *very* good with his hands—which made
him all the more dangerous to single mom
Lizette St. Hilaire. So how long could she
resist Chris's special brand of TLC?

Available at your favorite retail outlet!

MEN AT WORK™

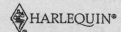 

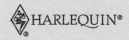 HARLEQUIN®

Not The Same Old Story!

 HARLEQUIN PRESENTS®

Exciting, glamorous romance stories that take readers around the world.

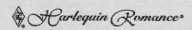 Harlequin Romance®

Sparkling, fresh and tender love stories that bring you pure romance.

 HARLEQUIN® Temptation.

Bold and adventurous— Temptation is strong women, bad boys, great sex!

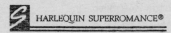 HARLEQUIN SUPERROMANCE®

Provocative and realistic stories that celebrate life and love.

 HARLEQUIN AMERICAN ROMANCE®

Contemporary fairy tales—where anything is possible and where dreams come true.

 HARLEQUIN® INTRIGUE®

Heart-stopping, suspenseful adventures that combine the best of romance and mystery.

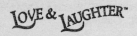 LOVE & LAUGHTER™

Humorous and romantic stories that capture the lighter side of love.

Look us up on-line at: http://www.romance.net   HGENERIC

HARLEQUIN®

INTRIGUE®

COMING NEXT MONTH

#481 MARRIED IN HASTE by Dani Sinclair
A handsome stranger swept McKella Patterson out of the way of a
speeding truck—then said her new husband was an impostor and her
life was in danger. Truth gleamed from his eyes, and McKella's heart
raced at his touch—but when the danger passed, would he disappear
from her life as quickly as he'd entered it?

#482 FIRST-CLASS FATHER by Charlotte Douglas
Return to Sender
Unresolved conflict had made Heather Taylor leave Dylan Wade, the
drop-dead-gorgeous cop she would always love. Desperation forced
her to return. Despite their past, Dylan *had* to save her kidnapped
baby—though she could *never* tell him the child was his own.

#483 NEVER CRY WOLF by Patricia Rosemoor
The McKenna Legacy
Donovan Wilde was a lone wolf who had no use for his McKenna
blood, or the legacy that accompanied it. But when Laurel Newkirk
showed up claiming to have been engaged to him—or someone
pretending to be him—he knew he couldn't escape Grandmother
Moira McKenna's legacy....

#484 ONLY A MEMORY AWAY by Madeline St. Claire
Were Judd Maxwell's recurring nightmares actually memories of a
crime of passion? Beautiful social worker Karen Thomas wanted to
help him unlock the memories—and his heart. But once unleashed,
what would his memory reveal?

AVAILABLE THIS MONTH:

#477 UNFORGETTABLE NIGHT
Kelsey Roberts

#478 PRIORITY MALE
Susan Kearney

#479 THE RUNAWAY BRIDE
Adrianne Lee

#480 A ONE-WOMAN MAN
M.L. Gamble

Look us up on-line at: http://www.romance.net